A Lady's
Handbook of
Espionage

ALSO BY KATRINA KENDRICK

His Scandalous Lessons
Tempting the Scoundrel
A Bride by Morning
A Touch Wicked
The Wayward Duke

A Lady's Handbook of Espionage

KATRINA KENDRICK

HEAD
of ZEUS

An Aria Book

First published in the UK in 2025 by Head of Zeus,
part of Bloomsbury Publishing Plc

9 7 5 3 1 2 4 6 8

A catalogue record for this book is available from the British Library.

ISBN (PB): 9781837931576; ISBN (ePub): 9781837931545

Cover design: Jessie Price
Typeset by Siliconchips Services Ltd UK

Printed and bound in Great Britain by
Clays Ltd, Popson Street, Bungay NR35 1ED

MIX
Paper | Supporting
responsible forestry
FSC® C018072
FSC
www.fsc.org

Bloomsbury Publishing Plc
50 Bedford Square, London, WC1B 3DP, UK
Bloomsbury Publishing Ireland Limited,
29 Earlsfort Terrace, Dublin 2, D02 AY28, Ireland

Head Of Zeus Ltd
5–8 Hardwick Street
London EC1R 4RG

To find out more about our authors and books visit
www.headofzeus.com
For product safety related questions contact productsafety@bloomsbury.com

For the survivors.

AUTHOR'S NOTE

Dear Readers,

While all of my work touches on darker themes, this book includes scenes that may make some uncomfortable. *A Lady's Handbook of Espionage* frankly addresses intimate partner violence (not between MCs) and grooming. While most of this occurs off-page and is spoken about in dialogue, there are a few scenes with the villain that require this content note. Please proceed with caution. A full list of notes is available on my website.

All my love,

Katrina

1

NEW YORK, 1869

Trouble had a way of finding Ronan Callahan. Usually, it came in the form of a fist aimed at his jaw or an informant with an itch to turn on him. But tonight, it was a blonde woman wearing emerald silk.

They were in some uptown mansion he couldn't be arsed to remember the name of, some railway tycoon's ostentatious monument to his wealth. She moved through the crush of Manhattan's elite, pretending to be just another debutante. But Callahan saw beyond the practised smiles. He'd made a career out of seeing what others missed.

She called herself Abigail Smith.

It was, by Callahan's meticulous accounting, her thirteenth name in two years.

The newspapers dubbed her the Spectre. The *Fantôme*. A ghost drifting through the lives of the rich to steal anything shiny and valuable. He'd tracked her exploits for months, a bemused admiration in the dispatches he sent winging back to Whitehall. Hard not to marvel at the fucking audacity of her grift.

And the cleverness, if he was being honest. She treated it like a game.

Oh, they had that in common, the pair of them. That understanding that the world was a board, and they had pieces to be played. Toffs and street thieves, Quality and guttersnipes – all people wanted the same things. Wealth. Status. Power.

The only difference was that he went for the straighter way of taking it. He'd beat it out of someone if he had to. Callahan had been born in the rookery, made in the image of dockside taverns and narrow alleys. Forced to make his way with fists and cunning when Whitechapel finally spat him out. He'd tried going straight once – clerk work, factory labour. His hands itched the whole time.

Too wild for honest work.

Too impatient for business.

Too damn mean for the church.

Left one path: government-paid thief. Spy, they called it, like the word made it cleaner.

But *her*? She worked the room like she knew this world well. Made men fall in love before she vanished with their fortunes. Never left bruises, just broken hearts. She bent her head as she laughed at some young swell's tepid wit. Fluttered her fingers against another's bejewelled lapel with a blush colouring her cheeks.

Every movement was calculated.

There was a certain art to her cons. A poetry that only someone versed in the same could appreciate. Her methods were prettier than his, to be sure, but a mark was a mark, whether you rolled them with a kiss or a fist. And Callahan made a study of her light-fingered exploits. He'd followed her across countries, lost her trail, and thought he'd never find it again. Now, here they were, in the same Manhattan residence.

Kismet, Callahan might've called it, if he believed in that sort of thing.

He waited for his moment. Spectre drifted towards the ballroom's perimeter, pausing to admire the view outside the open terrace doors. Callahan abandoned his whiskey on a footman's tray and intercepted her path. There was something almost fated about it. The inexorable tug of two bodies locked in opposing orbits, destined to collide.

"Lovely evening," he said. "Seems a shame to waste it on dancing and small talk."

Up close, she resembled a figure out of a Rossetti painting, with irises the colour of absinthe and hair like molten gold. An elegant nose. A mouth made for sin and secrets. Her skin looked soft enough to bruise under his fingertips.

Her attention didn't waver from the immaculate gardens beyond the terrace, but he'd wager she'd clocked his every feature and stored it away in her clever brain.

"I find these gatherings quite entertaining. Perhaps you'd find a gaming table more to your taste?" A smile, faintly mocking.

Christ, but she was a cool piece of work.

"Ah, see, I make it a policy never to gamble if I can help it. With cards or dice, at least. I prefer more unorthodox contests of chance."

"Such as?"

"Seeing how long you can keep this up before that accent slips." He leaned in, letting his voice drop low. "I'd lay odds that fetching little voice is meant to mark you as

3

a new money debutante, possibly visiting New York from Philadelphia for a match. But the Seine still shows through when you say certain words. A bit sloppy for someone with your reputation."

That earned him a swift, startled look. Her eyes flicked over him, cataloguing the austere lines of his evening kit, the hair he'd slicked into submission.

"You've a discerning ear," she allowed. "Mr . . . ?"

"Ronan Callahan, at your service." He swept her a bow. "And I've an ear for many things, Miss Abigail Smith. Tell me, did you come up with that all on your own, or did you borrow it from a headstone?"

"I haven't the faintest idea what you mean." She turned to face him fully.

"I'd say we can do away with the pretence. We're neither of us much suited for it." He caught her fingers on the pretext of brushing a kiss across her knuckles. Her hand tensed in his grip. "I know you're no more an American heiress than I am the Archbishop of Canterbury."

She tilted her head. The smile she gave him was practised. "My goodness. Do you approach all innocent women with such outlandish claims? Or am I special?"

"Come now, darling. There's not an innocent stitch on you." He glanced at her neck. "That's quite the rock weighing down your décolletage. Shame it doesn't match the ones dripping from your ears."

A hitch in her breath, quickly suppressed.

"A small inconsistency," she said. "My maid has been distracted lately."

"Funny thing about that diamond. The Duchess of Westchester's been missing it since last spring. Clashes dreadfully with the Countess of Harrington's diamonds dangling from your lobes. A lady of your discerning tastes should know better than to mix stolen goods from different heists."

He had the pleasure of watching that placid expression ripple.

"You're quite free with your accusations."

"Am I? I call it being observant. Comes with the territory in my line of work."

"And what work might that be? Professional ballroom lurker? Defender of the idle rich?" She raked him with a look. "But no. You've the appearance of a man accustomed to more utilitarian dress. And no taste for the useless chatter of the Quality. I suspected someone might be following me when I boarded that steamer to New York."

Clever minx. But he'd expected nothing less. "What do you say to a turn about the floor, Miss Smith? I promise I'm lighter on my feet than I appear."

"I promised the next set to Mr Avery."

"He's losing at the card table and won't notice if you've run off to Paris by morning." Callahan offered his arm. "One dance. I won't bite unless you ask nicely."

"How gentlemanly." But she laid her hand on him. "I suppose one dance couldn't hurt."

He had her now. Tension thrummed through her, that stillness of a creature poised to flee or fight. But there was curiosity there, too, and the faintest edge of excitement. The thrill of the game.

He knew it well. Lived for it, in fact.

The orchestra struck up a waltz, and he splayed his palm over the small of her back.

"Lovely form," he said, leading her through the turns. "But I shouldn't be surprised. Thieves need good footwork, don't they?"

Her nails dug into his shoulder briefly. If he hadn't been paying attention, he would've missed it.

"And spies don't?" she countered. "Crown agent, I assume? You're a long way from London."

He led her in a graceful turn, using the movement to study her face. "What makes you so certain of my loyalties? I could be Prussian." The words came out in flawless German.

"*Ihre anzug kommt aus London*," she replied, her German as perfect as his. "Narrow cut on the lapels, higher buttons." Her nail traced the line of a button, and his lungs forgot how to work. "That subtle curve here" – her touch skimmed his chest – "only comes from Savile Row. Fine hand stitching emphasised by a country that values delicacy over durability. And English wool has a unique feel under my fingers. The weaving technique, you see. Softer. Lighter."

Good God.

"Well spotted."

She patted his shoulder. "Your accent's slipping. Did I hear an Irish lilt just now?"

"Maybe." Callahan dipped his head, his lips grazing her ear. "How's my accent now, darling? Idle curiosity."

"American," she said, a bit breathlessly. "Manhattan born and bred. There aren't many men who can slip into different skins so seamlessly. Tell me your background."

"Dublin by birth, London by way of a misspent youth."

She smiled. "And what is your fine talent for observation telling you about me?"

"You walked in exactly forty-three minutes after the dancing started. Late enough to make an entrance, but not so late to be remembered as rude. You danced with Henderson first – old money. Then Parkington, whose wife is conveniently visiting her mother. Both men who wouldn't notice if you took their wallets, their watches, and their dignity all at once."

He skated his hand down to settle at the base of her spine. "But that back of yours," he continued, "it never relaxes. Not even when you laugh. I'd wager you've practised that delicate blush in the mirror for hours. Three times tonight, same downward glance." He lifted a brow. "How close am I to the mark?"

Surprise flickered in her face. She huffed a little laugh as they swayed. "You *have* been watching closely."

"I don't suppose you'd do me the very great honour of sharing something real? A name, a favourite flower, your preferred *nom de guerre*. Let's have a proper introduction."

"Names are just sounds people make to get your attention. Mine have all served their purpose."

"That so, Miss D'Aramitz?"

Her eyes flared. "You have me confused with someone else. Flattered as I am by your attentions."

"The thing about lies is that they multiply. First there's one, then three, then twenty. Soon, you need a ledger to keep track of them all. But I can always list them for you, if you'd like. The diamonds in Barcelona. The pearls in Vienna. We could talk about the heiress in Rome or the countess in Prague. Every few months, there's been a new woman with a new story. Different names, different hair colours, different languages. It's a remarkable collection of faces you've acquired."

A muscle ticced in her jaw. "Do you have a point to make, or do you just enjoy the sound of your voice?"

"My point is that I know you better than anyone else in this room. I've been following your trail across two continents. We're old friends by now."

Her expression was cold and assessing. "You do have a way with words."

"So I've been told. Most people mention it right before they try to knock my teeth out."

"You don't need to worry about violence from me. Unless that's what you're hoping for."

"I'll keep it in mind. You haven't answered my question."

"Which one? You've made so many baseless insinuations that I'm afraid I've quite lost track." She slanted a look at the open terrace doors. "Best if we resume this *tête-à-tête* somewhere more private, hmm?"

Callahan gave a nod. "After you."

The glass-paned doors clicked shut, and he backed her against the ivy-covered wall, both hands braced on either side of her head. She met his stare, back straight. As regal as a queen.

"Well?" she asked mockingly.

"Your name." He lowered his head until their faces were inches apart. "The real one."

She smiled slowly. "Spectre."

"And I'm the fucking Prince of Wales."

"You're not nearly blue-blooded enough to reach that high. What do you want from me?"

"That's the question, isn't it? See, I've got a bit of a quandary on my hands. There's a rather princely sum being offered for information leading to your capture. Enough to keep me in tailored suits and passable whiskey for years to come."

She didn't flinch from the threat. "Then why haven't you clapped me in irons already?"

He reached out to wind one of her curls around his finger. "We're having such a fine time, I thought I'd savour it."

He didn't see it coming. One second, he was looming over her, the next, his back slammed against the wall. She pressed a knife to his throat. Where had she even hidden that thing?

Her cheeks were flushed, chest heaving. He'd never seen anything so terrifyingly beautiful.

"Problem, Agent?" She grinned. "Not quite how you imagined the evening progressing? What will you do now, I wonder?"

The blade bit deeper.

Callahan kept very still. "I'm open to suggestions."

"Don't play games you can't win, Ronan Callahan," she whispered, lips brushing his.

"Who says I'm losing?" His voice came out rougher than he'd meant it to.

A heartbeat passed. Two. The orchestra hit a crescendo behind the glass.

The blade scraped over his skin in an idle caress. "I applaud your dedication, truly. As charming as this has been, I really must dash. Places to be, people to scandalise; you know how it is. It's been a rare pleasure, Agent Callahan.

But what fun would it be if you caught me so easily? I'd be disappointed if we never danced again."

Then she eased the knife away and slipped into the ballroom, vanishing into the crowd.

2

ATHENS, 1870

Isabel Dumont walked through the agora.

Sweat-slicked bodies and livestock crowded the ancient market. She inhaled the scent of spices, ripe fruit, and the faint aroma of smoke as she passed customers haggling with vendors. Their voices rose in a mix of Greek and Turkish, English and French. She spotted a gull attempting to make off with one of the fresh Aegean sardines from a stall.

It was chaos.

But Isabel savoured it: the heat and the noise and the freedom of travelling without Favreau hovering over her shoulder. She anticipated the jostling elbows and swinging trays, the absentminded steps back and sudden swerves. The key to remaining unseen was understanding the current of movement.

Today, invisibility meant the difference between victory and failure.

Just get the coin, she reminded herself as she headed for the Numismatic Museum presently housed at the University of Athens.

The bruises on her wrists had barely faded from Favreau's last demonstration of what happened to thieves who failed him. An American client of his wanted a rare antique coin. Favreau wanted to please the American.

And Isabel? She just wanted to survive.

All she had to do was steal it and disappear. A convincing performance of a bumbling American tourist, a quick sleight of hand, and she'd be bound for Paris. She'd deliver her prize to Favreau and lie low until his black mood passed.

A simple plan. Elegant.

All she wanted was to go home. Use a victory to distract Favreau for a few days so she could slip away and see her sister.

Emma still lived in the dingy flat they'd secured after the Duke of Southampton cast them all out. His mistress and two bastard daughters meant nothing once they became inconvenient. Disposable.

And then *Maman* fell ill.

Isabel still remembered it all – that wet, hacking cough. The doctor's face when he named his price. Their father's dismissal when Emma pleaded with him for money to pay for medicine. And later, the cold calculation in Isabel's heart when she realised what she'd have to do.

Poverty made people desperate. And desperation left you vulnerable to the wolves.

Emma never asked how Isabel earned the funds to pay for the doctor. She never asked why some of the coins came bloodstained, or why Isabel moved gingerly some days.

She never asked why Isabel didn't stay more than a night to catch her breath.

Emma never asked questions because Isabel always lied.

She refused to admit that she learned pretty girls had their own currency. It was part of the bargain she'd struck with Favreau – her body and service in exchange for training.

"Do this, and you'll never go hungry again," Favreau had promised, his hands in her hair. "Do this, and I'll teach you to take whatever you want."

He'd lied about the second part. Isabel had learned to take, but only what he wanted her to.

And *Maman* died anyway.

Isabel kept stealing. It had become something else by then. A mission. A vendetta. She wanted to hurt the rich and take their precious things. Empty their safes. Make them feel a fraction of what she'd felt when her father – a duke with more money than he knew what to do with – had abandoned them all to die. Aristocrats believed they could take and discard without consequence. Left behind their *inconveniences* to be chewed up and spat out by men like Favreau.

The coin, she reminded herself.

Because her master was never far from her mind.

The white marble face of the Central Museum loomed ahead. She just had to slip in—

"*Stop! Thief!*"

Isabel whipped around towards the source of the commotion – and felt the ground drop out from beneath her.

Through the parting throng of shoppers charged a half-naked man. Bronzed skin glistened in the harsh Grecian sun, muscles flexing. Dark hair, storm-grey eyes, striking features – he could have been Ares in the flesh, stepped down from his plinth to unleash chaos.

Ronan Callahan.

Because of course it was.

He vaulted over an upturned barrow and kept running. Feathers rained as squawking chickens exploded from their toppled cages. Baskets overturned, sending fruit rolling underfoot. Curses in a dozen dialects chased his heels. And he ran on, shirt torn halfway off and blood streaking his ribs – and still outrageously gorgeous.

If the deities of Olympus had conspired to pluck the most exasperating temptation from her past and plant him square in her path, they could not have set the scene more perfectly. Only Ronan Callahan could transform her simple smash-and-grab into a drama of epic proportions.

Isabel's mind bellowed at her to leave. To turn her back on this maelstrom masquerading as a man and salvage what she could of the day's agenda. That's what any rational woman would do.

Then she saw who was after him: six brawny men armed with blades. Callahan's odds looked grimmer by the instant.

Strangely, that decided her.

Isabel swore and lunged for the alley where she prayed Callahan was headed. If she timed it right – if she gauged his trajectory without being spotted by his pursuers . . .

She skidded around the corner just as Callahan's grey eyes locked onto hers. They widened, a single thought written across his face.

You.

"This way!" she hissed, snatching his wrist.

She yanked him into the shadowed backstreets.

"What the hell are you doing here?" Callahan demanded.

"Shut up and run!"

An order he obeyed without argument. They scrambled over crumbling walls and careened around corners. Isabel rifled through her hard-won mental map of the city, the boltholes and dead-end alleys. They needed to catch their breath and hide—

There.

A courtyard tucked between decrepit buildings and concealed by a curtain of wisteria. Isabel hauled Callahan into the tiny refuge.

The space barely qualified as a courtyard, truthfully. More a forgotten corner slumbering behind its veil of flowers, the stone walls bearing scars of past skirmishes long since lost to memory. But it would serve for now.

Isabel stepped back to assess her companion – and the inadvisability of the last fifteen minutes crashed over her.

What possessed her to intervene in Ronan Callahan's disaster *du jour*? Why had she risked herself? One glimpse of his stupid, beautiful face and all her instincts for self-preservation scattered.

She was many things, most disreputable, but she'd never fancied herself an idiot.

Until now.

Callahan braced his hands on his knees, chest heaving as he caught his breath.

Despite him being sweaty, bloody, and exhausted, Isabel couldn't help but stare. In New York, she had decided Ronan Callahan was the most beautiful man she'd ever seen. His black hair fell over his forehead and begged to be pushed back. When he opened his eyes, they were a grey so pale that they resembled quicksilver.

The few sorry scraps of shirt still clinging to his shoulders exposed far too much bronzed skin. Too many flexing muscles and old scars, each mark telling a story Isabel itched to unravel. He looked like Ares the moment before battle lust consumed him. Magnificent. Dangerous.

Frankly, he was an affront to decency.

Callahan straightened, a faint wince the only acknowledgement of the wound on his side. His scowl promised retribution. Ah. Not gratitude, then. Hardly a shock. The man would probably spurn divine intervention if it arrived without the proper paperwork.

"Now that we're alone, I'll ask again. What the hell are you doing in Athens?"

She shrugged. "Some sightseeing. Taking in the local colour. Some of us can travel without turning it into an international incident."

"Right," he said flatly. "Because you're so sodding circumspect."

"I'm the very *soul* of discretion."

Callahan looked like he'd tasted something unspeakable. "You're the soul of chaos."

"Why, Agent, it's almost as if you aren't overjoyed by my timely assistance. Such ingratitude for the woman who spared you a messy gutting. You're welcome, by the by."

She crossed her arms, absently noting her sleeve was now smudged with dirt and . . . was that rotten fruit? Lovely. Yet another thing sacrificed on the altar of Ronan Callahan's calamities.

"I assume you have a good reason for attracting the violent attention of what appeared to be half the criminals in the Plaka?"

His scowl deepened. "I had it handled."

"Yes, clearly. That's why a pack of cutthroats was baying for your blood."

"It's nothing I can't deal with. You didn't need to get involved."

For God's sake. Callahan would drag himself bloody and broken from the underworld itself before admitting he needed aid, let alone from her.

"I'm sure you'd have figured something out," she said. "Probably around the time they'd carved that lovely body into a more portable parcel."

He shot her a baleful glare that she ignored in favour of examining the alarming crimson stain seeping through his tattered shirt. Her smile slipped.

"That's a lot of blood."

"It's barely a scratch. A flesh wound at most."

She arched a brow. He'd probably describe a knife to the kidney as a *minor inconvenience*. "Your 'barely a scratch' is starting to drip onto my boots."

"They'll survive." But he glanced down at the injury. "It's nothing."

Isabel debated the wisdom of her next words, but in for a penny, in for the whole bloody pound. She'd already involved herself in this mess. Might as well see it through.

With a sigh, she said, "Remove those rags before you collapse and undo my efforts to haul your troublesome arse out of danger. Let me look."

He gave her a wicked smile that kindled some warm and reckless emotion in her chest. "If you wanted me undressed, darling, all you had to do was ask."

"Don't flatter yourself, Agent."

But she'd be lying if she claimed some part of her didn't sit up and take notice as he stripped off the shirt.

Nom de Dieu, the man was a masterpiece. Lean muscle, tanned skin from time spent outdoors. Even more scars and bruises across his torso. The inadvisable urge to follow those lines with fingertips and lips washed over her.

Not now.

Swallowing hard, Isabel dug through her skirts for the little tin she kept stocked with unguents and salves. Callahan tracked her every movement. She was keenly aware of his size and sheer physical presence.

"Be a love and hold still," she muttered. The scent of medicinal herbs cut through the wisteria's sweetness. "This will probably sting."

She scooped some of the salve onto her fingertips and reached for him, smoothing it over his injury with a touch far gentler than his wretched ingratitude warranted.

He hissed in a sharp breath, the muscles of his abdomen tensing. "Bloody hell."

"Don't be a baby."

"Has anyone told you that your bedside manner is shite?"

"Has anyone ever told you it's rude to bleed all over the person who just saved your worthless backside?"

A surprised laugh left him. "My apologies. How can I make amends?"

"Don't get stabbed."

She fished a roll of linen from her pocket. Her fingers trembled slightly as she wound the bandage around his torso. Everything about Callahan addled her wits.

"Why did you do it?" he asked quietly.

She glanced up and immediately regretted it. The look he slanted her was pure Callahan – intense and incisive, as if he could flay all her secrets bare if he pressed hard enough.

She added a last unnecessary fold to his bandage to buy herself a moment. "Do what?"

"Help me back there. Don't get me wrong – having a beautiful woman patch me up in a hidden garden is a fantasy come true. But it makes me curious."

He thought she was beautiful? If the heat and sun hadn't already reddened her skin, he might have noticed her blush. Because one compliment from Ronan Callahan made her forget all the reasons why she shouldn't be alone with him.

"Does everything need to have an ulterior motive?"

"With a thief like you?" He caught her wrist before she could draw away. "Yes."

He turned her captured hand over, thumb dragging across her palm. Isabel's breath stuttered as he stroked a callus born of lock picks and balanced blades.

"Perhaps I have a soft spot for hard-headed spies with more courage than sense." Her voice was husky.

"And here I thought I was special." He tugged gently, reeling her in with the barest pressure until she swayed into him. "To be singled out for rescue by the elusive Spectre herself. What alias have you decided on here in Athens?"

His eyes. God. This close, they weren't just grey. They had so many shades. The colours of storm clouds. Smoke. Steel.

And that little freckle at the corner of his mouth . . . She bit her lower lip at the sudden urge to taste him. To *bite*.

"Allison Marks," she said, switching from her usual, slightly Parisian accent to an American one. "Tourist from Boston."

"Well, Allison Marks, tourist from Boston." He said her fake name like he was tasting it. Testing it. "What's your price for helping me?"

"A future favour, maybe," she said. "Having one of Her Majesty's best in my debt could prove useful. A marker to be called in someday."

"So I'm to be a gem in your crown, little thief?"

She twisted her wrist, breaking his hold with a move she'd practised a thousand times.

But she didn't pull away.

Instead, her hand slid up his chest. Warm skin. Hard muscle. Her fingertips traced ridges and hollows and scars. She memorised him through touch, climbing higher – shoulder, neck, until her fingers tangled in his dark hair and—

Tugged.

Just hard enough to pull his head back. Isabel felt more than heard his sharp inhale, the shudder that chased through him.

"What are you doing?" he asked, voice rough.

"Thinking that maybe I'd rather have you in my bed than be a gem in my crown," she murmured, just to see how he'd respond. "I've been told I have deviant tastes and an abnormal appetite for pretty men. Tell me, how hard do you fuck, Agent?"

His eyes darkened. Something shifted in his expression – hungry and angry and wanting. Ah, good. Let him feel what it was like to be the one off-balance for once.

"I'm not a man you get to play with, Trouble."

"Trouble?" She raised an eyebrow. "We're using familiar names now?"

"If it fits. And you? You're nothing if not an ocean of trouble."

Isabel almost smiled. That meant he'd never forget her. She hoped he thought of New York as often as she had. Fantasies of his body against hers during that dance had kept her steady under Favreau's hands. Kept her sane. On more fanciful nights, she'd wondered what would have happened if she'd kissed him.

His attention dropped to her lips. Did she imagine it, or did he lean closer?

"You're a walking apocalypse, in fact," he whispered. "I shouldn't be surprised you have deviant tastes and a vulgar mouth."

She smiled. "Afraid I'll corrupt you, Agent?"

"Are you eager to try?"

Yes. But then, above the courtyard walls, she noticed the museum's roof. The coin she needed to steal. The man waiting in France and looking for any excuse to hurt her.

She couldn't afford distractions.

"Not today," she said reluctantly, releasing his hair. "But it's been lovely seeing you again. Now I have *touring* to do."

Callahan's brows snapped together. "You really expect me to let you walk out of here?"

She blinked at him. "Whyever not? I did just save your life."

"And as you admitted, it wasn't out of the kindness of your heart. You wouldn't know benevolence if it bit you on the arse."

"You've been contemplating my arse? I'm flattered," she said. "And most men would be grateful to have a beautiful lady save them from being murdered."

"Most men are idiots, and you're not a lady."

"And thank the good Lord for that. It sounds dreadfully dull." She started walking towards the wisteria curtain. "Next time I'm liberating something shiny, I'll think of you while I'm fencing it," she called over her shoulder with a wave.

She didn't look back as the flowers swayed shut behind her, though she felt his stare.

Because as much as she wanted to stay and amuse herself with Ronan Callahan, her circumstances allowed no dalliances. No emotions. No weaknesses. Favreau's possessiveness ran bone deep. To him, Isabel was a belonging. A precious bit of chattel that he'd invested years in collecting.

And Favreau did not share his toys.

❧ 3 ❧

HONG KONG, 1871

The stench of the Sheung Wan gaming hell clung to Callahan. He hated places like this. They set him on edge, made his fingers itch for the familiar weight of a pistol. But he was here to gather intelligence, and like every other job, he sublimated discomforts in favour of cold practicality.

Callahan moved through the press of bodies. He dodged drunkards and overeager gamblers and servers. The din was an overwhelming cacophony of shouts, the clatter of mahjong tiles—

He froze.

Across the smoky hall, a woman leaned over a gaming table.

Spectre.

Figures she'd be here. An unpredictable variable tossed into the equation of his already complicated evening. No matter how many months or miles stretched between each encounter – a year since Athens, two since New York – he could never seem to brace himself for impact. He studied her, cataloguing details: the blonde hair twisted into a demure coiffure, the low dip of her black silk bodice, the elegant arch of her neck.

For a moment, Callahan considered retreating – but then Spectre's gaze snapped to his. He grinned as her lips mouthed a curse.

With a derisive snort, she tore her attention away, focusing on an older gentleman with a thin moustache and eyes glazed from drink. No doubt she'd selected him for maximum malleability. Get the poor sod drunk, take him for every quid in his pockets, then scarper quick as a blink before he even realised he'd been had.

Callahan walked over and leaned in. "Fancy meeting you here," he whispered in her ear. "Bit far from your usual hunting grounds, isn't it?"

A tremor rippled through her, slight enough that he might've imagined it. "I'd tell you to go to the devil," she said, "but I imagine you'd interpret it as an invitation."

"More a challenge, really. I'm fond of insurmountable odds."

"What are you doing here, Agent?"

"Reconnaissance. You?"

"Winning." She glanced at her mark, who remained happily oblivious to their exchange. "Or I was until you came blundering in."

Callahan had seen that expression on cornered informants and spies who'd found themselves on the wrong end of a pistol: a feral gleam that heralded unwise decisions.

"From where I'm standing, you look to be treading a very fine line, Trouble."

Her fan flicked closed with an agitated snap. "I suppose

that would depend entirely on one's point of view. Now, if you'll excuse me, I've a game to finish."

Callahan's hand clasped her elbow. "I need a word."

Spectre set her jaw, but she allowed him to guide her to a dark alcove.

He braced a palm on the wall above her head. This close, he could count the freckles scattered across the bridge of her nose, see the darker flecks of emerald in her irises.

"What kind of shite have you stepped into?"

Spectre bristled. "You think that's the only reason I'm here?"

"Please. You belong in ballrooms with stolen diamonds dripping from your neck and rich idiots fighting for your attention. So, yes."

"Stop talking like you know me," she snapped. There it was – that flash of something in her eyes. Fear. She glanced toward the door. "Some of us don't have the luxury of a government purse and a licence to kill to fund our frivolities. You've never had to—"

"Fuck men old enough to be my father, just to keep my body stitched together for one more day?" He gave her a grim smile, taking a certain vicious pleasure in her flinch. "You've no idea the depths I've plumbed to survive, little thief. The things these hands have had to do. So tell me why you're in an opium den in Hong Kong trying to rob drunks."

Her lips thinned. "Change of scenery. Coin for the lifestyle to which I've grown accustomed. Not that it's any of your business."

He tipped her face up, forcing her to meet his gaze.

"Here's what I think," he said, very softly. "Judging by the way you're trembling, you're in a bit over your head, and someone with deep pockets and a distinct lack of humour has put a price on you. So you're trying to rustle up whatever money you can before they catch up, and that old bastard you're with" – he jerked his chin at her mark – "is tonight's lucky target. How am I doing so far?"

She sighed. "Must you always assume the worst?"

"You're an unrepentant thief. Been at it since you could toddle, I'd wager. Your first word was probably 'mine'. Your first complete sentence was probably instructions for a con. In the years since we've met, you've swindled, burgled, and bamboozled your way across half of Europe. At last count, you've got authorities in five countries searching for you. Six, if the Spaniards ever figure out what happened to some of their royal collection. So you'll forgive me if *assuming the worst* is just common sense."

She scowled. "If you're going to stand here listing my sins all night, I'm leaving."

"No. Come with me."

Spectre froze, blinking up at him. "Why in God's name would I do something as daft as that?"

"You want the whole list alphabetically?"

"I can't just—"

"I know a hunted creature when I see one," he said. "And you, darling, are running on nerves and instinct right now. How long since you've slept? Or had a proper meal?"

"That's immaterial."

"The fuck it is. When you're glancing at every shadow crosswise, that's when you make mistakes." He squeezed her shoulder, ducking to hold her gaze. "You've got two choices here, Trouble. You can keep hoping that gent over there will be too pissed to notice when you take a runner with his coin purse and anything else that isn't nailed down, or you can come to my hotel, sleep in a bed for the night, and figure out your next move in the morning. No strings, no expectations."

Spectre's lips parted. He could see her turning it over – where was the catch? What trap lay beneath his offer?

Because in a thief's world, kindness always came with strings.

Finally, her shoulders drooped in resignation. "I'd call you ten types of bastard if I thought it would do any good," she muttered.

Callahan's mouth twitched. "Oh, it does wonders for my self-importance, I assure you."

"You're a pox."

"I endeavour to please."

He guided her from the crowded gambling hall. It was slower going than he'd like, having to weave through the nighttime crowds of Sheung Wan. They stepped onto the Praya, the broad stone quay that swept the circumference of Victoria Harbour. The night breeze off the water was a welcome reprieve from the stench of the alleys, carrying the briny sea scent. At the far end stood the Hongkong Hotel.

Spectre followed him into the building and upstairs to his suite. The sitting room was sumptuous, full of green brocade and mahogany, complete with a pianoforte in the corner. Floor-to-ceiling windows offered a sweeping view of the harbour.

"Goodness," Spectre said. "Her Majesty certainly knows how to cosset her pets. Is that actual Aubusson carpet?"

Callahan slipped off his coat and tossed it over the back of a bergère. "Even we lowly civil servants appreciate a bit of luxury on occasion. I'll be sure to pass along your compliments to the Crown representative who secured these lodgings. He does so love decor feedback from wanted criminals."

Spectre glared at him but continued her circuit, trailing her gloved fingers along the carved marble mantelpiece.

"There's a spare dressing robe in the washroom if you want to get out of that gown before it squeezes the life out of you," he said.

Christ, he sounded like a surly innkeeper dismissing an undesirable tenant, not . . . whatever they were to each other now. Adversaries still, to be sure. But adversaries didn't save each other from assassins in Athens, pluck each other out of Hong Kong opium dens, or offer their beds as sanctuary.

Spectre paused before the wide bay window, stripping off her gloves. Each slow tug was an act of ritual disarmament. Once finished, she reached up to unclasp the heavy garnet pendant nestled at the hollow of her throat, tucking it away into some hidden pocket within the folds of her skirts.

Shedding pieces of her armour.

"I can feel you boring holes into my back with that stare," she said without turning around. "One might think you've never seen a woman before."

"Just appreciating this novel display of civility between us. Makes for quite the refreshing change, you and me playing nice."

And it did. There was something profoundly intimate about seeing her like this. Something tantalising about how the lamplight gilded her skin and picked out glints of gold in her blonde hair. She seemed almost . . . approachable.

"Careful, Agent." The corner of her mouth curved up as she glanced at him. "That almost sounded like sentiment."

"Don't get the wrong impression."

"I wouldn't dream of it. Since we're being so friendly, would you mind helping me with my buttons?"

Bloody hell. She'd likely meant it to sound coy, a bit of light needling. So why did it feel like a gauntlet thrown at his feet?

He crossed the room, fingers finding the row of pearl buttons between her shoulder blades. It should've been an easy enough task, but once he realised she wasn't wearing anything under the gown, *easy* became *exquisite torture*.

He fumbled with the last fastening, his knuckle grazing the dip just above the flare of her hips.

"There," he said, scarcely recognising his own voice. "Unwrapped."

She turned, and the movement made her bodice gape. A silvery scar carved a path over the rise of one breast. She had others on her back. A cartographer's dream of puckered knots and slashes – mementoes of her bloody trade.

"Thank you," she breathed.

Then the dress slithered to the floor as she sauntered into the washroom, giving him an eyeful of creamy skin and gentle curves before the door clicked shut.

Callahan muttered a strangled curse and waited for his pulse to slow. For sanity to return. He was clearly losing his mind to even contemplate whatever fool notion his cock was entertaining.

Bloody disaster, this. Nothing but trouble ahead.

He paced the room twice, then stopped cold when the washroom door creaked open.

Spectre's hands fidgeted with the tie of her – *his* – dressing gown. "I don't suppose you have a spare blanket for the settee? That would be adequate for my needs."

"I'll be taking the settee," he said. "You're in the bed."

A little crease appeared between her brows. The one he'd noticed in Athens when she was concentrating on bandaging his wound. "Don't be absurd. A big lad like you won't get a wink of sleep on that thing. You'll be knots from nape to knee come morning."

"I've slept on worse." Whitechapel alleys. Prison cells. Places a child shouldn't have had to call home. "The bed's yours. I insist."

"How noble, but there's more than enough room for us both." She drifted closer. "Unless you fear for your virtue."

He couldn't help but chuckle. "Sweetheart, my virtue is buried in an unmarked grave."

"Well then. What are you waiting for, Agent?"

He blew out a long, slow breath. God, he was going to regret this. He knew it in his bones.

"Get in the bed, Trouble. Before I toss you in it."

Her smile sharpened as she settled on the mattress. "Coming?"

Jesus wept.

As he undressed, Spectre studied him, lingering on the scars and bruises that mapped his history across his skin.

"You've a collection of new scars since Athens," she observed. "Exactly how many people try to kill you in any given year, Agent?"

"Enough that an attempted stabbing is what I'd call a normal Tuesday. You're looking at thirty-two years of rough living, little thief."

"Thirty-two?" Her cheek dimpled. "Practically ancient."

Callahan shot her a dirty look. As if he needed to be reminded that she was probably more than a decade younger.

Wearing nothing but his smallclothes, he slid under the blankets beside her.

Stripped of her mask and usual armour, it was tempting to believe the illusion – that Callahan knew this woman. That the dangerous yearning inside him was more than a passing madness.

The oldest lie whispered in the devil's voice.

"This is a terrible idea," he said.

"Oh, undoubtedly," Isabel agreed. "But aren't those always the most fun?"

Callahan snorted. "Your definition of fun and mine differ."

"Come now, Agent. Where's your spirit of adventure?"

"I left it in England. Along with my common sense and self-preservation instincts, apparently."

The bedsheets rustled. She turned to face him, one arm tucked beneath her head. "I have questions."

"Christ." Callahan fixed his gaze on the ceiling's scrollwork. "Course you do. Fine. Ask."

She chewed her lip. "Did you follow me here?"

"To Hong Kong?" He barked a laugh. "God save me. Contrary to what your inflated notion of self-importance might lead you to believe, my existence doesn't revolve around chasing your thieving arse across the globe like a lovelorn suitor."

"Hmm. And what business brings the esteemed Agent Callahan to the Pearl of the Orient, then?"

"Nothing that concerns you." When she continued to watch him expectantly, he sighed. "You're not the only one with pressing affairs that demand attention. Even errand boys must eat."

"Don't you ever tire of it? Being the government's weapon? Risking your life for people who would cross the street to avoid you?"

The question hit too close. Callahan had asked himself the same thing on countless nights. He'd spent his early years in Dublin, grown up as an orphan in Whitechapel. A street rat despised by the very society he now worked for. His old friends – Nick Thorne and Leo O'Sullivan – were currently building their own empire in the slums they'd survived. They'd nearly disowned him when he'd taken Wentworth's offer to join the Home Office.

"It puts food on my table," he said. "What's it to you? Does the Queen of Thieves morally object to how others earn their keep now?"

"Not at all. But I envy you the choice to leave your cage whenever you want. I'd be remiss if I didn't encourage you to take advantage of that freedom during our temporary armistice."

Something was off in her voice. Callahan studied her – the shadows under her eyes, the wariness in her expression. What had driven the infamous Spectre to a Hong Kong gambling den, trying to fleece marks for quick quid? Who was she running from?

"Want to talk about it?" he asked gently.

Spectre blinked. "Why do you care?"

"You saved my life in Athens. I owe you a debt."

"Ah. What happens tomorrow, I wonder? After this interlude expires? There must be a substantial bounty on me by now."

"Last I heard, a thousand pounds."

Her brows shot up. "That much? I'm flattered." She paused, considering. "Well, here we are. Your most wanted thief caught at last. Are you going to haul me in for Her Majesty's justice?"

"Not tonight," he said.

"And tomorrow?"

"I make no promises about tomorrow."

Before he could think better of it, he reached out, knuckles skimming along her throat. Her pulse raced beneath his fingertips. She wasn't as calm as she appeared.

"Do you want to kiss me, Agent?" she whispered.

No. That's what he'd say if he were thinking clearly. But sense had gone right out the window. His chest felt tight. And when her teeth caught her lower lip, his mind went blank.

I want to bite that lip, he thought. Then panicked at how much he meant it.

"Would you let me kiss you?"

Her breath hitched. "Yes."

Warnings blared through his head, ethics and regulations and boundaries crossed – but when his lips touched hers, his thoughts went quiet. Clear. The kiss was soft, questioning rather than demanding. He gave her room to pull away.

She didn't.

Instead, she opened to him, kissing him back with a hunger that matched his own. No performance, no calculation. Just raw need and a yearning so intense it hurt.

Callahan had kissed many women over the years. But none of them had tasted like danger and promise and something he couldn't name but wanted desperately to keep.

It was the first honest exchange they'd ever had.

His hand slid up to sink into her hair. God, he wanted her. Had since New York. Since she'd aimed that knife at his throat with steady hands and confident eyes. Since Athens, when she'd patched his wounds and saved his life. He wanted her every damn time he saw the name Spectre in the broadsheet.

This woman was going to ruin him.

"We shouldn't be doing this," he murmured against her mouth. "We should stop."

But his hands told a different story, one palm sliding up her neck, the other still gripping her hair like he'd die if he let go.

"You're the one with morals, Agent. So why aren't you stopping?"

Callahan groaned. "God, I don't fucking know."

And he didn't. He only knew he couldn't get enough of her taste. That he'd imagined this for longer than he cared to admit. His mouth found her neck, hot and hungry. Her skin was soft beneath his lips. He sucked hard at the tender spot beneath her jaw, deliberately marking her.

She gasped, gripping his arms. Not pushing him away. Pulling him closer. A savage satisfaction coursed through him at the thought that she might want his marks on her. His bites.

Tonight, she was his.

And he was going to hell for this.

He tugged at the sash of her borrowed dressing gown. The silk parted. She was beautifully shaped. Strong and lithe like one of the Imperial Ballet dancers he'd seen in St Petersburg. Small, perfect breasts, flat stomach, long legs.

But he wondered who dared to mar all that perfection. Her pale skin was marked by a constellation of scars, some old, faded to silver. Others newer. One slash was still red and puckered along her ribs.

Questions rose. *Who did this to you? Who am I going to have to kill for it?* But the warning in her eyes silenced them.

Not tonight.

So he pulled back to strip off his smallclothes. When he was finally naked before her, he paused. The sight of her spread out on his bed made his chest ache with want.

"You're staring," she whispered. Something almost vulnerable flickered across her face as she began to draw her knees together.

Callahan caught her thighs before she could close them. "Don't. I like looking at you."

He dragged his hands higher, watching goosebumps rise across her pale skin. She was so damn soft. Made him think of silk sheets in rich men's houses he'd broken into as a lad.

Things he wasn't supposed to touch.

"Just thinking you have the prettiest pussy I've ever seen," he whispered.

There it was – a blush. Not the practised coyness she used when playing a mark. All that fire and fight and careful calculation was gone.

This was something real.

"Filthy words, Agent."

"I save my fancy words for people who matter less." Callahan settled his weight between her thighs, savouring how her breath caught. "Poetry is for toffs and politicians. All I've got is the truth – you're the most infuriating, impossible woman I've ever met. And I can't get you out of my head."

Her smile was soft. Warm. Genuine. "Why would you want to? This is so much more entertaining."

"Which part?" He positioned himself against her, one hand sliding beneath her knee to lift it higher. "The part where we pretend to be civilised?" He pushed inside just enough to make her gasp. "Or the part where I fuck you until we both forget why we're supposed to stay away from each other?"

When he finally thrust deep, she cried out. "Oh, God—"

"That's what I want to hear, little thief."

She was perfect – tight and wet. He pulled back slowly, watching the pleasure ripple across her face before shoving in harder. The headboard slammed against the wall as he found a rhythm. Fuck hotel neighbours. Fuck everyone in Hong Kong. Nothing mattered outside this room.

Callahan gripped her thighs hard enough to bruise, fighting for control. He wanted this to last. Wanted to remember every second of having her. She met him stroke for stroke, her body rising to meet his. Demanding more.

"Harder," she moaned. "Fuck me harder."

Callahan couldn't help but laugh. "Now who's got a filthy mouth?"

She bit his neck in response.

"Jesus," he hissed, hiking her leg higher over his hip, changing the angle. The new position let him sink deeper.

"Yes," she gasped. "There. Right there."

He liked this – watching her. The way her small tits bounced with each thrust. The way she bit her lip when he hit that spot inside her just right. All the little whimpers she tried to hold back, but couldn't. This was the secret language of her ecstasy.

Powerful. That's how it felt seeing Spectre come undone.

Nothing existed but this. Not her enemies. Not his duty. Just skin on skin and the sound of their bodies coming together.

She clutched at him, greedy, her thighs tightening around his waist to pull him deeper. This wasn't a dream or a fantasy he'd conjured during lonely nights. This was real. She was here. Under him. Around him. Taking what she wanted.

Taking him like she was made for him.

But she'd always been a thief, hadn't she?

Callahan slipped a hand between them, seeking the bundle of nerves between her thighs. Circling once. Twice.

With a soft cry, she buried her face in the curve of his neck as she climaxed. His rhythm faltered as his own release crashed through him. His grip on her hip went slack.

For several minutes, they just lay there, tangled and sweaty. His heart slammed against his ribs so hard he wondered if she could feel it.

"Well," Spectre finally murmured, "that was . . ."

"Temporary madness?" he said before he could think better of it.

A minute flinch. "Of course. Simply working through the tension between us. And now it's—"

"Been worked," he finished. "Thoroughly."

The temperature in the room seemed to plummet. He

suppressed a wince. Open mouth, insert foot. A defensive reflex to build the walls back up before she could use it against him. Shagging her didn't change the fact that she was a thief, and he was an agent of the Crown.

"Right."

Spectre pushed him off, gathering the sheet to cover herself.

Callahan opened his mouth, though what he meant to say, he had no earthly idea. What came out instead was a gruff, "Go to sleep. We'll get you on the steamer tomorrow."

She turned away, presenting him with the rigid line of her back. "Goodnight, then."

He listened to her breathing even out as she succumbed to exhaustion. With a sigh, he rolled onto his side and shut his eyes.

The cadence of her breath lulled him to sleep.

Callahan woke to morning light falling across his face.

The other side of the bed was empty, no sign of Spectre beyond the imprint of her head on the pillow and a scrap of paper left behind. He snatched it up and read.

Agent,

The ledger is balanced, the debt repaid in full. Our business is concluded. Enjoy Hong Kong. -S

"Damn it all to hell." Callahan surged upright, ready to tear through the city to find her—

Only to freeze at the sight of the wardrobe doors flung wide open and empty.

Every last stitch of his clothing had vanished. His suitcase was gone.

Fuck.

He lunged for the window, nearly tumbling as the sheet tangled around his legs. Down below, the Praya was already awake for business – trundling handcarts, peddlers and street hawkers bargaining and bartering in a dozen different tongues.

And a familiar figure cut through the tangle with *his* suitcase clutched in a dainty hand.

Callahan sprinted from the room clad in nothing but his bedsheet, caution and dignity be damned. Gasps and scandalised giggles nipped at his heels as he barrelled through the lobby. He scarcely registered a shout over the roar of blood in his ears.

He burst into the street. More shouts followed.

Spectre glanced over her shoulder at the commotion. Her eyes widened before crinkling in amusement, a mocking grin flashing across her face.

Then she hiked up her skirts and dashed off.

That fucking thief.

He took off after her. Early morning light gilded the Praya's cobblestones as he sprinted down the road. The blasted sheet hampered his stride, but he pressed on. He should have tied her to the damn bed.

She reached the waterfront and, to his horror, popped the latch on his case—

And upended every last one of his belongings over the seawall.

Callahan could only watch in slack-jawed disbelief as shirts, trousers, smallclothes, and travel papers rained down to be swallowed by the waves. She had the bloody cheek to throw him a jaunty wave before spinning on a heel and melting into the crowd.

Leaving him alone. A panting, wild-haired madman in a toga.

Nearly naked in front of half of Hong Kong.

Damn her eyes, damn her quick fingers, damn every last infuriating, intoxicating *inch* of her—

A hand landed on his shoulder. "Here now, sir. What's all this about?"

Callahan turned to find an officer of the Hong Kong Police looming over him. The man's gaze flicked down over Callahan's heaving chest, the bedsheet barely preserving his modesty, then back up. Disapproval radiated from him.

"Well?" the officer barked. "Out with it, man. You're making an unholy spectacle of yourself."

Callahan opened his mouth and then shut it with a snap. What could he say? That he was a spy for Her Majesty's government? That he'd just been soundly fucked and robbed by his nemesis? That he'd allowed her to lure him into a dalliance, strip him of every possession and stitch of clothing, and then watched her vanish into the fetid circle of hell from whence she'd come?

No. Better they think him a cuckold than a complete incompetent.

Callahan tamped his rage into something approaching civility. When he trusted himself to speak without cursing, he drew himself up to his full height.

"Just a minor misunderstanding," he gritted, "with my

wife. You know how they can be, yes? Changeable as the weather. My apologies for the disturbance. It won't happen again."

The other man's eyes narrowed. But after a long moment, he shook his head, clearly washing his hands of the whole sordid affair.

"See that it doesn't. I'll let you off with a warning this time, but Hong Kong has standards to uphold. You'd do well to remember that, sir."

"Noted." He snatched for the sheet pooling around his ankles, wrapping it about himself once more. "If you'll excuse me?"

The officer gave him a last hard look but allowed Callahan to limp away with the battered dregs of his pride.

By the time he stumbled into his rooms, he was nearly blind with fury. When he found her again, she would pay for this.

But first, he needed trousers.

🍃 4 🍃

LONDON, 1872

Six months later

The pounding at Callahan's door dragged him from a restless slumber.

He groaned and clamped the pillow over his ears. Hadn't he snarled at his landlord that he was not to be disturbed unless the fires of hell were devouring the building?

The banging continued, an auditory assault worming its way through his whiskey-soaked brain.

"Mr Callahan!" The voice was female and infuriatingly familiar. "I know you're lurking inside like some foul-tempered bear in winter hibernation. Answer the door at once, or I'll break into song!"

Callahan's eyes snapped open, horror mixing with the beginnings of a truly spectacular headache.

Lady Alexandra Grey. Sister of the Earl of Kent. The Almighty, in His twisted sense of humour, had seen fit to conjure the one woman in all the world capable of rousing him from his self-imposed exile.

Because that's what this was. An exile. A chance to lick his wounds after Hong Kong in peace. He'd thought himself safe here, tucked in this shabby corner of Whitechapel. Thought he could while away the hours in a haze of cheap whiskey and regrets until the sting of humiliation faded.

More fool him.

Calling Alexandra a pebble in his boot would be a kindness. The woman was a thorn in his side on her best days, a pox on his entire existence on the bad ones. She possessed the tenacity of a barnacle and the survival instincts of a pheasant. If he ignored her, she'd simply break in.

Callahan hauled himself upright, the room tilting as he gained his feet. A quick glance in the mirror made him grimace. He looked like something that had crawled out of the Thames – rumpled, unshaven, and reeking of last night's indulgences. Good. Let Lady Alexandra see him in all his dissolute glory. Perhaps it would disabuse her of whatever harebrained notion had brought her to darken his doorstep today.

He wrenched open the door with a snarl, fully prepared to unleash a tongue-lashing that would send her scurrying back to Mayfair.

Only to pull up short.

Alexandra beamed up at him. Not a flaxen curl was out of place, her hair swept up into an elegant coiffure. She wore a gown of lavender trimmed with lace, the very picture of a proper young lady. Until one noted the flash of mischief in her expression.

But it was her companion who grabbed his attention. Petite and delicate, she regarded him with wide green eyes and an uncertain smile. Honey-gold curls framed her heart-shaped face.

Something twisted in Callahan's chest, a flicker of unnerving familiarity that vanished as swiftly as it came. Ever since that disastrous night in Hong Kong, he'd taken to seeing shades of Spectre in every woman who crossed his path. It was bloody inconvenient.

Not to mention pathetic.

"Mr Callahan! How lucky to find you at home," Alexandra trilled, pointedly ignoring the black look he speared her with.

"God, what fresh hell have you brought me now?" He sighed. Nothing good ever came from her surprise visits. "Don't tell me, let me guess. You've a corpse to bury, and it wouldn't be sporting to dump the poor bastard in the Thames unmarked? Sorry to disappoint, but Monday is my day for dismemberment."

Alexandra's grin never wavered. "Mr Callahan, while I always applaud preparedness, today's errand is far more benign. A trifling matter requiring your specialised skills."

Callahan's scowl deepened. He knew better than to trust this woman's assessment of any situation as *benign* or a *trifle*. She had a rare talent for understating the gravity of problems, usually right before they careened into catastrophe.

"I'm busy," he said, pushing the door closed. He had no desire to be drawn into whatever mess Alexandra had stumbled into this time. "Don't you have a list of hapless sods to torment? Puppies to kick? Men to set on fire?"

"You wound me. I would never mistreat an innocent puppy, and you're my *favourite* hapless sod to torment. Setting men on fire is debatable, but that's beside the point."

Alexandra slapped her hand against the door to block it. She leaned in, that dangerous smile still firmly in place. "Let us into that flat."

One of these days, he was going to strangle her with her own bustle.

"Go home," he growled.

"Oh, certainly. But before I go, idle curiosity. What's this I heard about a spy, name rhymes with *Ballahan*, being forced to run stark naked through Hong Kong after his clothes were thrown into Victoria Harbour? Would your superiors happen to know anything about that, by any chance?"

Humiliation rushed back – the shock of cold air on bare skin, the gawping stares, the jeers of the crowd. The memory of Spectre's grin as she vanished into the throng with the last of his dignity.

No, he wasn't going to think about that. Not now. Not ever again if he could help it. He'd sworn off women the moment he'd stumbled aboard the steamer back to England.

He was going to become celibate. Or something. Maybe. Thinking about her still got him hard, and that was the most wretched thing of all. His cock was confused. For the last six months, he'd been getting himself off every damn morning with angry climaxes.

Fucking pitiful.

Only a handful of people knew what had happened on the Praya. And none of them were the sort to gossip idly about the Crown's business, not if they valued their lives. Which left only one possibility: Alexandra had bribed a colleague. Or perhaps wheedled the story out of them with her wiles and charms. She collected secrets like a magpie hoarded shiny baubles – the darker and more scandalous, the better.

"How did you hear about that?" he demanded.

He'd spend the rest of the day plotting someone's murder.

Alexandra's grin widened. "You're not my only source of information. Now let us in."

Better to get it over with.

With a long-suffering sigh from the weary depths of his soul, Callahan opened the door just wide enough to admit them. Alexandra made herself at home perched on the edge of his desk while her companion took in his flat with wide eyes. He fought the urge to wince as her gaze settled on the detritus of his current existence – the empty bottles, the scattered papers, the piles of books. He'd been drinking himself stupid since his return from Hong Kong.

"Now then, Mr Callahan," Alexandra said. "What might you tell us about finding missing persons?"

"Depends on who you're looking for, what information you have, and whether I'd get shanked for tracking them."

Missing persons could mean any number of things in his line of work, from runaway heiresses to political dissidents in hiding. The people he was hired to find often didn't want to be found.

Alexandra waved a hand dismissively. "We need to find my friend's sister. Surely you can handle one missing woman without getting knifed."

Callahan's flat stare conveyed precisely what he thought of that assertion. In his experience, women could be just as deadly as men – often more so because people underestimated them. He'd learned that lesson the hard way.

In fucking Hong Kong.

"It always depends on the woman," he said, thinking of green eyes and a blade pressed to his throat.

The blonde spoke up. "Her name is Isabel Dumont. Last seen in Paris before she beat a rather hasty retreat. Presumably across the Channel here to London."

Paris. He should have known. That blasted city brought him nothing but trouble. He decided to hate Paris.

"Have you considered the possibility that your sister isn't interested in being found? Wherever she's landed, chances are she's started a tidy new life free of meddling siblings."

"Pay that no heed," Alexandra interrupted. "He's incapable of grasping familial affection."

Miss Dumont drew in a deep breath. There was a quiet determination in her eyes.

"Do you have siblings, Mr Callahan?" she asked. "Anyone whose safety concerns you?"

Memories flashed of the other lads in Whelan's gang huddled together for warmth on cold nights. Not related by blood, but the closest thing he'd had to family after his mother died.

At his silence, she pressed on. "If you cared for someone, and they disappeared after sending what amounted to a farewell, are you telling me you wouldn't move heaven and earth to ensure their safety?"

Something tightened in Callahan's chest. "Sometimes the trouble isn't that they don't wish to be found. It's the danger in finding them."

He'd told himself that a thousand times over the years, late at night when the whiskey flowed a bit too freely and memories clawed at him. There was a reason he kept to himself these days.

"If my sister is in danger, I want to know," Miss Dumont said quietly. "I won't sit idle imagining her lost or dead without at least trying to learn the truth."

Every instinct screamed at him to walk away, to wash his hands of this. Get back to drinking. But when he noticed the determined set of her jaw and the desperate hope in her eyes, he felt something splinter.

Damn it. Bugger. Shite.

With a sigh, Callahan dragged a hand through his hair. "What does she look like? What's her occupation? What are her interests?"

Miss Dumont hesitated. "Darker hair. More petite. She has something of a knack for languages. And assuming identities."

Callahan's eyebrows rose at that last bit.

The woman cleared her throat, a faint blush creeping up her neck. "And employing legally ambiguous methods for acquiring funds."

Ah. There it was.

"Oh, so she's a criminal. Bit of an important thing to leave out, considering the circumstances. You prepared to face some uncomfortable realities if I turn up proof she's alive and well?"

"I just need to know if my sister is safe. Can you help me or not?"

"I'll ask around. Tap a few sources. Can't make any promises."

For a horrifying moment, Callahan thought she might hug him. He took a hasty step back, just in case, because the last thing he needed was an armful of emotional woman.

He turned his attention to Alexandra. "And you. Try

anything to interfere with my work, and I'll toss you straight into the bog out front."

Alexandra placed a hand over her heart. "No tricks from me. Just compensation for services rendered. Fifty pounds."

Miss Dumont's jaw dropped. He could practically see the calculations running through her head, the realisation that such a sum was far beyond her means.

But right now, she wasn't his mark. The lady was.

His mouth curved into a sardonic smile. "Double it. I have expensive tastes."

It was a lie, of course. Callahan lived simply, and most of his earnings supported the network of street children and informants he'd cultivated over the years. But Alexandra didn't need to know that.

The noblewoman's eyes narrowed as she surveyed his threadbare flat. "The evidence of it appears to be absent. Sixty, you extortionist."

"This flat is a front, and I have mouths to feed. Seventy-five in advance."

"Seventy," Alexandra argued. "Half in advance, and no more arguing."

Well. Seventy *could* fund plenty of whiskey for future brooding, at least.

"Wait." Miss Dumont's voice was tinged with panic. She grabbed Alexandra's arm. "I can't pay that much. Surely we can find someone less expensive—"

"Consider it a gift between friends. It's nothing." Alexandra turned back to Callahan. "Well? Do we have an accord?"

He rolled his eyes. "I suppose so."

Alexandra propelled Miss Dumont towards the door. Finally.

"We'll leave you to it, then," Alexandra called over her shoulder. "Send word if you learn anything."

She paused on the threshold, spearing Callahan with a look that could have stripped paint from walls. "And remember, if you even think of cheating my friend, I'll tell your superiors about Hong Kong."

Callahan's jaw clenched. "I said I'd find her. Now get the hell out of my flat, you wretched harpy."

Then he slammed the door in their faces.

Time for another drink.

5

Callahan wove through the tangle of Whitechapel's night-dark streets.

Light spilled from the taverns and brothels crammed on either side of the narrow lanes. The chill air hung heavy with soot and stale ale – scents as familiar as breathing.

This was the only place he'd ever felt at home.

Faces peered at him from darkened doorways and alleys, looking for any hint of weakness. Any opening to lighten his purse by a few coins.

But he'd grown tall and strong and vicious in this festering corner of the city. Earned his scars in these streets. Bled and bartered for the right to stride through hell's antechamber unmolested. The wolves knew better than to nip at his heels.

The Brimstone loomed ahead, its doors gleaming in the glow of the gas lamps along its façade. This was no ordinary gentleman's club. Here, the aristos brushed shoulders with the dregs of the underworld – secrets to ruin lords if the price was right.

Callahan slipped around the back and rapped sharply on the delivery door. A moment later, the door opened.

"Well, I'll be damned. Look what the cat dragged in."

Leo O'Sullivan propped a shoulder against the doorframe. A grin curved his mouth as he surveyed Callahan, gilded curls tousled around a face that belonged on a Renaissance painting.

"Thought maybe you'd finally found a ditch to die in," O'Sullivan drawled. "Be still my heart. Our lad is home. And here I assumed you'd be too busy these days licking the Home Secretary's boots to cavort with us common folk."

Callahan's history with Nicholas Thorne and O'Sullivan was a battered, bloody thing forged in the cutthroat crucible of the streets. No matter his job or how far he travelled, he'd always end up right back here.

He shouldered past O'Sullivan into the Brimstone's staff quarters. "I need your contacts. Missing person."

O'Sullivan clapped him on the shoulder, steering him deeper into the club. "I'd offer my services without trouble, but Thorne's been asking after you. Might want to brace yourself."

Callahan envisioned the variety of rusty implements Thorne would probably threaten to shove into his most delicate crevices.

"I don't suppose you'd care to give me a hint as to what sort of garrotte I'm walking into?"

"Not a chance. I'm just the messenger."

Sound and scent crashed over him as they traversed the main floor. Expensive perfume twined with cigar smoke. The discordant melody of laughter, clinking glasses, and lilting strains of music from the pianoforte all blended into a wall of noise.

This was the dark, pulsing heartbeat of London's seedy centre. For all that the Brimstone dripped with luxe trappings – gilded mirrors, mahogany panelling, plush velvet upholstery – at its core, it remained a place for society's every desire to run rampant.

O'Sullivan manoeuvred them through the crush until they reached a set of double doors. In there were the true power players. The men who came to the Brimstone to make deals and broker secrets.

"Cheer up, mate," O'Sullivan said. "You look like you're being dragged to your own hanging."

"Feels apt enough. Dealing with Nick always puts me in the mind to pen my will."

"Need a minute to ready your bollocks?"

"I doubt my bollocks are safe either way."

With a chuckle, O'Sullivan swung open the doors. The dim, smoky room was dominated by a massive gaming table occupied by half a dozen aristocratic men in the middle of a game of Vingt-et-un.

And at its centre sat Nick.

Finely made evening clothes hugged his lean frame. Not a dark hair out of place or a wrinkle marring his ruthless perfection. He'd always worn arrogance well. These days, he draped himself in authority and vicious elegance.

A lifetime ago, Nick, Leo, and Callahan had run these streets. There wasn't an alley or rookery they hadn't marked – with brawls and battles and all the dark deeds men did to survive. Thorne had parlayed those early years into a vast network of influence that spanned London. There were few pies in the City that didn't have his fingers stuck well within the filling, whether the baker was aware of it or not.

Nick's black eyes flicked up at Callahan's approach. The familiar weight of the dagger in Callahan's coat was a cold comfort, as was the knowledge that O'Sullivan would step in if things turned ugly.

Probably.

"Ronan. How good of you to drag your mangy arse to my club after all these months."

The assembled players glanced between them with avid interest. Scandal was the only currency that never depreciated.

"Clear the room," Thorne said, setting down his cards. "My old friend and I have matters to discuss."

Grumbling, the lords threw down their cards and slunk out. The heavy doors thudded shut.

Nick leaned forward, forearms braced against the table. "I've heard some interesting news, Ronan. The sort I've taken great pains to stay informed of. Would you care to hazard a guess as to its general theme?"

"You know I'm rubbish at riddles," Callahan said. "Why don't you spit it out and save us both the time?"

"Imagine my surprise," he replied, "when I learned that the estimable Agent Callahan had a visitor yesterday. *Two*, in fact. And one of them happened to be *my fucking wife*."

Oh, shite. Bollocks.

Fuck.

Of course, Thorne knew about Lady Alexandra's visit. The bastard was so entrenched in the intimate workings of Whitechapel that a mouse couldn't shit without him knowing. Someone had probably sent up a signal the instant Lady Alexandra and Miss Dumont set their dainty feet onto the cobblestones. Thorne guarded his estranged bride every time she came into these streets.

From afar, of course.

Callahan braced for impact. "I'm just doing a favour for her friend who had a sister go missing. They hired me to help."

Thorne's hand curled into a fist. "You mean to tell me," he said, each word precise, "that you are now in the employ of my wife. Who hasn't deigned to speak to me in nearly four years. Who wouldn't cross the street to piss on me if I was on fire. She asked for you. *Specifically*. Perfectly content to darken your doorstep and beg favours."

Alexandra was Nick's bruise. He'd lied to her, tricked her into marriage to get his hands on the fortune in her trust, and she'd tossed him over the moment she learned the truth. Still, that money had all been put into making Thorne one of the most powerful men in England.

Callahan held up his hands as if he were trying to gentle a rabid dog. Which honestly wasn't far off. He might dress like a toff, but this was still the same Nick Thorne who fucked and fought his way from the Nichol, honing himself into a walking weapon. He was as feral as they came. Especially for his woman.

"She knows I've got connections that might track the chit down," Callahan said.

"Fascinating." Thorne's expression was cold and flat, and that's when he was most dangerous. "And how *did* my darling wife become intimately familiar with your connections?"

And there was the blade sliding home. Callahan winced, glancing helplessly at O'Sullivan. The other Irishman just shook his head, mouthing, "You're buggered, mate," with entirely too much relish.

Callahan blew out a gusty sigh, dragging a hand through his hair. "I may have availed her of my services a few times. She uses sources from the East End for that bleeding heart crusade she calls journalism. I thought if I made myself available and kept an eye on her, she might be less likely to end up with her throat cut in some piss-reeking alley."

Thorne's eyes narrowed. "How noble of you. And how long have you been *availing* yourself to my wife?"

Another wince. He'd been hoping to avoid this particular confession. But Nick had always had a way of sniffing out a man's sorest spot and digging in his claws.

"Two years now," he admitted. "It started just after some nasty business involving a nobleman. She came round looking for something she could use to pin the bastard's bollocks to the wall."

The other man stared at him for a long moment. Then, in a blink, he launched across the room.

Nick's fist smashed into Callahan's face. He had half an instant to lick the blood off his lip before the other man slammed him into the wall hard enough to make his teeth rattle.

Christ, but he'd forgotten how strong the bastard was.

"Tell me," Thorne snarled, leaning in. "Do you service her in other ways as well?"

"Fuck no," Callahan said. "Christ, Nicky—"

"So instead of turning her away like any sane man would, you decided to become her pet scrounger. Slipping her information that could get her killed ten times over if she barks up the wrong tree."

Well. He wasn't wrong. But reasoning with his wife was also like trying to argue with an obstinate, mouthy rock, so what the hell else was he supposed to do?

"Put the man down, Nick," O'Sullivan said calmly from where he was pouring himself a drink at the sideboard. "You're going to kill him, and I don't want the lads to have to clean his guts out of the carpet."

A thread of sanity in the maelstrom. Callahan dragged in a relieved breath as Thorne's grip loosened.

"I want an answer from him, Leo," Thorne said. "I destroyed my wife for all of *us* to get out from under Whelan's boot. So he owes me a fucking explanation."

Callahan's own temper was clawing at its fraying tether. Not to mention the headache from overindulgence and Nick's fist. "I gave her just enough to keep her from winding up a bloody corpse in your streets. If I turned her out on her arse, she'd only run straight to someone with fewer compunctions about keeping her in one piece."

Something flashed across Thorne's expression at that. His throat worked as he swallowed, gaze cutting briefly to the side. "I assume you've kept our shared past from her."

"Of course I have. I'd like my liver to stay where it is. As far as your lady is concerned, I'm selling my expertise for a few coins to line my pockets."

And it was an excellent way to keep his ear to the ground regarding the nobles and their scandals. Lady Alexandra had a rare knack for collecting secrets that made useful leverage.

A subtle tension eased out of Thorne's shoulders. "Good.

Best we keep the details buried because the second she finds out, she'll decide you're the last man in London worthy of trust. She'll probably fling herself into something even more reckless. Better the devil she knows, I suppose." He took a long breath before releasing Callahan's shirt and stepping away. "The woman she's got you hunting. What's her story?"

"A Frenchie by the name of Isabel Dumont. If she takes after her sister, she's petite with green eyes. Dark blonde hair, according to the description. Has quite the knack for adopting new identities and stealing money. Last seen in Paris before she bolted, best guess puts her here in Town now."

Callahan tried not to consider how that description resembled Spectre in all her troublesome glory. That would be too much of a coincidence. Too much like fate taking the piss at his expense.

No, best to assume this was like every other woman who got herself in a spot of trouble with nowhere to turn except thievery or selling her body.

"You've just described a quarter of the doxies in Whitechapel alone," Thorne said. "Anything else?"

"Probably looking for a bolthole to lay low in until the dust settles."

The other man looked thoughtful. "No doubt she'll need to unload whatever she's nicked. That takes contacts. Specialised ones."

The kind of contacts that populated the Brimstone's smoky back rooms, though neither of them needed to say it aloud.

"You've found people on less," Callahan said.

"Fine. I'll put a discreet word out with my sources. See if anyone's heard whispers of a new woman with quick fingers and a pretty face." He cut a glance at O'Sullivan. "Leo? You've got a few avenues of your own to explore, I'd wager."

O'Sullivan drained the last of his whiskey. "I'll rattle a few cages, see what scurries out."

"Good man." Thorne returned his attention to Callahan, amusement fading. "Don't think for a moment we're finished discussing my wife's little meetings with you."

"You might want to kiss and make up with her before you toss around those proprietary nouns, Nicky."

"Watch your mouth before I put my fist back in it."

"Brave talk for a man too craven to confront his woman. You lied to her, swindled her, and you've yet to apologise. Bend your knee on her doorstep if you want my advice. Grovel. She'll probably cut off your bollocks, but at least you can say you made an effort."

Something dark moved behind Thorne's gaze. "I don't want your advice," he said softly. "You ought to take more care with your words. I've killed men for less."

A chill slithered across Callahan's skin at the eerie calm in the other man's voice. He'd witnessed the brutal efficiency of Thorne's rage too many times to doubt the veracity of that threat.

He forced his face to blankness. "Then I suppose it's a good thing we're such dear, dear friends. Aren't we, Nicky?"

"If one hair on Alex's head comes to harm, I'll carve pieces off you until even the rats can't recognise the scraps, friend or not. Nod if you understand."

There was nothing yielding in Thorne's expression, not

so much as a flicker of doubt. Only the flat certainty of a man who'd spent a lifetime dealing in blood.

"Noted." Callahan knew where the lines were drawn as well as anyone; he wasn't stupid enough to cross them. "Can I go now, or did you want to wave your cock about a bit more first?"

Thorne's smile was vicious. "Oh, you can go. I'm sure you've all manner of important skulduggery to be about. And the next time Alex ends up on your doorstep with a job, I had better hear from you."

Callahan didn't have to be told twice. O'Sullivan fell into step beside him as he walked out the door.

"Aren't you glad you stopped by?" the other man drawled. "An evening with Nick always does wonders for my disposition."

"Fuck off," Callahan snarled.

O'Sullivan ignored that. "If you ask me, this little side venture is the best thing that could've happened. You're going soft. A good chase is just the thing to put blood back in your cheeks."

"When I want your opinion, I'll bash my head against a wall until I'm witless enough to ask for it."

O'Sullivan's laughter chased him down the stairs.

6

The ropes bit into Isabel's wrists. She'd lost track of how many hours she'd been bound to this chair, locked away in some forgotten corner of London's underbelly.

Her captor knew his knots.

She'd made a mistake, letting down her guard enough to sleep. A fatal, foolish error born of desperation and exhaustion and the kind of weariness that came from always looking over her shoulder. One of Favreau's men had broken into her little bolthole and tied her up.

Across the room, the Butcher stood by the door. She'd heard all about this man. That he liked to cut his victims up into small pieces and send them to loved ones over weeks and months. A finger. A toe. A foot. Each gift more gruesome than the last.

By the time he sent the head, his marks went insane.

Favreau loved the Butcher's methods. *D'une manière animale*, he'd said.

In an animal way.

The Butcher looked almost bored as he cleaned his nails with the point of a blade. His eyes, when they sliced towards her, were flat. Empty. Twin grey stones plucked from the bed of a river that had drowned its share of screaming victims.

Shark eyes. Dead and cold and utterly without mercy.

"Comfortable?"

Isabel gave her most dazzling smile. The one that had charmed tidbits of information from tight-lipped marks and made Favreau's face gleam with hunger.

"Exceedingly. I especially appreciate the ropes. You're very good at knotwork."

But not better than her.

She flexed her aching fingers behind her back, testing her bonds. She'd started to slip her wrist out millimetre by painful millimetre.

"I confess," she continued, "I wouldn't have thought playing watchdog was quite your style. Don't you have some fingernails to pull out somewhere? Kneecaps to shatter? Is being a nursemaid truly the best use of your prodigious skills?"

She'd known men like him before. Had the scars to prove it, written on her body in a brutal cipher.

"Keeps my knife sharp," he said. "Been a while since I had a live one to practise on. And you?" His stare raked over her, taking in her coat and men's trousers. "Oh, I've heard *you're* a thing of beauty when you bleed."

Isabel's heart tripped over itself. Cold sweat prickled along her nape and the small of her back.

Cold hands, cold voice, cold blade on her skin, and she wants to scream, but her throat won't make a sound—

She held back a flinch as the Butcher pushed off the wall.

He stalked towards her, each thudding footfall echoing like a drumbeat.

Somewhere, in a distant corner of her mind walled away behind steel and ice, a younger version of her started to cry.

Weakness, Favreau would croon as he fucked her. *It has no place in our line of work, ma petite. Even monsters have standards.*

For an instant, she was back in his bed, his dagger tracing idle patterns over her skin. Leaving the ugly latticework of scars he'd loved to make.

Take it, ma petite. Let the hurt shape you. Better a weapon than a woman, non? Weapons don't flinch when you use them.

Ruthlessly, she shoved the memory down deep. Isabel had learned long ago how to smile through her hurts and wear her scars like armour. All those inconvenient human things that had no room in this life she'd made.

She was a blade, and blades didn't break.

"If you think," she said, holding the Butcher's dead gaze, "that Favreau will let you take liberties with his property before he's done with it, you're more of an idiot than you look. And that, quite frankly, strains the bounds of credulity."

It was dangerous to play with a man like this. A fine line between restraint and provocation. Too little, and she'd never get what she needed from him. Too much, and, well . . . men like the Butcher seldom required more than the flimsiest excuse to indulge their baser instincts. She was not afraid of pain, had made an art of smiling through torments that would crush another woman.

But she did so hate wasting her time.

His face darkened, fingers tightening around his knife. "What makes you think he's got any use for you now? You're damaged goods. Maybe he's planning to put you down. Cut his losses now that you've gone and grown a conscience."

The cold certainty of it knifed between her ribs. Because there was truth in the Butcher's words.

She'd betrayed Favreau. Betrayed the Syndicate. Committed the unforgivable sin of killing his men, escaping Hong Kong, and sending him on a chase for six months. Now, the devil was on his way to collect his due.

She'd be damned if she made it easy for him.

Isabel pushed her wrist out of the rope by another degree.

"Oh, I'm certain Favreau would love nothing more than to put me in the ground at the right moment." She leaned forward as much as her bonds allowed until the blade kissed her cheek. "But since you bound me to this chair in one piece, I assume he wants me breathing."

"Breathing don't mean I can't make you sing," he said softly. Dangerously. "Reckon the famous Spectre screams just as pretty as any dumb pigeon when she's getting bits sliced off."

A rough scrape of his thumbnail along her jaw. She breathed through her nose, willing herself still. She'd endured worse at the hands of better.

She pushed the rope down her wrist again, holding back a flinch as it rubbed her raw skin.

"You're right," she mused. "It has been a while since I had a proper scream. Better men than you have tried and failed to inspire one. Although not for lack of trying."

He moved suddenly, the edge of his weapon pressing to her jugular. Old terror rose. The helpless animal part of her remembered every hand pinning her down. Every violation written on her skin.

"Shut it," the Butcher hissed. "Keep that tongue behind your teeth, girl, or I'll carve it out and feed it to you."

Isabel's smile never wavered. "You're welcome to try if you're that eager for a gelding."

The Butcher went still. She tracked the ripple of rage, the clenching of that brutal jaw – a fracture in his control. And with it came a warning of a hundred other women he'd killed. The ones who'd screamed and begged. The ones who hadn't been able to keep their skin intact.

Isabel had no intention of joining their ranks.

"Go ahead," she purred, tilting her head to expose her throat. "Slice me open and let me bleed. See how loudly you squeal when Favreau puts you on your knees for it."

Isabel's heart slammed against her ribs. Silence stretched. And then—

The bright, blooming sting of parting flesh. But she never flinched. Never shied from the blade, even when a thin trail of blood slid down her chest.

She'd die before she'd scream for him. The pain at her wrist as she wrenched the rope down the heel of her hand grounded her. Blood pooled in her palm.

"Women who don't know when to shut their mouths get cut," he said, almost gently. The flat of his blade scraped her skin, smearing blood in its wake. "Final warning, dove. Keep that" – a flick of steel towards her lips – "quiet, or I'll take my chances with Favreau's temper."

"I don't think so, *monsieur*. Because you're not just a

killer; you're a dog. And dogs don't bite the hand holding their lead."

Then she burst from her bonds in an explosion of movement. She threw herself at him, her hands clamped to either side of his head.

And she sank her thumbs into his eyes.

The Butcher bellowed, trying to fling her off. His blade clattered to the floor as he reared back.

It wasn't enough. She smashed her forehead into his nose, satisfaction surging through her veins at the sharp crunch.

Ah, there it was. *His* turn to scream. And it was every bit as pathetic as she'd expected from a man who only ever took lives. Who thought that gave him power.

"Where are your threats now?" She dug her fingers harder into his eye sockets. "Where's that swagger?"

Isabel drove her knee into his groin. The Butcher crashed to the floor, and she followed him down. Merciless. Her thighs clamped around his neck as she cut off his air. Squeezed and *squeezed* until he scrabbled weakly at her hips, her waist. Trying to pry her loose as she choked the life from him.

"I've made men more dangerous than you piss themselves and beg for their mums," she hissed. "Men who can take pain, who don't flinch easy. And do you know what I did to them?"

He made a wheezing sound, and she tightened her thighs around his neck.

"I broke them. Took them apart an inch at a time until there was nothing left. But you? You aren't worth the effort it would take to make you scream."

Then she rolled off him, grabbed his knife, and slit his throat.

He convulsed once, twice. A long, rattling exhalation. Somewhere nearby, a rusted pipe dripped. One. Two. Three.

And then he went limp.

She knelt over him, chest heaving. The din of her pulse crashed through her skull. From some distant corner of her mind, she could feel the girl reeling back, hands pressed to her mouth.

The crack of a hand across a tear-streaked face, pale eyes like sleet—

Take it, ma petite, fold it up and tuck it away.

Isabel pushed to her feet. She made herself look at the corpse sprawled before her, the ruin of his throat. Her handiwork.

Sloppy, Favreau would've said, clucking his tongue. *Too much wasted energy. Killing is a precise art. Like surgery.*

Her torn wrists screamed as she flexed them, but the pain grounded her. Sharpened her resolve. She'd leave her kill for Favreau to find – a message from the servant to her master.

So she kicked the Butcher's limp hand out of her path and left the flat.

7

R onan was having a shite day.
    It was the kind of day that made a man contemplate
hurling himself into the Thames. But that would deprive him
of the vindictive pleasure of imagining all the creative ways
he could murder the two women at his front door.

Lady Alexandra Grey and Miss Emma Dumont were
the very last creatures he wanted invading his domain.
Especially when he was sleep-deprived.

"I said I had a lead," he growled. "I didn't ask you to
come."

O'Sullivan had arrived the night before with news, and
Callahan had dashed off a note to Alexandra like a proper
gent getting paid seventy quid.

Damned fool that he was, he'd thought it might buy him
a bit of peace. Should've known her ladyship would use any
excuse to come barrelling through his door.

The woman in question breezed past him into the flat.
"Oh, Mr Callahan. Charming as always. As you'll recall, I
paid you a small fortune in advance. Therefore, I have every

right to ensure it will be put to good use. Now, what's this about a lead? Out with it."

Callahan smothered the urge to throw her out and focused on Miss Dumont. "A female matching your sister's description was seen leaving a property near Charing Cross."

"Well, then. What are we waiting for?"

He blinked. "*We?*" he repeated. "I'm not taking you."

Images of Nick Thorne's retribution danced through his mind. That ruthless bastard would spend an afternoon happily sifting through Callahan's guts if anything happened to his estranged wife. And Callahan was rather fond of all his bits remaining attached and in working order, ta very much.

"Don't be obstinate," Alexandra said. "I paid for results, and I mean to see them."

With a noise of exasperation, he snatched up his greatcoat.

"Christ alive," he muttered. "Fine, come to some rat-infested rookery. But this is against my better judgment."

He nudged his unwanted companions towards the door, trying not to think too hard about all the ways this was sure to end in misery, maiming, and a long, messy demise.

The journey to Charing Cross passed in blessed silence, for which Callahan was profoundly grateful. Sparring with Alexandra always left him feeling like he'd gone three rounds with a vicious alley cat.

The building Leo told him about was unremarkable. Just another red brick structure huddled among its equally dilapidated fellows. Inside, the air was thick with the stench of mould.

Callahan led the way up the rickety staircase. They

reached the landing, and he paused before a door already ajar.

He eased it open.

Darkness greeted them, barely penetrated by the wan light from a narrow window at the end of the cramped corridor.

Miss Dumont lifted a hand to her nose. "*Sang de Dieu.* What is that foul odour?"

Callahan didn't bother with a response.

Death had a smell. A taste.

He withdrew a box of lucifers and a candle from his greatcoat. The small flame illuminated a scene that would have given even the most hardened criminal pause.

Blood. So much blood – spread beneath the body of a man sprawled across the floor. His throat had been slashed.

A gasp from behind him reminded Callahan that he wasn't alone. Miss Dumont swayed on her feet, her face pale. He grasped her shoulders to steady her.

"Take her out of here," he said to Alexandra. "I need to search the premises."

Callahan shut the door on their retreating backs and turned back to the body, jaw tight.

The cut was clean and precise – one swift slash from ear to ear. Poor bastard had bled out in moments. This was the kind of skill that spoke of practice. Of cold efficiency. He'd trussed up enough of his own over the years to recognise a professional's handiwork when he saw it.

Callahan took a look around the flat but only found a rope discarded on the floor. He glanced at the body with renewed interest. Well, well. Seems the gent here tried his hand at tying up the elusive Miss Dumont and found his throat slit for the trouble. Other than that bit of evidence, she'd left nothing behind. Not a scrap of paper. Not a piece of clothing.

Just the brutalised body lying there like a letter written in blood.

By the time he exited the flat, Miss Dumont seemed to have collected herself somewhat, though her eyes were still glassy with shock. She gripped Lady Alexandra's hand.

"No sign of anyone else," he said. "But if your sister slit that man's throat, she aimed to send a message. Precise work. He bled out fast. Can't have been more than an hour or two. Rigor hasn't fully set in."

Callahan watched as understanding dawned on Alexandra's face, her eyes widening.

"A message?" she repeated. "What makes you think—"

"She wanted this death witnessed. Found. Whoever your sister's got herself tangled up with, she just declared war on them."

Emma met his gaze. "The Syndicate. Isabel betrayed them."

Callahan went very still. In his line of work, there were certain organisations, certain nasties you simply Did Not Fuck With. And the Syndicate? They weren't just on that list. They were at the top.

"Come with me," he said. "Now."

Less than a half hour later, Callahan ushered the women up the narrow stairs and into his rooms.

"A trifling fucking problem, that's what you told me this was," he growled, rounding on them. He pointed an accusing finger at Alexandra. "The Syndicate is *not* a trifling problem."

"Well, how was I to know?" Alexandra asked, defensive.

"I'm not the one gallivanting about with international spies. You ought to tell me these things."

Callahan ignored her, turning his glare on Emma. "*You*. Tell me everything you know about your sister's involvement, or I am tossing you out on your arses this instant. I will throw every pound of that money right after you unless you start talking. How did your sister get involved with an international crime ring?"

Emma's breath quickened as she struggled to find the words. "I don't – I don't know. After our mother died, she started frequenting the gaming hells and private clubs where aristocrats gathered. We're the bastard daughters of a duke, and she . . . wanted to settle scores. Ruin them. Take their money."

Callahan said nothing, merely gesturing for her to continue. After a weighty pause, Emma took a shaky breath and pressed on.

"I didn't know the details of what she got herself into. It was just last night I heard mention of the Syndicate from an ally of Isabel's."

Callahan scrubbed a hand over his stubbled jaw, his mind racing. "If your sister gathered information on aristocrats, she would have attracted the Syndicate's notice. They doubtless sought to recruit her skills." He gave a dry, humourless laugh. "Fuck me, this venture keeps getting better and better."

"Isabel did what she needed to survive when no one else gave a damn whether we lived or died," she snapped. Her eyes flashed with anger. "Our mother was sick, and we had no money. You've no right to judge either of us, Mr Callahan."

Callahan's mind drifted back to his youth, to the dark alleys of Whitechapel where he'd learned to pick pockets and break into homes. He'd done what he needed to survive, just as Isabel had.

"Go on, Mr Callahan." Alexandra smoothed her skirts over her knee. "Tell us about the Syndicate. What is it?"

"An underground network that originated in Russia. They started smuggling opium. But their reach has expanded, and they've branched out." He crossed his arms over his chest. "They've assassinated diplomats. Rival gang lords. Meddled in international affairs. I told you both that you might not want to hear the uncomfortable truths about who your sister aligned herself with."

He'd seen what the Syndicate did to traitors. Bloated bodies fished from the Thames, mutilated corpses left as warnings in dark alleys. Body parts delivered to enemies in boxes. Nasty work, even for a man of his experience.

"If she were dead," he continued, "the Syndicate wouldn't have left her to rot in the shadows. She would have been displayed as a warning to other traitors. You'd know about it."

He saw Emma flinch. "Will you help her, Mr Callahan? If you find Isabel?"

Callahan kept his expression neutral. Necessity had taught him to guard his tells and shutter stray emotions. He was treading a fine line with the Office right now after his cock up in Hong Kong. Sticking his neck out for a Syndicate thief might be more trouble than she was worth. Still, if she could be squeezed for information . . .

"That depends," he said with ruthless practicality, "on whether she proves useful."

He didn't have the privilege of making promises he couldn't keep.

Callahan crossed to the battered desk shoved into one corner. He rifled through the drifts of papers and empty ink bottles until he found a small notebook beneath the detritus.

"Got a mate or two still in Paris. Ones who might've caught wind of your sister's exploits before she hopped the Channel. I'll send them a wire, tell them it's urgent. I want you to tell me what you know about her. Background, old haunts, *everything*. Leave nothing out."

"All right. Thank you."

"Thank me if I find the chit with her head still attached."

❧ 8 ❧

The abandoned distillery was dark. Shafts of moonlight knifed through gaps in the decrepit roof, just enough to illuminate any assailant trying to sneak up on Isabel. She crouched in the deepest corner and fought not to fall asleep. Each sound scraped along her nerves. She'd spent too many nights awake. Not enough real rest.

Just a few days more. Then she'd board the steamer bound for Le Havre at first light and put the stinking cesspool of London at her back. Hopefully, crossing the Channel would throw Favreau off her scent. Then she'd—

A scuff sounded past the shaft of light.

Isabel's heart seized behind her ribs. She pressed deeper into the blackness, straining to listen past the thunder of her pulse.

There it was again – a careful footfall.

Isabel eased her weapon out of its sheath. Her gaze raked the darkness as a large silhouette detached from the shadows.

She launched herself at the figure, aiming straight for the bastard's jugular.

He twisted at the last second, but her blade bit deep into his shoulder.

His bellow echoed through the distillery. She ripped her dagger free, but before she could strike again, his arm clamped around her middle. He yanked. Spun her. The air punched out of her lungs as her back collided with a wall of hard muscle. Then the bastard hauled her off her feet.

"Bloody, buggering fuck, Trouble. Must you lead with the stabbing?"

The familiar timbre crashed through her wild panic. She knew that voice, whiskey-rough and insolent. Had heard it in her dreams.

"Agent Callahan," she said. She'd never admit aloud that she was glad to see him. She'd missed that voice. Missed *him*. "Fancy meeting you here. I'd say it was a pleasure, but . . ." She writhed in his crushing embrace, an exaggerated wriggle that pressed her backside to his front. "It's rather difficult to exchange pleasantries while being so aggressively manhandled."

He grunted and twisted his hips aside. "Stop rubbing your arse against my cock," he snapped.

"Just testing whether it's possible for a man who just got stabbed to still get hard. And look, the answer is yes."

"Doesn't erase the fact that you just tried to take off my damn arm."

Good. If he was angry, he was distracted. Anger made men stupid and more prone to mistakes. And she would once again have to wiggle out of Ronan Callahan's clutches.

"You snuck up on an armed woman in an abandoned distillery in the dead of night. What in the devil did you expect? Squeals of maidenly delight? Swoons into your manly arms?"

"I expected you to be holed up in the finest suite Claridge's had to offer, not dressed in the clothes of a filthy little street lad and scuttling through the arse-end of Whitechapel like a sewer rat."

It shouldn't have mattered what this man thought of her. She'd forfeited the right to care about anything so fragile as pride the day she'd first let Favreau press a priceless necklace into her palm and a possessive kiss to the inside of her wrist. When she'd weighed her precious scruples against her family's needs and made her choice.

And damned herself in the choosing.

"Sorry to disappoint. I'm afraid I'm all out of feather beds and champagne at the moment." With a sharp twist of her hips, Isabel broke his hold and danced out of reach. "I know my hospitality leaves something to be desired at present, but needs must."

Callahan glared at her, his hand clamped over the bloodstain spreading across his shoulder. Even in the dark – dishevelled and radiating murderous intent – he was so damn beautiful it hurt to look at him.

Callahan's icy gaze raked over her. Isabel tried not to fidget. She was aware she hardly looked her best these days. There were dark circles under her eyes, a gauntness to her cheeks. She'd lost weight. Each mark was a tally of the slow, brutal war she'd been fighting. The cost of betrayal was etched across her body.

The woman he'd fucked in a Hong Kong hotel room had eroded piece by piece until only this remained – a cornered, feral thing.

"Christ, Trouble. You look like a stiff breeze would knock you arse over teakettle. When's the last time you had a proper meal and not just the memory of one?"

"Why, Agent, I didn't realise you cared. Here I thought you were only interested in collecting the bounty on my head and hauling me in front of a magistrate."

"Among other things." His eyes narrowed. "Tell me. When you scarpered off with my clothes in Hong Kong and left me bare-arsed in the street . . . is that how you treat all the men foolish enough to fall into your bed?"

She couldn't exactly tell him that it had killed her to leave him like that in Hong Kong. That playing the part of the confidence artist withered a small corner of her heart.

But so had hearing his words.

Temporary madness. That's what he'd called fucking her. As if they hadn't been circling each other like two predators in the woods for years.

But she donned that mask again because this man was her walking ruin.

"Oh no. You're special," she said, winking. "I've never taken my pleasure without an escape route planned."

Callahan didn't smile. His hand drifted down to toy with the blade sheathed at his hip – an unsubtle warning. "Careful," he said softly. "This time, I won't hesitate to use it."

"What happened to that famous English chivalry?"

"Must have left it in my other coat. The one you chucked in Victoria Harbour."

She shrugged. "Then I suppose we're even. And you've long since ruined any chance at getting me on my back again."

The way his pupils flared said he remembered every filthy,

glorious second of having her naked and spread beneath him.

"Don't look at me like that," she snapped, a flush crawling up her neck.

"Like what?" Now, he gave her that grin that made her heart give a little stutter. "Like I've already had you? The memory of you coming on my cock is seared into my brain, Trouble."

He was lethal. The way he wielded seduction like a weapon.

"We both know you're not here for a tumble," she said.

"Alas, business before pleasure. I'm on the hunt for a person of interest. An Isabel Dumont, to be precise. Dark blonde hair, green-eyed, and petite. Looks and behaviour resemble an internationally notorious thief of my intimate acquaintance, come to think."

Non. Non. Non. Bon Dieu.

Hearing her real name on Ronan Callahan's lips sent a jolt of dread through her. Because of course, he was tenacious enough to discover her identity. Of course, he couldn't leave it alone. *Of bloody course*, he'd show up again at exactly the wrong moment when she needed to run as far and fast as possible.

This was why she'd left him in Hong Kong. Caring was an extravagance she couldn't afford. Not anymore.

Breathe. Shove up the walls.

Pretend like you always do.

She arched a brow and kept her tone flat. Bored. "And what has this Miss Dumont done to inspire Her Majesty's hound to chase her through London?"

His eye twitched at the words *Her Majesty's hound*.

"Got herself into a spot of bother, I reckon. The kind that ends with corpses rotting in unsavoury corners and a sister worried she'll be collecting body parts from the Thames. One Emma Dumont paid for any news of her wayward sister's whereabouts. Poor chit's near sick with dread over it."

Isabel swallowed. She hadn't spoken to her sister in nearly a year. A few months ago, she'd written a terse letter promising she was still alive and sent it through channels she prayed were still secure.

But what choice did she have? This was the only way to keep Emma safe. Isabel had only ever managed to keep two secrets from Louis Favreau. The first was her meetings with Callahan.

The second was the existence of her sister.

"How much is peace of mind going for on the open market these days?" she asked, as if she didn't care about the answer.

"Seventy pounds. Enough to keep my whiskey cabinet well-stocked for the foreseeable future." He grimaced. "And I'll be adding a stabbing surcharge."

Seventy pounds? Sainte Mère de Dieu.

Where in damnation had Emma beggared herself to scrape together that princely sum? With the squalor they'd been abandoned to after their father's desertion, they'd survived on the funds Isabel obtained after Favreau took the lion's share of her heists. Last she heard, Emma found work dressing and tutoring courtesans and actresses. And now she was tossing a small fortune at Ronan Callahan's feet?

Damn. Bloody hell. *Nom de Dieu de putain de bordel—*

"How valiant of you," she gritted out. "Well, I hope you

track down this wayward woman, Agent. If she's half as hardened a criminal as you seem to think, she'll either slit your throat in your sleep, or you'll be sending her to the gallows. What a treat for her sister, wouldn't you say? Now, if you'll excuse me, I think I *will* go see what's on offer at Claridge's. Have a nice bath, let a bottle of claret breathe on the sideboard—"

He prowled towards her. She'd seen that coiled menace in him before. In Hong Kong, right before he'd pinned her to the hotel sheets and fucked her until all she could do was pray he never stopped.

Now, all that barely restrained brutality was focused on her again. This was the hunter who'd tracked her halfway around the globe. This was the blade at her throat.

"Drop the act, Isabel. Your sister's in knots over you." His voice lowered, turning soft. "That man you left to rot in Charing Cross. He was Syndicate muscle? One of Favreau's dogs?"

In a blink, she was back in that abandoned flat, with her thumbs in the Butcher's eye sockets. His blood had been warm when she'd slit his throat.

Monster. Villain. She was those things.

Her fingers skimmed over the raw ligature marks ringing her wrists. Trophies from the Butcher's tender care.

"What I do and who I kill is my business," she said. "The minute details of my sordid life story aren't yours to collect for my sister or as some contest with the men who want me dead. You've found me. Tell Emma I'm fine, and offer her condolences that you stumbled across my little mess. Apologies for you finding the corpse I left. It wasn't meant for you."

His expression went cold. "And no messages of devotion to relay, I take it? You could send a note. She's employed as a maid by the Earl of Kent. I imagine you're familiar enough with Pall Mall to know where he lives."

She couldn't believe Emma was in *England*, of all places—their father's homeland—and playing servant to their father's peers. What had put such a foolish notion in her her head?

Isabel shook off the thought and snapped her attention back to Callahan. "I don't know why you care. I've disappointed everyone foolish enough to rely on me since approximately 1850, and I'd hate to break such a winning streak."

He stepped closer. Too close, his chest brushing hers. So warm and tempting.

"Why is the Syndicate hunting you, Isabel?" he asked softly.

Please, please stop. They'll use you to get to me. They'll use anyone.

Better he believe her to be an indifferent, callous bitch. Then maybe he'd leave her alone.

"I'm sure you'd love to slap me in manacles and ask your questions in some ghastly interrogation room. But do us both a favour and stop chasing it. And stop chasing *me*."

Please.

But he reached up and skimmed his knuckles over her cheek. "Hong Kong. I'd wager it's the last time you managed a decent night's sleep, isn't it? Secure in my bed."

The question knifed through her. She had no right to safety. To rest. Her life was calculated in debts, paid for in blood and sweat and pieces of her soul, and there'd be no respite until those scales finally balanced.

Or they buried her.

"Go home, Agent," she said quietly, resisting the urge to lean into his touch. "Collect your fee. Give Emma my love. And pray that this is the last time we cross paths." Her eyes drifted to his shoulder. "You'd best tend to that before you bleed out. I promise you, I'm not worth dying over."

She shoved him away. In the breathless moment before he recovered, she turned and fled.

9

Isabel pulled her cloak tighter against the damp as she walked.

After so many years, London was almost as familiar as Paris. She knew who had warm beds and who didn't ask questions. The taprooms that opened their doors to her and the shopkeepers who'd accept a few coins to hold their tongues. The madam in Mayfair who granted Isabel a bed when she needed rest. But none of that mattered now because Favreau would have men watching all those places.

She needed to board a steamer.

Get to Emma. Then the docks. Then anywhere but here.

Her boots clicked against the wet cobblestones as she strode towards Pall Mall. The houses loomed ahead, their windows glowing warm with lamplight. For days, she'd lurked in these shadows, observing her sister from a distance and protecting the only family she had left.

A scream sliced through the night – the kind she recognised. *Terror.*

Isabel froze. Then a desperate, choked shout came that sent ice through her veins.

She knew that voice.

Emma.

Bolting forward, she reached for the knife strapped to her thigh. She rounded the corner in time to see a man's fist connect with Emma's jaw. Her sister crumpled against the wall, blood staining her pale hair.

Isabel recognised the attacker's stance immediately – shoulders squared, weight forward on the balls of his feet. Syndicate training.

Isabel didn't think. There wasn't time for thinking.

She launched herself at the man. Her blade slashed once, twice, biting deep into his side. He was stronger, but Isabel was faster. Favreau had taught her how to use an opponent's size against them. How to find the vulnerable spots. How to end a fight before it truly began.

She feinted left, then slipped behind the man as he lunged. Her arm snaked around his throat.

"You picked the wrong woman's sister," she hissed in his ear.

Her knife opened his throat in a ruthless slash. Isabel released him, letting the body fall with a dull thud. It was a faster death than he deserved, but Isabel couldn't draw it out, not with Emma on the ground and barely conscious.

She rushed to her sister, kneeling.

"Isabel," Emma's voice was a thin rasp.

She hesitated, torn between staying and fleeing. But she knew what would happen if she remained – questions she couldn't answer, dangers she'd bring to Emma's door.

Footsteps pounded against the cobblestones. A man's voice shouted Emma's name – the Earl of Kent. Isabel had to trust that he would take her home.

Go. Go now.

With one last look at her sister, Isabel turned and sprinted out of the alley.

Isabel struck a lucifer and lit the cigarette pinched between her lips. Smoke curled upwards as she leaned against a tree, focusing on the townhouse across the street.

Three days since Emma nearly died in that alley. Three nights of rain and cold and hunger. The earl had whisked her sister away to his brother's fancy townhouse in Belgravia, and Isabel hadn't moved from this spot since.

Her muscles ached. Her stomach growled. She ignored both.

She'd missed the damn steamer to France and her chance to put London at her back. Leaving Emma was out of the question.

Favreau was a patient man. Now that he knew Isabel's weakness, her pressure point, he'd never stop hunting Emma. He'd use her sister to force Isabel's hand.

Leaving wasn't an option anymore. Not until she figured out a way to keep her sister safe.

A flicker of movement in the townhouse's window caught her attention – a man's tall, broad-shouldered silhouette. The Earl of Kent. He was handsome, she supposed. Earlier, when she'd spied on them, she'd noticed a curious softening in his face when his gaze landed on Emma. It thawed some of that aristocratic reserve.

She didn't like that look.

It was the same expression the Duke of Southampton gave when he'd pulled *Maman* into his lap. Isabel had been little more than a girl then, peeking around the doorframe of their lavish Parisian flat.

But then, years later, when disease had ravaged Marie Dumont's body and Southampton's ardour had cooled, his expression changed. There had only been disdain. He'd tossed a fistful of francs at *Maman's* feet before tossing them out of their flat.

Then he left his bastard daughters to rot in the streets.

A twig snapped. Isabel whirled, knife already in hand.

"Easy, Trouble. It's just me."

Callahan emerged from the shadows. He'd traded his usual greatcoat for a jacket, the fabric straining across the breadth of his shoulders. The light from the gas lamps caught his face, all hard shadows and sharp edges. He looked like the kind of man that mothers warned their daughters about. A rogue who'd fuck a woman and leave her heart bleeding.

Isabel's fingers fell away from her blade. But she kept her weight balanced on the balls of her feet, battle-ready. Just in case.

"Agent." She took a deep drag on her cigarette. "I should've known you'd be stalking me."

"I'm always up for a bit of recreational stalking. Someone's got to keep an eye on you. Wouldn't want that devious mind getting into mischief without proper supervision."

"Don't you have actual crimes to solve? Monarchs to defend from the terrifying prospect of stolen unmentionables? Murderers to catch?"

"Like you haven't been leaving behind corpses, Dumont."

"Don't know what you're talking about," she said with a shrug.

"Of course you don't. But I go where the job takes me. And lately, that seems to be whichever festering rathole you've tucked yourself away in. If I had a shilling for every time I've had to track your scrawny arse, I'd be a wealthy man."

"If you had a shilling for every time I've been tempted to stab you, you'd be the richest corpse in London."

Snorting, he plucked the cigarette from her fingers. She watched as he raised it to his mouth, his lips fitting over the space where hers had been a moment before. Something fluttered low in her belly at that indirect caress.

"Always a delight conversing with you," Callahan drawled around a mouthful of smoke. "Like pulling teeth, only less pleasant."

"I do try." She snagged the cigarette back, ignoring the way her fingers brushed his in the exchange. "So tell me, how did you track me to Belgravia? Bribing street urchins? Shrubbery skulking? Carrier pigeons?"

"Nothing so cunning. Didn't take a genius to deduce you'd be keeping watch over your sister after that unpleasantness in the mews. Had a few informants do a bit of nosing about, and *voilà*." He swept out an arm. "One thief located."

Isabel grunted. "How's your shoulder?"

"Still attached despite your best efforts."

She chuckled. "I've many skills, Agent, but gentleness remains elusive."

He held her gaze, their history stretching between them. Suddenly, she was back in that Hong Kong hotel room. His damp skin against hers. Their limbs tangled. Those rough hands learning every inch of her as if she might disappear.

I like looking at you.

And she liked him looking at her. So hungry. So warm and alive. He'd made her feel beautiful, scars and all.

And she rewarded him by doing what she always did: taking what he had and leaving chaos in her wake.

"So," she said, looking away. "What do you want with me? Or did you simply miss my voice?"

"You have me all figured out, don't you? Yes, I pine without that insolent mouth to enliven my days. Must be why I'm out here freezing my arse off watching you sulk in the shadows. Brooding doesn't suit you, you know."

"Oh, and I suppose you're the expert on what does suit me?"

"I've watched you for years, haven't I? Seen you work ballrooms and gambling dens where men can't take their eyes off you. And now I've had the dubious pleasure of cleaning up your messes. Seems everywhere you go these days, a man ends up with his throat slit."

"I've denied any involvement."

"Oh, you deny it," he said, a little mocking. "Tell me hypothetically, then. What other deadly talents have you been hiding up those sleeves?"

She glared up at him, refusing to step back. Refusing to give ground. "What if I told you I hypothetically strangled one of those men with my thighs first?"

That shut him up. His mouth fell open, and for once, the great Ronan Callahan had nothing to say. Ten seconds ticked by while his gaze dropped to her legs, encased in the tight trousers she'd stolen to pass as a lad in the dark.

She felt it then – that liquid heat pooling low in her belly. The one that only ever appeared when he looked at her like this. Like he wanted to consume her.

"Picturing it, Agent?" She smiled.

He let out a slow breath. "Thinking there are worse ways to die."

The air between them crackled. Isabel almost reached for him, almost gave in to the urge to grab his shirt and pull him into the shadows. Almost.

"I'll keep that in mind," she said. "I only kill when I have to. If I hadn't acted, you'd be scraping what was left of my sister off those cobblestones." She nodded toward the townhouse, needing to change the subject before she did something stupid. Like touch him. "What do you know about the people keeping Emma?"

Callahan shrugged. "Decent, as far as the Quality goes. The earl is sharp. Keeps his hand in at Parliament, from what I've gathered. His brother's got charm enough to coax a nun from her habit, but he's not soft. And their sister—" A hint of what might have been genuine amusement lurked at the corners of his mouth. "She's got a mind like a razor. Fancies herself a journalist, much to her brothers' despair. Goes swanning about in the East End interviewing pickpockets and scriveners and God knows what else. She's the one who put up your finder's fee."

She thought of the earl's expression when he looked at Emma earlier. "Kent and Emma. Are they lovers?"

"His sister's maid, as far as I know. But I can't say I make a habit of poking my nose into an aristo's romantic entanglements. Too much drama, too little profit."

"Spoken like a true pragmatist."

Another beat of silence, another drag on her cigarette. The slow curl of smoke in her lungs fortified her.

"Is there a reason you're worried his intentions towards your sister might be less than honourable?" Callahan asked.

Of course, he'd caught that. He might look like a pretty ornament, but Callahan's mind proved inconveniently sharp.

"Pretty promises from a nobleman's lips always turn to ash," she said shortly. The last thing she wanted was to discuss her background with him. "But my larger concern is the state of his brother's defences. That terrace might as well be an invitation for any halfway competent thief, and the servant's entrance is a jest."

"You've an eye for weakness."

"Of course I do." She gave a bitter chuckle, dropping her cigarette to the ground. She crushed it with a boot. "Favreau trained me to find the cracks in every fortress."

The memories of his brutal training never faded with time. She still recalled the punishments. The realisation that he liked the way blood looked on her skin.

Like paint on a canvas. Do try not to fail so often that I'm forced to sully it.

Callahan went quiet, considering. When he finally spoke, the words were careful. Measured. "I have a proposition for you. A job." At her sharp look, he explained, "Under my supervision, you could put those skills to work. What was it you called it? A government purse and a license to kill to fund your frivolities?"

A sharp pain spread through her. Was that what he wanted? To have the Spectre under the government's boot?

"A generous offer," she said. Her tone conveyed precisely

how much she detested it. "And you're proposing this out of the goodness of your heart, I'm sure."

"I'm proposing it because we both know that Syndicate bastard in the mews won't be Favreau's first attempt at using your sister as leverage. He'll twist the knife in any soft place he can find."

"Is that it, then? You'd make me your collared hound to point at whichever target the Crown deems a threat?" She stepped closer, right up into his space. "Or is it because you're hoping to scratch that itch you've been nursing since Hong Kong?"

He went very still. "You should be careful taunting sharks, little thief."

"Don't pretend you're the only shark here, Agent." She traced a fingertip over his chest, and his heartbeat spiked beneath her touch. "How many nights have you lain awake aching for the chance to have me? Bending me over and putting me on my knees as much as you want." She brushed her lips over his jaw. "You want me to be your *good girl*? Or do you just want to fuck me again without worrying I'll pick your pockets after?"

When he spoke, his voice was low and rough. "You have an inflated sense of your own appeal. And a filthy mouth."

"That wasn't a denial. I'll tell you what I think of your offer – I've had enough of men claiming their chains are for my protection. Men who'd put me on my back and call it salvation, who'd shove a knife in my fist and tell me it's a mercy. Your precious Home Office is no different from the Syndicate. The Crown sees our kind as disposable. How does that feel? To have the Home Office's collar so tight around your throat, you can barely breathe? Knowing they'll use this pretty body up until it gives out?" She moved closer. "What does that make you, Agent? Go on, tell me. Nothing wrong with being a whore, but call it what it is."

She saw the instant her words hit their mark. He stiffened, going rigid as if she'd slid her knife between his ribs.

His hands shot out, clamping around her biceps in a bruising grip. "You think you've got it all figured out. The poor little street rat with the tragic past. Always lashing out, always on the run. Too busy feeling sorry for yourself to see a rope when it's thrown at your feet."

It would be so easy to yield. But she couldn't. Her failures, her inadequacies, had nearly cost Emma her life. She had to keep this man as far away from her as possible. Had to make him despise her, revile her, because the alternative—

It was unthinkable.

"Let me speak plain," she said, very softly. "I've already sold my body for survival. I don't want a keeper, and certainly not one chained to the Office. You were a pleasant diversion in Hong Kong. A nice big cock to ride and a purse to lighten. But your utility, like your charm, has reached its limit."

He flinched. She saw it the moment before his expression smoothed out, and his hands fell away.

She wanted them back. She wanted to erase those words and tell him she was sorry. That if she had any softness left in her, he'd been the one to tease it out in Hong Kong, in Athens, in New York. And that was why she could never keep him.

Softness got people killed.

"Right," he said flatly. "Right then. Suppose that clears things up quite concisely."

He straightened his shoulders. Rebuilt his ramparts and bulwarks and all his impenetrable barricades. When he spoke again, he might have been carved from marble for all the emotion he betrayed.

"If the lady declines the offer of assistance, who am I to press the matter? Consider this my sincere apology for wasting your valuable time, Mademoiselle Dumont. It won't happen again. Enjoy the rest of your evening. I'm sure you have places to be. People to rob. Throats to slit. Good evening."

Isabel watched him go, that earlier stabbing pain spreading through her body. Tears scalded her eyes, but she blinked them back.

This was for the best. The kindest cruelty.

Sentiment is a noose, Favreau had told her once. *Give someone a piece of your heart, and they'll always betray you.*

The only way to survive was to cut those vulnerable parts out. To pack the wounds with ice until nothing could touch her.

Nothing and no one.

❧ 10 ❧

Isabel paced the lanes of Belgravia while keeping an eye on the townhouse.

Callahan hadn't come back. She wondered if he'd watched her at all from the shadows. If he even wanted to bother.

He'd probably washed his hands of her. Decided she wasn't worth the trouble. What good was a thief who let herself get tracked down, anyway? Who became exhausted enough to let her skills atrophy?

She'd tried to start a new life after Hong Kong. She went back to Paris to leave that note for Emma and tie up any loose ends. It had seemed so easy to convince herself that she'd wiped her trail clean when she'd left. New name. New face. Not a fugitive, not a traitor, but just another unremarkable urchin scuttling amid London's faceless masses.

Such a sweet, comforting lie.

Those lies were for marks.

She'd spent too long conning herself. Her face was

known, thanks to Favreau's singular talent for description and the money lubricating his every demand. There'd be no sanctuary for Spectre on either side of the Channel.

"*Stop it*," she snarled at herself, picking up her pace.

A shadow moved at the mouth of the alley.

Isabel reached for the sheath at her thigh, but not fast enough. Someone sprang out of the darkness. Arms clamped hard around her middle.

Her head snapped back, her skull connecting with a satisfying crack. Her captor let out a low grunt of pain, but his arms cinched tighter.

A strange calm descended. Gone was the frantic thud of her heart – only the familiar fury remained, cold and clean.

If she was going down, it would be fighting.

She drove her elbow back into his gut, fuelled by desperation and the clawing animal need to *breathe*.

"Bitch!"

She hit the cobbles hard.

"Fuck Favreau," he snarled. "I'll kill you myself."

"*Va te faire foutre*," she growled.

Then she bolted. The slap of her pursuers' boots echoed off the walls. *One, two* – she flicked a glance over her shoulder.

More. Christ, it was like an entire battalion bearing down on her, cutting off her avenues of escape one by one.

Panting, she slowed to a stop. The only way out was the way she'd come in, but that was no longer an option.

Isabel gripped her knife hard.

The men slowed to an arrogant, swaggering walk as they blocked her in. Even in the guttering flicker of the one lone gas lamp at the mouth of the passage, she could see the sly twist to their lips as they took in her panting breath, the rapid rise and fall of her breasts.

Oh, they'd enjoy this. She'd enjoy this more.

She bared her teeth at them in a feral grin. "Come on then, you bastards."

The first one came at her low and fast. He twisted to avoid her slash, but the point opened the skin of his cheek.

She didn't spare him another glance, already whirling to meet the next attack. They fell on her like a pack of starving dogs.

Had it only been a year since Favreau ran her through drills like these? Dancing between blades as he barked corrections? His fingers had dug into her bruised flesh later as he praised her, rewarded her, sharpened her into the weapon he wanted.

Nothing existed now but the hammer of her heart. The burn in her muscles as she pivoted and lunged. A knife skated along her ribs, parting fabric and flesh. A fist cracked across her cheekbone.

Isabel fell to her knees. A wheeze lurched from her chest. Hands wrenched her upright, and with a snarl, the man drove his fist into her stomach. Once, twice, until she couldn't even gasp. Black stars swam at the edges of her vision.

Through the high-pitched ringing in her ears, she could make out the distant murmur of voices. "Careful, idiot! Boss wants her alive."

"Just making sure the message sticks," came the response, punctuated by a sharp sting in her midsection.

Isabel tried to scream, but all that emerged was a breathless keen.

Rain kissed her upturned face. A strange lassitude crept over her then, smothering thought, feeling. It would be so easy to just . . . drift. Surrender to this seductive darkness rising to claim her.

Then, clarity pierced the grey haze. A single thought.

Emma.

They would go for Emma.

Biting back a groan, Isabel rolled to her belly. One breath. Two. She levered herself up on wobbling elbows, then to hands and knees.

A boot landed between her shoulder blades and shoved her back down. Her cheek smacked the wet stones.

"Look, mates, she's still got some wiggle in her. What do you say we make her dance more before we truss her up for delivery?"

More hands on her, in places they had no right to be. Palming the curve of her arse, dipping between her thighs.

The void rose up to meet her. A siren song luring her into the cool, dark depths, an endless sea of forgetting. It would be so easy to sink beneath the surface. To close her eyes and let oblivion take her. Maybe this time, she wouldn't have to resurface, wouldn't have to drag herself back to a world determined to break her.

Favreau's face swam out of the shadows behind her lids. Not smiling, for once. Grim and intent.

Get up, ma petite, he murmured, stroking a finger down her cheek. *Pain is nothing to creatures like us. Show them why you're mine.*

Her eyes snapped open. The guttering embers of her fury stirred. Coalesced.

Became an inferno.

Her fingers closed around the hilt of her fallen blade, and she buried it in the bastard's thigh.

He reared back with a bellow, his grip loosening. She tore away and staggered to her feet, ripping the knife free.

Her legs shook, barely willing to hold her weight. Black streaked through her vision. But she locked her knees. The buildings wavered as she stumbled out of the alley. Direction had lost all meaning, the world smearing in her periphery. An endless stretch of pain and putting one foot in front of the other. She had to get off the street. Her new bolthole was too far, an impossible distance in her current state.

But Emma . . .

No. It was too dangerous. She wouldn't risk leading Favreau's men to her sister's doorstep.

Her shoulder collided with a wall, the impact igniting fresh agony along her left side. She bit back a whimper and blinked hard to clear the black fog crowding out her vision.

No choice, then.

She needed Emma to contact Callahan. She didn't know where he lived, and his offer was the only way she would survive.

Isabel pushed off the bricks and stumbled forward, her battered body moving on pure instinct. She couldn't remember going to the townhouse. Couldn't recall navigating the twisting streets and alleys. But soon, the elegant façade of Kent's brother's home loomed out of the murk.

There. The second floor. Emma's bedroom window.

Her shaking fingers found holds in the cracked mortar between the bricks as Isabel heaved herself up the wall. Determination propelled her onwards.

Emma, Emma, Emma.

At last, her groping fingertips located the sill. She hauled herself up and over, tumbling into the darkened room beyond. Pain exploded through her body as she hit the floor.

Distantly, she heard a gasp. The clatter of a fallen candlestick. Then gentle hands were smoothing over her shoulders, turning her onto her back. "*Isabel.* Isabel. Open your eyes. What happened? How did you find me here?"

Isabel grimaced. "Ambush . . . barely escaped this time. Watched you . . . to make sure you were safe."

She might have slipped into unconsciousness then, but Emma gave her another shake.

"Stay with me, Isabel. Look at me."

With a soft groan, Isabel forced her eyes open once more. "Didn't know where else to go."

❧ 11 ❧

Isabel had almost died three times in her life.

The first time, she was fifteen years old, huddled in a Parisian alley. She remembered how the cold had seeped into her bones, how the world had faded to a hazy grey, and then ... nothing until Emma's frantic voice had pulled her back.

The second time, she was seventeen. Favreau's knife had slid between her ribs in punishment, but she'd clawed her way back to consciousness days later.

The third time was now.

Or perhaps it had been yesterday. Or the day before. She drifted in and out of awareness, caught between waking and dreaming. Sometimes, she thought she heard voices – Emma's soft murmurs, unfamiliar tones laced with concern. At one point, she'd groaned a protest as the perfunctory touches of a doctor examined her.

The faint rustle of fabric nearby drew Isabel's attention. She cracked an eye open, wincing at even that small movement.

Emma.

"Em," Isabel managed.

"Don't strain yourself," Emma said, grasping her hand.

Isabel swallowed hard. "You called . . . a damn doctor. Annoying."

"My sister was bleeding all over the rug. That cancelled any promises I made to you."

"You sent the Home Office after me."

"Ah, well, that was my doing." This from the other side of her bed, where a blonde woman sat. Lady Alexandra, Isabel had gathered from watching Emma over the last few days. "In fairness to your sister, she didn't know the man was a spy at the time."

Isabel grunted. She shifted her focus back to Emma. "And you fell in with an earl."

"I see we're going through a list of my betrayals," Emma said. "Of course."

"I'll kill him . . . if he uses you."

Isabel saw the flicker of understanding in Emma's eyes. Their shared history, the father who didn't even want them.

Isabel forced her gaze once more to Alexandra. She took in the fine silk of the woman's dressing gown. Despite her weakened state, Isabel's mind began to calculate, familiar habits rising to the surface.

"I could sell that for a decent meal."

Alexandra's eyebrows rose. "Do you think so? How decent?"

Isabel considered that, mentally tallying the potential value against the current rates in London's seedier districts. "A month's worth of the best meat pies, and pocket the rest for knives."

A grin spread across the other woman's face. "Oh, I like you. Alexandra Grey, at your service. I had to meet the infamous Isabel Dumont in person."

"Infamous." Isabel's cracked lips twitched. "Bleeding lout . . . in a guest room. Not my finest first impression." She sucked in a ragged breath. "Suppose I'm retired now. Tell Callahan . . . I accept his offer."

Emma's eyes widened. "To work for the Home Office?"

"Better them . . . than the Syndicate."

Alexandra spoke up. "I'll tell him. Would you like me to convey any threats?"

"I like her," Isabel murmured to Emma.

The splintering crack of wood shattering rent the air.

Isabel surged upright, ignoring the searing agony that ripped through her at the sudden movement. Her hand closed around the knife she kept at her ankle for emergencies.

Three men burst into the room, faces obscured by dark fabric. Moonlight glinted off their blades.

They'd found her.

"Stay in bed," Emma ordered, as if Isabel were in any state to do otherwise.

"Let me handle it," Isabel gritted out, even as her vision swam.

The first assassin lunged, blade raised. Isabel's arm snapped out. The knife left her hand in a graceful arc, singing through the air before burying itself to the hilt in the man's throat.

A gurgling cry escaped him. He stumbled, hands scrabbling at the blade as he crashed to the floor.

One down. Two to go.

The second assassin charged, but Emma brought her heel down on the man's instep. He rounded on her. Backhanded her across the face. Emma grabbed the fire poker and swung hard.

The third assassin went for Isabel and pinned her to the mattress. His hand closed around her throat, choking off her air. Stars burst in her vision as she clawed at his grip.

Just as the darkness began to close in, the man's fingers loosened, and Isabel sucked in a desperate inhale. Alexandra lunged from the shadows, snatched the fire poker from Emma, and brought it down on his head with a crack. He went limp and collapsed to the floor.

Alexandra rose to her feet. "You know, I don't believe I've ever struck a man with a poker before. It's remarkably satisfying."

A ragged burst of laughter escaped Isabel at that.

The thunder of approaching footsteps drew her attention. She tensed, preparing for another fight, but it was only the Earl of Kent and his brother.

They skidded to an abrupt halt. Mr Grey – the brother – looked almost comically disappointed. "Don't tell me I missed a chance to shoot someone."

Alexandra arched a brow. "Perhaps if you'd hurried a bit faster, you might have been useful." She turned to the earl, beaming with childlike enthusiasm. "James, did you know I got to hit a man with a poker tonight?"

Isabel's vision blurred again as the earl fussed over Emma.

"Don't mind me," Isabel rasped. "I'm only bleeding to death over here."

Emma rushed to her side. "You seemed robust enough to fling a knife with deadly accuracy."

"Small mercies." Isabel collapsed back into the pillows, exhaustion washing over her. "Send for your Home Office spy, please. I'd like to see the dawn."

⤜ 12 ⤛

Callahan stood before the hearth in the safe house with his hands braced on the mantelpiece.

Behind him, hushed voices sounded – Emma and Kent sat beside each other with their heads bent together in some private conference. Isabel perched on a chair to the left of her sister, looking like she might bolt at any second. She hadn't spoken a single fucking word to him since they'd arrived.

When Lady Alexandra's messenger had shown up at his flat with news of Isabel's surrender, he'd laughed. Actually fucking laughed. The same woman who'd looked him dead in the eye in Belgravia and said—

You were a pleasant diversion in Hong Kong. A nice big cock to ride and a purse to lighten.

His fingers dug into the mantelpiece.

But your utility, like your charm, has reached its limit.

She hadn't come for him. That much was clear. She was here because the Syndicate wanted her head on a spike, and he was her last resort. When the doctor examined her knife wounds, she'd stared at the floor like he wasn't even in the room. Hell, she'd looked everywhere but at him when he showed her where she'd sleep for the night.

Like he was poison.

Just put her on a fucking boat and get rid of her.

Callahan turned, his face carefully blank. "We'll have new identities sorted for both of you. Complete with travel papers. Then it's a nice trip across the Atlantic to throw off the Syndicate's trail."

"Oh yes, a holiday is just perfect," Isabel said, examining her nails. "I do so hope you plan to travel with us, Mr Callahan. Just imagine the stimulating conversation over newspapers and weak tea each morning. The excitement is mounting already."

She was pushing him away with both hands, throwing up walls of jagged glass and metal.

He understood. It was what they did, people like them. The walking wounded, the ones who'd learned early and often that caring was weakness.

But that didn't make her rejection sting any less.

"I won't be staying," he said. "After we disembark, I'll be handing your arse off to another poor sod. I'm allergic to attempted murder at close quarters. But I assure you the arrangements will be most comfortable, given that I'd rather leave you bleeding out in a ditch."

Isabel's eyes narrowed. "Comfortable," she repeated. "I hope that includes booking us passage on separate ships since I'm allergic to overbearing jailers with delusions of control."

How does it feel, Agent Callahan? To have the Home Office's collar so tight around your throat, you can barely breathe?

"I'm certain you'll find the quarters perfectly adequate," he said. "Her Majesty's government does occasionally spare expenses for ungrateful but useful harpies. After which, you will haul yourself back to England to do your job. And if you even attempt to flee, I'll find you and put a noose around your neck myself."

Isabel surged up with a snarl. Emma's hand shot out, grabbing her sister's shoulder before she could launch herself at Callahan. He made a mental note to thank the younger Dumont later, preferably when Isabel wasn't within earshot or throwing distance.

"I said I'd work for you," Isabel growled. "But it will be on my terms. No chains and no nooses. And tell your superiors that I want another handler. Not you."

"The preference is mutual. What about you?" he asked Emma, his tone softening. This sister was easier. She was sane, for one thing. "Any name in mind for your alias, Miss Dumont?"

Emma gave a wan smile. "I suppose I'll leave that to you. Choose whichever name you think is best."

Before Callahan could respond, Kent cleared his throat. "Whatever name and identity you assign her, make it fit for the future Countess of Kent."

Emma's head whipped towards Kent, her expression slack with shock. Even Isabel seemed momentarily thrown.

"Christ." Callahan pinched the bridge of his nose. He was getting a damn headache. "Of course, you both had to go and needlessly complicate things." He loosed a sigh. "I'll send word when it's time to depart for the steamer."

He stalked out of the parlour, leaving the Dumonts and Kent to sort themselves out. The boards creaked beneath his boots as he navigated the narrow halls of the safe house for the cramped study that served as his makeshift headquarters.

Damn Kent and his romantic declaration. The earl had just doubled Callahan's workload. Creating a false identity for a thief was difficult enough. Creating one for the future Countess of Kent? That required craftsmanship and time, which was in short supply.

He shrugged out of his coat and tossed it over the back of his chair. Dropping into the seat, he tugged a sheaf of papers close and unscrewed the cap of the inkwell. He couldn't have said how long he sat there with his head bent over his work before a pointed cough broke his concentration.

Isabel against the doorframe. "Plotting my demise? Or doodling little hearts around my name?"

"What do you want, Trouble?"

"Just making sure you're not saddling me with some ghastly *nom de plume*. No Scarlett O'Harlots, if you please. I have a reputation to maintain."

"And what a sterling reputation it is. Tell me, do you prefer 'infamous thief' or 'traitor to international crime syndicates' on your calling cards?"

"I was thinking more along the lines of 'peerless acquisitions specialist.' It has a certain ring to it, don't you think?"

A smile tugged at the corner of his mouth before he could stop it. Then memory crashed in – her mocking voice in Belgravia.

Nothing wrong with being a whore, but call it what it is.

The almost-smile died. "I'll take it under advisement. Was there something else, or did you come to make my life more difficult than it already is? Because there's no need. You're doing an exceptional job of that by existing."

Her chest expanded on a breath. Something flickered in her eyes – an emotion that might have been hurt – and then she shook her head.

"Good," he said, standing and reaching for his coat. The room suddenly felt too small. Too hot. Too filled with her. "If you'll excuse me, I have work to do. Arranging aliases and safe passage for ungrateful thieves is surprisingly time-consuming."

Callahan moved to exit, but Isabel stepped into his path. Close enough to touch. To take.

"Move," he growled.

"Why?"

"Why what?" He sidestepped; she matched him. "You'll have to be more specific. My list of questionable life choices is extensive."

His list started with her.

Hell, it ended with her, too.

"Why are you helping me?" she asked. "After everything I said in Belgravia? After Hong Kong?"

Callahan fixed Isabel with a look. He was struck by how young she looked beneath the bravado and the scars. Young, and very, very tired.

"You're an asset. A valuable one when you're not actively trying to be a liability. And I'm in the business of acquiring and maintaining assets."

Her lips thinned, but she said nothing.

Let her think what she wanted. Being a cold-hearted bastard suited him fine. Better than the truth – that he couldn't get her voice out of his head even when he slept.

"And your sister is innocent in all this," he continued. "I'm many things. A bastard with the Home Office's boot on my neck, as you so kindly pointed out. But I'm not in the habit of letting innocents suffer for the sins of their degenerate siblings, Miss Dumont."

"Don't call me that," she said, her hands curling into fists.

"What?" Callahan knew he was pushing too far, but God help him, he couldn't stop. "*Miss Dumont?* Oh, I'm sorry, what would you prefer? Allison Marks? Mary Griffin? The esteemed Gräfin von Hohenstein? Or perhaps Ekaterina Mikhailovna—"

"That's *enough*." Her chest heaved, colour high on her cheeks.

"Why?" He gripped her wrist. Not hard enough to hurt, just to hold her in place. "Tell me why I shouldn't use the only real damn thing I know about you."

She trembled. Heat radiated between them like it always did when they got too close. Like striking flint against steel.

Christ. What was it about her? Years of this back and forth, years of her getting under his skin. And here he was, still losing his damn mind over her and wanting things he had no business wanting.

"Tell me one real thing," he whispered. "Just one, and I'll call you whatever you want."

There was something so vulnerable about the way her body seemed to curl into him. The way her forehead nearly touched his. A soft exhale left her.

But then she said, "There's not a single thing about me that's real. Not in New York or Athens. Not in Hong Kong. That's the truth."

Cold swept through him. Stupid, stupid bastard. He'd asked for this, hadn't he? She had one talent in abundance.

Spectre was a fucking liar.

Callahan released her wrist and stepped back. "I'll bring you clothes and new travel papers tonight. We leave for the steamer after dark." He straightened his coat. "I'm sure you'll be eager to be rid of me, since you've just been performing this whole time."

He walked around her and out into the grey London morning.

Whitehall loomed ahead, the pale stone edifices stark against the sky. Callahan shouldered his way through the doors for the Home Office, walked up the staircase lined with columns, and down several dark hallways and corridors.

He ignored the clerks and aides scurrying about their business and didn't slow until he stood outside his superior's office.

MATTIAS WENTWORTH, read the plate affixed to the door.

Squaring his shoulders, Callahan rapped and pushed open the door.

Wentworth sat behind his desk with his shirtsleeves rolled to the elbow and his dark hair spilled across his forehead. Despite being born to an aristocratic family, the spymaster was anything but soft. His forearms were corded with muscle, and his shirt strained over his shoulders. When his blue eyes rose to meet Callahan's, they were sharp. Flat.

"Out with it," Wentworth snapped, tossing aside his pen. *Ah, pleasant as ever.* "What've you fucked up?"

"Good afternoon to you, too, sir. I appreciate your faith in me. It's a balm to my soul."

Wentworth snorted. Stabbed a finger at the papers fanned across his desk. "Five minutes. That's what you've got before I ship you to the coldest corner of hell I can find. Start talking."

Well. Straight to it, then.

"I assume you're referring to my acquisition of a certain asset?"

"If by 'asset' you mean the thief we've been after since 1868, then yes. Imagine my surprise when I received a courier this morning informing me that not only had you secured her cooperation, but you intend to ferry her across the Atlantic without my authorisation."

Callahan shrugged. "There wasn't time to go through the formal channels. Favreau's men had already made an attempt on her life. I couldn't risk them succeeding. She's the most dangerous thief in Europe, has inside intelligence on the French arm of the Syndicate, and now she's ours. Forgive me if I thought that warranted expediency on my part."

"The only reason I don't have your bollocks in a vice right now," Wentworth said with a glare, "is because I know Spectre in the custody of the Home Office is better than her helping Favreau."

"Just so."

"I heard something about another woman involved."

"Our asset's sister. Targeted as leverage." Callahan ran a hand through his hair. "The Earl of Kent wants to marry her."

Wentworth let out an aggrieved sigh. "Christ. Nobody informed me Kent had taken up thinking with his prick."

"Didn't realise the depth of his affections, truth be told. She was his sister's maid, and you know how aristos are."

The spymaster gave a mocking smile. He was, after all, the second son of a viscount. "So I suppose I'm crafting some hidden heiress from Boston. How's her ear for accents?"

"If she's anything like her sister, decent."

"Let us hope so. Inform Kent that he needs to take a long honeymoon. Keep up the pretence of unfathomably falling in love with some American chit. The Syndicate can have no inkling of who she really is." He tapped a slim folder to his left. "I have three tickets for the Liverpool Express tomorrow morning. I'll put someone on the identities. Should be delivered to the safe house by nightfall." His stare sharpened with a look that absolutely, unequivocally communicated that he wouldn't hesitate to skin Callahan alive if this all went tits up. "I'm trusting your instincts on this."

"Understood, sir."

"Spectre will need a handler in Boston. Someone to keep her controlled and low profile. No reason you shouldn't take the position."

"She wants another handler," Callahan said, his expression a careful mask of indifference. "I think it best to grant the request."

One of Wentworth's dark brows winged upwards. "Oh? And why is that?"

"I believe our interpersonal friction could become a liability if allowed to continue long term."

His superior studied him. Callahan resisted the urge to fidget beneath that scalpel-edged scrutiny.

"You've fucked her, haven't you?"

Callahan couldn't quite suppress his flinch. There was no point in denying it. "Six months ago. In Hong Kong."

With a curse, Wentworth ran his hands down his face. "I'd ask what the hell you were thinking, but that would presume you were thinking at all. Christ, man, we've been trying to bring her to heel for years, and you tumbled the chit into bed?"

"Momentary lapse in judgment. It won't happen again."

"Damn right, it won't. I'll have the lads upstairs send a cable to Portia Vale and have her meet you both in Boston to take over guardianship. You are going to be the consummate professional, Agent." He jabbed his finger onto the desk to emphasise his words. "You'll keep your head down and your cock in your trousers, and you'll deliver Spectre into Vale's hands without any further complications. Do I make myself clear?"

"Crystal," Callahan bit out.

He could picture Isabel's sneer, could almost hear the mocking lilt of her voice whispering in his ear. *Such a good little lapdog.*

⋙ 13 ⋘

When Isabel was little, she dreamed of the sea.

Not that she'd ever actually seen it at the time. Paris was so far from the coast, and *Maman* had always been too busy to take them on a holiday. She shopped, visited the modiste, attended the theatre with the duke while he was in town. Isabel and Emma's days were spent in lessons – language, philosophy, deportment. Everything their mother decided they needed to navigate a world with little kindness for bastards and fewer options for women.

After Southampton threw them out, Isabel used to curl onto the floor in their new, cramped little flat and imagine the waves. *Maman* once told her the sea sounded like breathing, deep and endless.

Isabel liked that.

Later, when Favreau was on top of her, inside her, hurting her, she'd think of the ocean. Its rhythm, its vastness. A reminder that she existed beyond her skin and bones and whatever he was doing to them.

The first time she ever saw the sea, she'd been stupid enough to tell him.

Quelle innocence, he said, stroking her cheek. *We should make it a memory.*

That night, he gave her the first of what would eventually become a collection of scars.

She stood at the ship's railing with England fading into the distance. Her cigarette rested between her fingers, the smoke curling in the air. The waves rose and fell in a ceaseless flow, hissing and roaring with each swell before crashing against the hull.

She'd stopped dreaming of the sea years ago. Now, it just reminded her of knives. Of blood and constant running.

Find a distraction, she thought to herself.

She liked to find lovers on her travels. Ships were good for that, for confined spaces and temporary men with no names and no histories. Men who thought they were claiming her when she was actually using them. She'd spend a few days forgetting, letting herself understand that a cock could feel good and make her body sing. The more she fucked, the less Favreau owned her.

But there was only one distraction on this ship worth pursuing.

Tell me one real thing. Just one, and I'll call you whatever you want.

Let Ronan hate her. He didn't have to like her to bed her.

She ground out her cigarette and descended below deck, removing the pins from her hair as she reached Callahan's door. The lock yielded so easily.

Isabel slipped inside.

Callahan surged up from where he rested on his bunk, snatching his pistol from the bedside table and pointing it right at her chest.

"If this is a new interrogation tactic, it needs work," Isabel drawled. "What kind of agent lets a thief sneak up on him?"

"The kind who was expecting a knock."

Her gaze lingered on his muscular torso, at the bandage from where she'd stabbed him in the shoulder. This was the first time she'd seen him without clothes since Hong Kong, and somehow, he was even more beautiful. More devastating.

"I'm requesting an audience," she said, shaking herself. "I assume we can dispense with the formalities?"

She wasn't sure what reaction she'd expected – annoyance, maybe. Or wary resignation. She hadn't expected the way Ronan's stare swept over her in a slow, heated drag, as tactile as a physical touch.

Yes. He might detest her, but *that* look was hungry.

"Is this the part where you tell me you're here to complain?" Callahan asked. "Take issue with the thread count, perhaps? Or are the sightlines from your quarters not murderous enough?"

"Now that you mention it, I do have a bone to pick." She moved to the edge of his bed. "Something about a truly unfortunate alias I suspect may be your doing."

After unpacking the dresses he'd managed to procure for her on short notice, she'd opened the envelope with her travel papers to find his petty revenge staring her right in the face.

"Sweetheart, the bureaucratic wrangling required to pull those identities together would astonish you. And this is the thanks I get? I'm wounded."

"Oh, I haven't begun to wound you yet. Do I look like

a *Felicity Snodgrass* to you? It sounds like someone who faints at the sight of ankles."

"You're unbelievable."

"So I've been told. Often and with great enthusiasm."

The pistol lowered, but not before he dragged the cold barrel down her throat. She shivered despite herself.

"Why the hell are you really here?" He pressed the muzzle between her breasts, not gentle, not careful. "Got an itch that needs scratching, Trouble?"

She bit her lip. "If I said I did?"

His lips curved into a wicked smile. He set the pistol aside on the small table next to his bunk, then leaned back against the wall, his broad shoulders flexing as he slowly, deliberately, pulled down the sheet covering his lower half. Her throat went dry when it finally slipped past his hips. He was hard. Thick. Ready.

Waiting.

His hand wrapped around his cock, and he began to stroke, slow and taunting. "Go on, then. *Scratch*."

There was something obscene about his shamelessness. His head fell back, exposing the column of his throat, but his eyes stayed locked on Isabel's. Like he was fucking her with his gaze.

Look, but don't touch. Want, but don't have.

"Take off the dress," he commanded.

As if he had any right to be giving orders, sprawled there like a debauched king.

"Maybe I should punish you and just use my hand," Isabel said, as if she hadn't come in here looking for exactly this.

He grunted, moving faster now, the muscles in his

stomach flexing with each pull. "Can't have it both ways, Trouble. You break into my cabin in the dead of night, you don't get to pretend you're not gagging for it. So you have two choices. Either strip and ride my cock like we both know you're dying to, or watch me spend all over my fist like a sad little voyeur too craven to take what you want."

"There's always a third choice. I could leave. Find someone who doesn't think he owns me. Perhaps you're not the man to help me *scratch* this particular itch, after all."

"If you wanted someone else, you'd be in his bed. And I'd bet everything I own that if I touched you right now, you'd be dripping for me. So. Choose."

Insufferable, arrogant bastard.

Isabel reached for her fastenings. The weight of Callahan's gaze was a physical thing, searing through layers of muslin and boning, dark and fevered and ravenous. There was a savage sort of surrender in baring herself to him this way. A profane offering to be devoured or destroyed at his whim.

The dress fell. Her fingers shook when she removed her bustle. He kept watching. Kept stroking himself as she fumbled with her corset next, the front-busk style for women who dressed themselves.

She hesitated at the combinations, the thin cotton all that remained. His hand moved faster, his chest rising and falling, hair tumbling over his forehead.

Enough. She needed to wrestle back some power.

"Stop," she ordered.

He didn't. His cock was thick in his fist, and he worked it with lazy confidence. Lips slightly parted.

"Stop or I'll keep this on."

"If that stays on, this is all you get," he said. "I keep

going until I spend, and you get to crawl back to your cold bed, aching and empty."

This was always their problem. Him pushing, her retreating. Him demanding everything, her giving nothing. Except in Hong Kong. For a few hours, she'd forgotten who she was, who he was, and felt more alive than she had in years.

Give in or walk away.

In the end, the hunger won out.

She ripped at the ribbons, shoving the flimsy cotton down until she stood naked before him, flushed and panting and so very, very hungry.

Callahan's stare drifted over every imperfection. The scars all over her torso, the puckered starburst beneath her breast, the bandage at her ribs. All the broken, battered pieces of her offered in unholy sacrifice. She counted his breaths, waiting for disgust to cross his face. The light had been so dim in Hong Kong. Kinder. Maybe he hadn't seen the full extent of the damage. Maybe—

"Come here," he said, voice rough.

She stepped closer. He reached out, calloused fingertips skimming over the longest scar on her hip.

Isabel flinched. "Don't."

"Why not?" he asked, voice low.

"Just – not like that." Her jaw clenched. Gentleness was worse than cruelty. Gentle undid her.

But then Callahan's mouth pressed against the raised ridge of a mark, breath hot on her skin. When his eyes met hers, they burned fever-bright with longing – as if even her scars, her flaws, her myriad failings, only made him want her more.

Too much, too close, too intimate.

"Don't," she whispered again.

"Should I tell you how beautiful you are? Scars and all?"

Part of her wanted to shut her eyes against his words. Tell him *no* and *stop*. That his tenderness wasn't what she needed from him when the ocean waves were so loud, and Favreau's voice kept whispering in her memories.

But he stared up at her like she was a goddess, and she hadn't felt beautiful since Hong Kong.

Something splintered deep in her chest, the fissures spider-webbing *out* and *out*.

"I was expecting you to promise to slay my demons," she said. "Track down the monsters who gave me these marks and make them all bleed."

His fingers flexed. "But you don't want me to slay your demons, do you? You want me to fuck them out of you." A pause, heavy and charged. "So kiss me."

Something inside her snapped. She lunged forward, crashing her mouth against his. Her teeth caught his bottom lip, hard enough to hurt. Hard enough to make him grunt. Her nails raked down his back, drawing red lines she wished would scar. Let him carry her marks for once.

"Christ," he hissed, hands digging into her hips.

Callahan yanked her into his lap. His cock pressed against her, hot and hard, and a whimper escaped her before she could swallow it down.

Isabel ground down against him, desperate for friction. For release. For anything to drown out the screaming in her head. He kissed like a conquering warlord. Devouring, consuming, taking her apart and demanding her surrender even as he stole the air from her lungs.

He tasted like whiskey and sin. Like salvation.

"I need—"

His grip tightened in her hair. "That's right. You need. You want. You *take*. But not tonight. Tonight, it's my turn to take." Then his hand pushed between her thighs, and he plunged his fingers inside her. "Just as I thought. *Dripping* fucking *wet*. It's honestly shameful how much I've thought about this cunt. How it feels. How tight it is. Even after you stole everything and left me stranded with no clothes, no money, and no way home." His words were punctuated with another slick thrust of his fingers. "So tell me something, Trouble." His voice hardened. "Between us, who really deserves the punishment here?"

His fingers disappeared suddenly. Before she could protest, he grabbed her wrists in one large hand and slammed them above her head. Cold metal kissed her skin.

Click.

"What—" The fog of arousal cleared enough for Isabel to realise what had happened. Her eyes widened as she tugged at the restraints.

The bastard had cuffed her to his bed with darbies – which he'd obviously brought along for her.

"Something wrong?" He smirked.

"What do you think you're doing?"

"Taking my vengeance."

Isabel's expression darkened. "When I pick the lock on these—"

"Oh, little thief. That's not going to happen. Because these beauties?" Callahan flicked one of the cuffs with his finger. "I made these myself, patented and everything. Thought of you with every design modification. The nested locking mechanism with multiple tumblers." He kissed down her jaw. "Secondary internal locks in case of tampering . . ." A nip at her earlobe. "And a specialised fucking key, sweetheart. Because I want you to stay right where you are. No more running."

"*Agent*."

His teeth caught her bottom lip. "When my mouth is between your thighs, you call me Ronan."

Callahan began kissing a slow path down her body, as if he intended to torture her all night. Touching her everywhere. When he reached her breasts, he lingered, drawing one nipple between his teeth until she arched up, wanting more. But then his lips brushed over the scar beneath her left breast, the ones along her navel. All the little marks that existed as reminders of the things she'd done. All the ways she didn't deserve him.

"Look at me," he growled.

Her eyes snapped to his. Callahan shoved her legs apart, hooking her knees over his shoulders. The position left her completely exposed. Nowhere to hide, nothing to bargain with. Then his tongue licked up her pussy.

Isabel's head slammed back against the pillow. "*God!*"

Her hips bucked. The bastard just pressed her down harder, pinning her in place until she couldn't think. Couldn't breathe. Could only feel his mouth working against her, his tongue circling her clitoris with teasing, gentle pressure when she needed more. The soft licks made her strain against the cuffs until the metal bit into her skin.

"I think you owe me something," he murmured. His rough palms slid up her inner thighs, pushing them wider apart. "An apology. For Hong Kong."

"No," she moaned.

His eyes narrowed. "*Yes*."

Then he thrust two fingers into her.

Isabel cried out. Another thrust, harder this time, curling his fingers to stroke that spot inside her that made stars burst across her vision. If her hands were free, she'd grab him by his hair and force that smug mouth exactly where she needed it and ride his face until she came.

But she was trapped. Bound and spread open and completely at his mercy. He worked his fingers faster, mouth closing over her clitoris again, and Isabel felt herself spiralling higher. She was close.

Callahan pulled away.

She made a ragged sound. "Please, I need—"

He nipped at the skin of her inner thigh. "You need what? My fingers? My tongue? My cock? Be specific."

"Fuck me." Pride was a distant memory. All that mattered was the ache between her legs and what this man could do for her.

"Say you're sorry," he murmured with a soft kiss to her stomach. "That's all it takes."

Isabel turned her face away. Apologies were for the weak. For people who had something to lose. If she gave him even that tiny piece of herself, there'd be nothing left. No walls, no armour. Just her bleeding heart exposed for him to crush. He'd see everything – all the ugliness, all the damage, all the reasons she wasn't worth the trouble.

She'd rather die.

Instead, she wanted to shatter him open and strip him down to raw nerve until his composure fractured. Didn't he understand what she needed? His mouth on her, his cock inside her, distraction and distraction and distraction until all those ugly memories receded like the tide. His body was useful. She could manipulate it like a tool until it yielded and gave her what she wanted.

"Ronan." She used his first name in a calculated move.

His pupils expanded, swallowing the grey of his irises, and his lips parted on an exhale.

Yes. There we go.

"Give me my apology, Isabel." He was fighting fire with fire, using her own tactics against her. Rearing back and sinking his claws in. "Three words: *I was wrong*. And then I'll give you what you need. Come on, little thief."

She searched his face for any crack in his resolve, any hint that he might give in. But all she found was that same stubborn determination that made her want to fight him or kiss him until they both suffocated.

"*Va te faire foutre.*" The metal dug into her wrists, a sting she scarcely felt over the roaring in her blood. "You'll get an apology over my cold, dead corpse."

His eyes flashed.

That's it, she thought. *Break for me, damn you.*

But then his expression smoothed out – a mask sliding into place. "Have it your way," he said with a shrug.

Before she realised what was happening, he was off the bed, grabbing his clothes from the floor. Bored now. As if she were of no consequence.

"What are you doing?" Her panic disgusted her.

Callahan shot her a look as he buttoned his trousers. "Going out for a smoke."

"A smoke?" Her voice rose an octave. "You can't just leave me here like this!"

"Actually, I can." The calm in his tone was gone, replaced by something hard and sharp. "I gave you a choice, and you chose your damn pride over what you want." He yanked his shirt over his head and reached for his coat. "So get comfortable. Think about your sins. I'll be back when you've had enough time to reconsider."

"Agent!" She thrashed against the restraints. "If you do this, I swear to God I'll—"

The door slammed shut.

❧ 14 ❧

Callahan stared out at the water. The sky hung low and heavy, the fog rendering everything in shades of grey.

Grey water. Grey sky. Grey mood.

He lit a cigarette, watching the ember flare orange.

Isabel knew how to get under his skin; that was the real problem. The woman had a talent for finding the soft places, the weak spots. She reminded him too much of himself.

He took a deep drag, letting smoke fill his lungs.

Sex was just business for him. Always had been. After his mother died when he was eight – after Whelan took him in and told him he had to work or starve – he'd learned what bodies were worth. What they could buy.

Food.

Shelter.

Protection.

Joining the Home Office was supposed to give him back some control, but every scar he earned told the same story: survival had a price, and you paid for it with flesh.

He never fucked for pleasure. He fucked because it was useful, because it got him things he needed.

Hong Kong changed that.

Callahan saw Isabel across that crowded room and just ... wanted. No angle, no mission. Just her mouth, her hands, her body beneath his, the way he'd imagined after New York and Athens. Wondering if she'd be the first woman he actually enjoyed.

When she ran, she took something of him with her. Something he didn't know he could lose. Maybe that's why he couldn't forgive her; she'd pulled that raw need from him, then treated him like another mark.

"Shit," he muttered, flicking his cigarette into the water.

He shouldn't have left her chained up in his cabin, but he was tired of being used.

"Mr Callahan!"

Christ.

Biting back a groan, he turned to greet the approaching couple.

Emma Dumont walked towards him on the arm of her earl, a pleasant smile on her face. Kent, in contrast, was the very image of an aloof aristocrat – except when he glanced at his future bride. Then his features thawed into something like awe.

These Dumont women really did bring men to their knees.

"Lord Kent," he said in greeting. "Miss Dumont. To what do I owe the pleasure?"

"Have you seen Isabel?" Emma asked. "She wasn't in her cabin."

"I haven't seen her since dinner. Perhaps she's in the ship's library?"

The earl frowned. "At this hour?"

Shit.

Callahan scrambled for a plausible lie. Something vague. Something that didn't sound like "chained naked to my bed."

"Hmm. Maybe taking in the sea air, then," he offered, the picture of innocence. "You know how your sister gets when she's confined for too long."

She fixed him with a stare. "Alone? Days after nearly dying at the hands of an international crime syndicate?"

He could practically feel his bollocks trying to crawl up into his body cavity. There it was. That same relentless pursuit he knew so well from interrogations, from watching a mark, waiting for that telltale flinch. He'd just never expected to have it turned on him with such ruthless precision.

"Ah. Upon further consideration, I may have expanded the parameters of Miss Dumont's confinement."

Chin up, shoulders back. The quintessential agent, unshakable, immovable—

"I see." Emma's gaze could have drilled holes through a lesser man's skull. "And what necessitated these *expanded parameters*?"

Shite. Shit, shit, fecking shite.

"One can never be too thorough with security. Your sister has proven quite slippery in the past. It's for her safety that I've taken extra precautions."

Miss Dumont gave him the most unimpressed expression he'd ever had the misfortune to encounter. One he was beginning to suspect was a Dumont family trait.

"Mr Callahan. Perhaps you'd be so kind as to answer me plainly. Where is my sister?"

Callahan shot a helpless look at Kent, silently imploring the earl to rein in his diminutive fiancée before she eviscerated him and left his entrails for the herring gulls. But the earl merely stared back. The bastard was probably enjoying watching him squirm.

"She's in his cabin," Kent said. "Cuffed, I'd wager."

Of course, he fucking knew. Callahan thought of the reverent way he touched Miss Dumont, the quiet devotion in every look. He'd probably seen that same savage need reflected in Callahan's eyes when he looked at Isabel: the animal snarl, the white-knuckled restraint. The need to see her kneeling at his feet, wrists crossed at the small of her back, waiting for him to choke her on his—

"She's resting," Callahan said, shaking off his wayward thoughts. "Quite comfortably, I assure you."

Emma's lips pursed, but she said nothing. After what could only be called a silent threat to send him to the very depths of hell if anything happened to her sister, she turned on her heel and walked away. Kent cast one last glance over his shoulder as he followed, his own look promising unpleasantness.

Message received on both accounts.

Well. No sense dawdling above deck when he had a naked thief below. Of course, there was no telling what mood he'd find her in after leaving her to stew for hours.

Probably homicidal. The odds of him escaping their little encounter without bodily injury were slim.

Callahan paused outside the cabin door, reaching for the iron-clad control that had seen him through countless missions, innumerable brushes with death and damnation.

Right then. No more stalling.

He stepped into the room. The illumination from the lantern threw stark shadows over the figure splayed on the narrow bed.

Isabel. Asleep.

She twitched and shuddered against the sheets. Perspiration beaded her brow.

"*Non, s'il vous plaît*," she mumbled. "Just don't—"

Callahan crossed the room, his heart slamming against his ribs.

He was unequipped to handle this. Give him a pistol and an enemy to hunt, a code to crack or a mark to shadow – those he could navigate with ruthless efficiency. But Isabel thrashing in his bed, trapped in whatever hell her mind had dragged her to?

It was unfamiliar terrain.

He'd known Favreau was a cruel bastard. The kind who'd break what belonged to him just because he could. Callahan's eyes traced the silvery lines marking her skin, each one telling him exactly what kind of monster had caged and hunted her.

"*Non. Je serai sage.*"

Something twisted in his chest – an emotion he didn't have a name for.

With a muttered prayer to a god he scarcely believed in, Callahan reached out and let his fingertips graze her temple. The lightest brush, barely there. A tentative foray into gentleness from hands far more accustomed to violence.

Isabel flinched away from his touch.

"Trouble," he said. Low. Coaxing. "Wake up."

Another whimper. He'd seen men die, had murdered plenty, been through more pain than most. But this sound? This was killing him.

"Come back to me, little thief."

Her eyes snapped open, wild with terror, and for a brief moment, he saw everything she'd hidden behind that confident façade. Then the fear was replaced with fury.

"You bastard," she snarled. "*You left.*"

There. Anger was easier than vulnerability with this woman; he could work with it.

He shoved down the softness that had crept in moments before. "What's wrong?" He smirked. "Don't like being abandoned? Hurts, doesn't it?"

She yanked at the cuffs, the metal clanking against the bed frame. "Very clever. Point made. Now unlock these before I kick your teeth in."

"Hm. No, I don't think I will. Not yet, anyway."

Callahan dug in his trouser pockets and fished out his pre-rolled smokes and a book of lucifers. He took his sweet time lighting up and brought the cigarette to his lips.

"Maybe I like you this way," he said, exhaling a plume of smoke. "You paint quite the picture. Would take a stronger man than I to resist savouring it."

Isabel's upper lip curled in a silent snarl. "What next? Some vulgar comment about my mouth and what you'd like to do with it?"

Callahan's eyes narrowed. He lunged forward, one hand braced beside her head on the mattress.

Isabel went still beneath him, her cheeks pinkening.

"You'd love that, wouldn't you? If I fucked that infuriating mouth until you choked on my cock."

That flush swept down her throat. "Would you? Use me so ruthlessly?"

Callahan let his gaze wander down her body. The curve of her breasts, the taut stomach with its silvery scars and bandage, the way her chest rose and fell faster.

"Would you want me to?" he asked.

Her teeth scraped her lower lip, and he nearly groaned. It was so easy for her to make him forget all the reasons he shouldn't touch her. Want her.

"Uncuff me, and you can use me however you want."

Even naked and chained, she was negotiating. Trying to gain the upper hand. It was what made her dangerous.

"Business first," he said.

Callahan pushed off the bed. He took another deep drag of his cigarette, using the precious seconds to regain his composure. To tamp down the urge to pin her to the mattress and see that smart mouth take his cock.

"The Home Office needs intelligence," he said. "On Favreau and the Syndicate at large. We had a man on the inside of their Moscow arm before he got burned. Used a sanctioned hit as an exit strategy and promptly fucked off to retirement. We've been fumbling blind ever since."

He snagged the chair from the corner and straddled it backwards. "Let's start with the basics. How does Favreau run his operation?"

The ship rolled with a large wave. Rain pattered against the porthole window.

Finally, she spoke. "His inner circle is hand-picked young, and groomed for absolute loyalty." The metal cuffs clinked as she shifted. "The desperate ones are his favourites."

"Orphans?" he asked, thinking of Whelan and his collection of street children.

"No," she surprised him by saying. "He prefers those with family."

Isabel's gaze drifted to the window, watching the dark water slide past the glass. "When you're alone, you have nothing to lose. But family? Family can be used against you."

Callahan's grip tightened on the chair's back.

"You don't need to torture someone who loves their mother," she continued, quieter. "You just need to mention her name and promise to care for her. Then remind them what happens if they disobey. You don't run when he'll slit your family's throat for it."

"Christ," he whispered.

"I never told him about Emma or my mother. But I think he knew someone existed. He's good at finding weaknesses." She looked at him now. "Lonely girls will let a man fuck them. But desperate ones don't ever say no when he hurts them."

The question burned on his tongue before he could stop it. "How old were you?"

The cabin creaked around them. Seconds stretched by.

"Sixteen," she finally said.

Something cold and heavy settled in the pit of Callahan's stomach. His fingers twitched with the sudden, savage urge to wrap around Favreau's neck. He wanted the bastard's blood. Wanted to watch the life drain from his eyes. He'd make damn sure Favreau never touched Isabel again.

Callahan took a long drag from his cigarette, forcing the rage down.

"Go on, little thief."

"By the time I was eighteen, I was valuable enough that he kept me close. Being useful had advantages. The more he trusted me, the more freedom he gave me." Her lips curved into something too bitter to be a smile. "He'd let me travel alone for heists sometimes. Only when necessary, and always with his loyal men, but it was enough. I just needed him to believe I'd always come back."

"Hong Kong," he prompted. "You were fleeing?"

"Trying to." She tapped the cuffs against the bedframe in agitation. "I planned it for months. Made him think it was his idea to send me to Hong Kong. By the time I killed the men he sent to watch me, I'd be gone. I had papers arranged. Money hidden. But I needed more for passage and bribes." She exhaled slowly. "And then you walked in. Exactly where I didn't need you to be."

The gambling hall's smoky interior flashed in his memory – the scent of opium, the drunken laughter, and Isabel across the room, her face a careful mask that didn't quite hide her desperation.

"And fucked your exit strategy," he finished for her.

"Yes."

"You looked half-dead when I saw you there," he said, voice low. "Like you hadn't slept in months."

A sharp, humourless laugh escaped her. "Sleep isn't something you get much of in Favreau's bed. And after all that careful planning, you blundered in. I had to improvise."

"Improvise? Or simply choose a more attractive mark?"

Her eyes slid over him, taking her time. "You have your uses," she said finally. "But when you spotted me in Hong Kong, I ran out of options. Favreau would destroy anything in his path to get me back. Not just because I'm good at what

I do. Because I'm his." She blinked hard. "Do you want to know the worst part? The part that makes me hate myself?"

Lantern light caught on the shine of her hair, the curve of her throat. He couldn't speak. Could barely breathe.

He held himself still.

"Sometimes I miss him," she confessed. "His attention. His approval. I'd have crawled through glass and debased myself at his feet for a single scrap of regard. And whenever he graced me with it, I was pitifully, revoltingly *grateful*."

Callahan inhaled deeply, holding his breath until his chest burned, then slowly letting it out. Trying to control the rage building inside him.

When he looked up, Isabel was watching him. Waiting. Like she was ready for his judgment, his disgust. As if any decent man could look at her and feel anything but fury at the one who'd put that desolation in her voice.

She'd been so young – just like him.

He cleared his throat. "When I was a lad, I belonged to a bloke named Whelan," he said roughly. "Ran a pick-pocketing ring in the East End. Whelan taught us how to steal from the rich, but that wasn't enough for him. Men with money would come around and pay to use us however they wanted." He swallowed hard and gestured at his face. "Pretty boys fetch a price, and I'm more than aware of my appearance. So, believe me, I know what it is to trade your dignity and your body for scraps. You carry no guilt in this. None. Favreau saw a girl he could break, so he twisted you into something he could use."

Isabel was quiet. All that bravado and confidence was gone, replaced by the same vulnerability he saw when she woke from her nightmare.

She looked away first. "Do you plan to leave these cuffs on all night?"

He knew that voice – the one that said she'd retreated somewhere he couldn't follow. Behind walls he'd never be allowed past again tonight.

"No." He reached for the key. The lock clicked, and he eased the manacles from her wrists. "Your bandages need changing," he said softly. "May I?"

A pause, then a mute jerk of her chin.

Callahan soaked a rag in the tepid water in his room's basin and took the tin of salve out of his bag. Gently, he peeled the cloth off her torso.

"This was close," he said. "Luck seems to like you."

"Luck isn't a word I'd use to describe my existence thus far, Agent."

"You're still breathing, aren't you?"

"For now."

The rain beat harder outside. Callahan worked in silence, his fingers tracing a path around her injury, then the other marks – the faded lines on her stomach. Some were thin, others raised and jagged.

"How many of these were heists, and how many were Favreau?" he asked, following a mark curving over her hip.

"My scars aren't up for discussion."

Right. He knew when not to push.

The silence stretched between them, filled only by the distant slap of waves against the hull. He tended to her carefully – cleaned the wound, applied the salve, and added a fresh bandage. When he finished, he secured the end with a small knot.

"There. Should hold till morning."

She angled her chin at his shoulder. "Your turn. Let me see my handiwork."

Callahan held her gaze as he removed his shirt. He wasn't shy about his body, but something about the way she watched him made his fingers clumsy. His body had scars layered on scars until there was barely an inch of skin that wasn't filled with bullet holes, knife wounds, burns, and lash marks from Whelan's belt. Each one was a reminder of the endless bartering of blood, the slow erasure of self.

Annihilation, one scar at a time.

"We match," she whispered. "Don't we?"

Yes.

They were both fluent in the language of brutality and life's cruelties. The singular agony of knowing how it feels when your body belongs to someone else.

She focused on his shoulder. "Impressive needlework. The stitches are nearly invisible."

"Lady Alexandra patched me up. All those years embroidering pillows finally put to practical use."

He grabbed a roll of fresh linen, tore a strip with his teeth, and began rebinding the wound. He'd performed this ritual a hundred times, in a hundred rooms, but never with an audience. Never with every vulnerability laid bare.

"So," Isabel said, leaning against his pillow as if she belonged there, "am I to be your prisoner for the remainder of our voyage to Boston?"

Callahan tucked the end of the bandage, then looked up at her. Something dark and hungry unfurled in him at the sight of her naked in his bed.

He moved before he could think better of it, crawling

toward her until he had her caged against the headboard, his arms braced on either side of her. Her thighs fell open.

"Are you asking to be cuffed again, Trouble?" he asked.

Her exhale was shaky. "No."

"No?" He smiled. "I thought you had deviant tastes. Wasn't that what you told me in Athens when you tried to shock me with this vulgar mouth?" He grazed a finger over her lower lip.

"Maybe you're more depraved than I am."

"Am I? Because I think that one day, you'll offer me these wrists and beg me to bind them."

"Is that what you think?" Her voice was teasing. "That I'll wake up desperate to be at your mercy?"

"Not desperate. Eager." Her pulse jumped under his lips when he pressed them to her throat. "I'd take my time with you and find all the places that make you gasp. The ones that make you beg. And when you're shaking . . . when you can't remember your own name . . ." He brushed his mouth against hers, not quite a kiss. Just a whisper of contact that had her leaning toward him. ". . . I'll show you what it means to be worshipped until you forget you were ever anything but holy."

Her eyelids fluttered closed. For a moment, she surrendered. Softened beneath him.

And then he fucked it all up.

"Stay with me tonight," he whispered against her lips, "and I'll make it worth your while. For every question you answer about the Syndicate, I'll give you pleasure."

The change was immediate. Her entire body went rigid, and the softness in her eyes hardened.

Shit.

"Trouble—"

"Get off me," she said, shoving at his chest.

Callahan moved back. She scrambled from the bed and grabbed her clothes, yanking them on with quick, angry movements.

"I'm going to my cabin. If you try to chain me again, trust that I won't tell you a damn thing."

"That came out wrong." Callahan raked a hand through his hair. "I didn't mean it to sound like that."

"No." Isabel straightened, fully dressed now, and pinned him with a look so cutting he almost flinched. "You meant exactly what you said. I'm worth more to you as an informant than a woman."

She slammed the door behind her.

"Well done, you absolute fucking idiot," he muttered to himself.

❧ 15 ❧

Isabel paced the deck as the ship approached the harbour. For days now, she'd been avoiding Callahan. Every time he'd knocked on her cabin door, she'd slammed it in his face. She'd mapped the entire ship – every shadowy corner, every hidden alcove – just to disappear whenever she spotted him.

She hated to admit how much his words hurt her. The idea that he was just using her for information. For his *mission*.

But maybe she should be grateful, too. It was a reminder of who they were to each other.

Isabel leaned against the ship's railing, salt spray misting her face as Boston's harbour came into view.

A warm hand settled on her shoulder. "Izzy?"

The tension went out of her at Emma's voice.

"Are you all right?" her sister asked.

Isabel forced a smile. "I'm counting the minutes until we're off this floating prison."

Emma fidgeted, brushing her pale blonde hair behind her

ear. She wore a lovely pink travelling dress that suited her new alias and station – Genevieve, the soon-to-be Countess of Kent.

"You know James and I will be here for you, yes? Just say the word and—"

"No. We have to stay apart for your safety. As far as the world is concerned, you're Genevieve Hamilton, heiress eloping with an earl. No previous attachments." A cynical twist of her lips. "It won't be any different from when you didn't hear from me for a year."

Emma flinched. Hurt flashed across her face, but she said nothing.

At least her sister knew Isabel hadn't abandoned her. The year she went quiet, she'd been with Favreau, then Hong Kong, then fleeing wherever her feet could take her.

Keeping Emma safe had always meant pretending she didn't exist.

They both watched as the ship eased into its berth. The air filled with shouts and the creaking of ropes, the thud of gangplanks being lowered, yelling from the welcoming crowd on the shore. Passengers began to gather their belongings.

"I suppose this is goodbye, then," Emma said. Moisture gathered in her eyes. "Promise me you'll be careful and you won't do anything reckless."

Isabel snorted. "*Reckless* is practically my middle name. Along with *Danger* and *Poor Life Choices*."

Footsteps approached from behind.

"Emma." Kent's voice, deep and commanding. "Our carriage is waiting at the docks."

"Right. Of course." Emma hugged her, squeezing so tight it hurt. "I love you. Always. No matter what."

"I know," Isabel whispered. She looked at Kent as she released her sister. "Take care of her for me."

"I will," the earl said. "You have my word."

"See that you keep it. Or there's no corner of this earth you can hide from me."

He gave her a slight smile. "I'd expect nothing less."

Isabel squeezed Emma's hand one last time and watched them walk away. She remained at the railing for a few more minutes, gathering herself, then made her way towards the gangplank.

And nearly walked into a muscular chest.

"Careful, Trouble." Callahan's voice was a low rumble, edged with a familiar bite of mockery. "It'd be a shame if you went arse over teakettle before we've even left the ship."

She couldn't look at him. Couldn't meet that storm-grey gaze without remembering the sounds he'd dragged from her throat with lips and teeth and tongue.

"Maybe if you didn't insist on looming out of nowhere, I wouldn't be in danger of falling," she snapped.

"Maybe if you paid the slightest bit of attention to your surroundings instead of getting lost in your head, my 'looming' wouldn't take you by surprise."

There was a certain set to his mouth and a crease between his brow she'd learned to recognise – his frustration simmering just below the surface.

Good. At least she wasn't alone in her discontent and irritation. He ought to be every bit as miserable as she was.

"Are we going to depart? I'm eager to meet my new handler."

His lips tightened more. "After you. I already had your luggage collected."

A gleaming black carriage waited for them at the edge of the docks, drawn by a pair of matched bays. Neither spoke as they climbed inside.

Callahan's massive body made the space seem even more cramped, his knees brushing hers as he settled onto the bench opposite. Isabel angled away. She focused on the view out the window as the vehicle lurched into motion and winded through Boston's narrow streets lined with brick buildings. The air was thick with coal smoke and the mingled scent of the ocean. Vendors hawked their wares on street corners, their shouts blending with the clop of hooves and rumble of wheels on cobblestones.

"You've been avoiding me."

His voice cracked the silence like a whip. She didn't flinch. Didn't so much as shift her gaze from the window.

"Have I?" she asked coolly.

The bench creaked as he leaned forward. "You know you have. Ever since that night in my cabin, you've been slithering through every bolthole on that blasted ship like a scalded cat. Did you think I wouldn't notice?"

"Anyone ever tell you that you have a way with words? Be still my beating heart."

"Anyone ever tell you that sarcasm is the last refuge of the emotionally stunted?"

"I think you're confusing sarcasm with self-preservation."

"I think you're confusing self-preservation with cowardice."

That barb struck home, but she let the pain wash through her like a tide. It wasn't anything she hadn't already done before. In Hong Kong, when she ran away with his suitcase and threw his belongings in the harbour, she'd become an expert in pretending to be indifferent to him. Not letting her body betray how often he threw her off-balance. She just quietly rebuilt her walls and ramparts, wrapped them in thorns, and waited for him to crumble them all over again.

"I'm not a coward," she said.

"Could've fooled me. Ever since that night, you've been running so hard I'm surprised there isn't an Isabel-shaped hole in the hull."

"For someone so determined to analyse my actions, you seem remarkably obtuse as to their cause."

"Obtuse?" He scoffed. "That's rich, coming from you. It's a wonder anyone can parse your intent through that thorny tangle you call communication. You were almost bearable when you were chained to my bed."

"And you're almost tolerable when your mouth is shut. What a shame that's such a rare occurrence. Tell me, did you expect fawning gratitude when you offered to fuck me as a reward for information?"

Callahan winced. "I told you it came out wrong. I know you're used to closely hoarding any scrap of intelligence and making me claw it out of you."

Her chest burned. He was right; he did keep clawing it out of her. Picking and picking and *picking* all her scabbed-over wounds, things she'd buried deep. And one day, he'd ask her again about the scars all over her torso, and she was going to tell him because this man was her own personal apocalypse. Destroying her with tenacity and stubbornness and all those tender kisses. As if he *cared*.

Isabel curled her fingers into her palm. "I'm re-establishing boundaries. This is business. I think your superiors at the Home Office would appreciate my efforts to remind you that you are an agent of the Crown, and I'm an asset, and the moment you deliver me to my handler, I'm no longer your obligation."

His mouth closed with an audible click, expression hardening. "Of course," he said flatly. "I beg your pardon, Miss Dumont."

Miss Dumont. Said deliberately, as if he weren't scratching at her walls with his fingernails.

We're nothing. We can't be anything.

They jolted to a stop in front of a handsome brick townhouse. Callahan climbed out of the carriage, helped her down, and then pulled from her touch – cold, perfunctory.

Treating her like an asset.

The door of the residence swung open, spilling golden light onto the steps. A woman emerged – tall and lithe, with dark hair and sharp, angular features.

"Agent Vale," Callahan said, inclining his head in greeting. "May I present Miss Isabel Dumont?"

The woman – Vale – fixed Isabel with a piercing stare. Her eyes were a startling shade of amber, and Isabel had the discomfiting sensation of being dissected.

"Miss Dumont," Vale said. "Welcome to Boston. I hope your journey was uneventful?"

Frankly, Isabel wished it were less eventful.

"As uneventful as one might expect, given the circumstances."

"Indeed." Vale smiled and gestured to the open door. "Well, come in. No sense in lingering on the doorstep."

The townhouse's interior was elegant, filled with mahogany furniture, landscape paintings, and dozens of shelves lined with books. Isabel stored away each piece of information, learning about her new circumstances, her temporary home and handler. Vale favoured dramatic mountain scenes with colourful, wild strokes. The leather-bound books were primarily travelogues, indicating a spy accustomed to playing different regional roles.

Vale led them down the hall to a study and motioned to the chairs across from the desk.

Isabel tried not to squirm as she sat beside Callahan.

"I'll be frank, Miss Dumont," Vale said, leaning against the desk. "Your presence puts me in a delicate position. On the one hand, you possess valuable intelligence. On the other, you're a criminal with a history of betrayal and deception. So what I expect is your full cooperation. That means unquestioning obedience and discretion. Can you give me those things?"

For a long moment, Isabel said nothing. She could feel Callahan's gaze on her. Daring her to rear back and refuse. Isabel didn't, after all, take well to the words *unquestioning obedience*.

But she also wasn't in any situation to object.

"I can," she said. "But if there are any chains or darbies, my assistance ends."

She half-expected Vale to bristle at her defiance. "Fair enough," the other woman said. "You won't be chained, but you won't leave this house without my permission and escort. You will submit to daily debriefings, during which you will share every scrap of information you possess about the Syndicate. Simple enough?"

"I already agreed with Agent Callahan to these terms. I'm aware of the deal I've made."

"Excellent. Then if you'll excuse me, I'll telegram

Wentworth to let him know you've arrived. Callahan, please see yourself out."

She left the room.

Isabel curled her fingers into her dress as Callahan stood. This was it. He was leaving, and she was going to have to let him.

"Miss Dumont," he said, standing and walking to the door. "It's been a pleasure. Have a nice life."

"Wait."

The word slipped free before she could stop it.

His shoulders tensed, but he didn't turn.

There were so many things she wanted to tell him. An apology for Hong Kong. An explanation for why she fled the way she did. All the secrets she'd kept buried beneath her skin like shrapnel. How weeks after she ran, when her ship finally docked and she found what she was looking for, she'd spent three days huddled in a ball on a stranger's floor, bleeding and crying and so damn sorry for hurting him.

The words stuck behind her teeth. She couldn't say them aloud, not today. Maybe not ever.

But she could give him something else.

"You asked for one real thing," she said quietly. "And I was never honest during any of the times we met. But I wanted you to know that what happened in that bed in Hong Kong was real for me. It was the first time I'd—" She broke off, exhaling sharply. "You were the first man I ever wanted."

He turned and stared at her for a long moment. His eyes were storm-dark, hungry in a way that made her thighs press together. She knew that look. Had seen it in Hong Kong, in Athens, and over and over again in her dreams. Then he strode over to her and grabbed the front of her dress.

"Agent—"

His lips crushed against hers, stealing whatever she might have said next. Not gentle. Not sweet. His teeth scraped her bottom lip, and she tasted copper.

He murmured against her mouth, "Open."

She did.

Callahan's tongue slid against hers. He gripped her hair with his other hand until her scalp stung, but she didn't care. Pain, pleasure – they blurred with him. Always had.

She clutched his coat, fingers digging in as if she could somehow keep him there. Just a few more seconds. Just until she had control over herself and could let him go without breaking apart.

His kiss was almost violent in its intensity. Bruising. And she yielded, surrendering for this moment before he had to leave. She'd store this away with every other stolen memory between them – Athens, New York, Hong Kong, the pleasure he gave her on the steamer.

Her collection of things that weren't meant to be hers.

In two days, she'd hate herself for this weakness. In two hours, she'd stare at the ceiling and reimagine every second. But right now, with his heart pounding against hers, she couldn't bring herself to care.

Callahan's kiss tasted like goodbye.

His breath was hot against her mouth when he pulled back. Chest rising hard against hers. He leaned in, lips brushing her ear.

"Don't run from Vale," he growled. "Don't make me hunt you down, little thief. Because I'll find you. Always."

He pressed his mouth to hers one last time. Softer now. Almost gentle.

"Be good," he whispered.

The door closed behind him quietly, and Isabel touched trembling fingers to her bruised lips.

❦ 16 ❦

Five months later

Isabel's fingers tapped restlessly against the window as the carriage navigated London's streets.

Five months away, and nothing had changed.

She'd hated Boston at the beginning. Hated feeling like she was trapped and couldn't run. But somewhere between her morning briefings with Vale and the evening teas, she'd found a rhythm. A peace. A sense of safety that she hadn't felt since she was a child still ignorant of the ways the world broke girls.

It had been nice.

"You're quiet," Vale said, not looking up from her book.

"Just admiring the scenery."

That earned her a snort. Portia Vale wasn't a woman who bothered with pleasantries or lies. It was what she'd come to appreciate most about her handler – the brutal honesty between them. She never looked at Isabel like she was damaged goods. They weren't friends, but they'd become colleagues, of a sort. Vale, after all, had heard every deep, dark secret by now. Every job, every name, every drop

A LADY'S HANDBOOK OF ESPIONAGE

of blood spilled. She knew about where Isabel's scars came from. About Favreau's knife games.

Things she hadn't even told Callahan.

"He'll be there," Vale said, as if she read Isabel's mind.

Her face went hot. "Who?"

Vale just looked at her.

"I don't care."

"Yes, you do."

Yes, she did.

The carriage hit a rut, jostling them both. Isabel braced herself against the wall, her heart giving a stupid, foolish lurch at the thought of seeing Callahan again.

Somewhere in this city, he was going about his day, unaware she'd returned.

For months, she'd waited for him to appear at Vale's door with some excuse, some pretence. For him to show up on one of her walks with some bumbling American accent. To climb through her window, maybe. But he never did. Because she was a captured asset now rather than a target, and she gave him no excuse to hunt her down.

After years, Ronan Callahan had finally brought the notorious Spectre to heel – and then washed his hands of her.

"You never answered my question on the steamer," Isabel said. "Did Wentworth give any actual reason for dragging me back here? You told him I wanted to stay in America?"

Vale flipped a page. "I told him. He said no."

"Of course," Isabel muttered. "And the information I gave you? Has he done anything with it?"

"We wouldn't be in this miserable city if he hadn't."

*

153

Isabel shifted her suitcase in her hands as she followed Vale into the nondescript government building. Their boots clicked against the marble floor as they proceeded down the hall to a door labelled MATTIAS WENTWORTH.

Vale rapped twice.

"Enter." The voice from inside was deep, clipped.

The office was smaller than she expected. No grandeur, no display of wealth or power. Nothing to say, *Look how important I am*. Just functionality – a desk, three chairs, some bookshelves against one wall.

And him.

Mattias Wentworth wasn't what she'd pictured. Not some severe, grey-bearded official with liver spots, but a handsome, rugged man sprawled almost insolently in his chair. He was younger than she'd anticipated, perhaps only a handful of years past thirty. He had keen blue eyes and close-cropped brown hair. When he reached for a file, his forearm muscles flexed beneath his pushed-up sleeves.

Those weren't the arms of someone who shuffled papers for a living. He looked like he'd learned to fight before he learned to read; this was a man who broke things.

"That will be all, Vale," he said without taking his eyes off Isabel. "You can go."

"Sir—" Portia started.

"The return steamer leaves Friday." His tone left no room for argument. "Get some rest before then."

Isabel felt a flicker of panic as Vale's footsteps retreated and her last ally disappeared through the door.

Wentworth studied her. "So you're Spectre."

"And you're the one who's been reading about all my sins for the past five months."

His mouth twitched – not quite a smile. "Sit, Miss Dumont. Put down the suitcase."

She hesitated, then sank into the chair in front of his desk, her back straight like a lady. Like someone who hadn't killed men with hairpins.

"I trust you've settled well enough with Agent Vale these past months?"

"Well enough. Is my sister Emma all right?"

"*Lady Kent* has just returned to England. The Syndicate lost her scent months ago, her alias as an American heiress is holding up, and as long as there's no connection to her past, she remains safe."

The warning was clear – Emma's safety hung on the tenuous thread of her false identity. But she was alive and well with her new husband, and that was what mattered.

"I understand," Isabel said. "She'll hear nothing from me."

"See that she doesn't. Now. To—"

The door swung open without a knock.

Isabel's head jerked up.

Ronan Callahan filled the doorway, every bit as beautiful as she remembered. His black hair was damp from the rain, messy, as if he'd been running his fingers through it. Faint stubble coloured his jawline. When his grey eyes met hers, they went as dark as storm clouds over the sea.

Her heart kicked against her ribs. Even after months apart, her body still reacted to him as if he owned it.

"You summoned me, Wentworth?" His gaze never left Isabel.

That voice. Every time they were apart, she'd forget it a little – how deep it was, the way it seemed to brush over her skin like fingertips.

"Have a seat, Callahan."

She kept her attention on Wentworth as her personal plague dropped into the chair beside her. Her senses filled with him. The heat of his body, the scent of rain and leather, the edge of his boot touching hers.

It was torture.

Wentworth pulled papers from a drawer. "The information Miss Dumont provided about the Syndicate's operations has been useful. We intercepted communications about a man named Edmund Ramsgate."

The name meant nothing to Isabel. "Who is he?"

"A biochemist of some repute. Brilliant, reclusive. Lives in some decrepit country house most of the year, except when he emerges for scientific events. But we've had a look at his finances, and while there's no direct connection to Favreau, he's certainly quite flush for an academic hermit." He pushed a paper across the desk. "My men copied Ramsgate's research notes, and they're working on decoding them. But his sudden influx of capital coincides neatly with Miss Dumont's reports of expanded Syndicate activities on English soil. Look here." Wentworth tapped a row of figures. "Until a year ago, Ramsgate was up to his neck in gambling debts. He owed sums he had no way of repaying through legitimate means. Favreau wouldn't waste resources on a mere scientist unless he had something of value to offer."

"What's the play, then?" Callahan asked.

"The Marquess of Ripon hosts an annual symposium at Basil House for leading minds in the scientific community. Thanks to the Office's cordial relationship with Ripon, Ramsgate has received an invitation. I need you both to attend and find out what he's doing for Favreau without alerting the Syndicate or anyone else to our interest."

Callahan grimaced. "You want us to go to some posh scientific salon and make nice with the nobs?"

"As husband and wife," Wentworth said.

Isabel's stomach dropped.

No. No. No. *Zut alors.*

Husband and wife meant sharing quarters. It meant touching, pretending, acting like they belonged to each other.

Her gaze flicked to Callahan. He'd gone rigid, jaw clenched, but he said nothing. He was probably used to getting orders he didn't like.

Isabel spoke first. "Surely there's some other way—"

"There isn't," Wentworth interrupted. "Ripon's gathering begins in two days. You'll be reporting to Basil House tomorrow afternoon. A dossier with your cover identities and a wardrobe befitting your roles will be delivered to your flat in the morning before you depart, Callahan."

"Mr Wentworth, I really must . . ."

She couldn't seem to catch her breath. Her chest felt too tight, her skin too small, and the world tilted around her. She gripped her chair, trying to anchor herself against the rising surge of panic. Five months in America, and she'd almost forgotten what it felt like – this drowning feeling when the walls closed in, and she had no control over what happened to her.

"Miss Dumont."

Wentworth's clipped voice cut through the static. She lifted her head to meet his piercing stare.

"This is not a request. You come to me absent any leverage. If I have even an inkling that you intend to betray me to Favreau, there is nowhere on this earth that I won't find you. I will make the very short duration of your days agony. If you wish to continue drawing breath, you will adopt some humility. Swiftly."

Icy fingers trailed down her spine. She forced her lungs to work, to pull in air. "That won't be necessary. I understand what you require."

"Good. Callahan, I leave the rest to you. Don't disappoint me." Wentworth turned back to the papers on his desk in dismissal.

Isabel and Callahan left the office.

"Well," she said, slumping against the wall in the corridor. She tapped her fingers against her suitcase. "That went about as well as a jump from a burning building."

Callahan snorted. "Of course, you find this amusing."

"Not in the slightest. But I hardly see what choice we have in the matter."

"This'll end badly."

"No question. I'll probably stab you again."

"Good to know your smart mouth survived Boston intact."

He scrutinised her, attention moving from her face down to her shoes and back up again. Slow. Deliberate. After five months, she wasn't any more inured to that look, to the way it stripped her bare. Ronan Callahan had a stare like a rapier.

When she could take it no longer, she snapped, "You're staring."

"Just thinking that you look ... different." He cleared his throat. "Better."

Different how? Better than what? But she knew what he

meant, didn't she? She weighed more. Her skin had colour, the hollows beneath her cheekbones had filled in, and she'd finally had full nights of rest. She looked less like the half-starved creature he'd found in the abandoned distillery.

"Fascinating what happens when you're not constantly looking over your shoulder," she said. "Regular meals. Regular sleep. Regular . . ."

The word "life" died on her tongue.

Callahan's expression softened. "Where are you staying?"

The question caught her off guard. She hadn't thought past the meeting with Wentworth.

"I—" She hesitated, lifting her suitcase. "I came straight from the docks in Liverpool."

"Jesus, Trouble. What was your plan? Sleep in the street?"

"I didn't have a plan. Vale took care of everything in Boston."

"Fine. My place."

Isabel blinked. "Your flat? With you?"

"No, with the bloody Queen." He glowered at her. "Yes, with me. It's not Claridge's, but it's got a roof. And walls. A bed with a mattress. Unless you'd prefer I track down Vale and beg her to delay her departure?"

"No." Isabel had encroached on Portia's kindness enough. "No, that's not necessary. Lead on."

Callahan lived in Whitechapel.

The building leaned slightly to the left. Soot-stained bricks crumbled at the corners, and the front door hung crooked, its paint flaking off, with a knocker so rusted it probably hadn't moved in years.

As they stepped into the building's foyer, the smell hit her first. Not filth exactly, but the particular odour of sweat and ale and coal smoke. Isabel said nothing, just followed Callahan up the stairs. It wasn't as if she hadn't slept in worse while on the run from Favreau.

Two floors up, Callahan fumbled with the lock at a door that looked like someone had tried to kick it in at least once.

The key stuck, and he jiggled it roughly. "Damn thing."

"Let me." She set down her suitcase and nudged him aside, feeling the way the lock caught. A delicate touch, a slight lift upward, and it clicked open. "There."

He stared at her, then pushed the door wide without a word.

Isabel trailed him inside. His home wasn't as unkempt as the rest of the building. Small, yes. Cluttered, definitely. But it was clean and cosy and she rather loved the piles of books and the worn furniture. The windows were spotless, catching what little grey light London had to offer.

"Well? What's the verdict?" he asked, taking her suitcase from her and setting it beside his couch. "Does my modest abode meet with mademoiselle's approval?"

"I expected rats. And more whiskey bottles."

"The rats are on holiday, and I finished my bottles in the aftermath of Hong Kong."

She bit back a laugh. "Well. It's very atmospheric. I thought being in the government's employ paid better, though."

"It pays fine. But I like being surrounded by reminders of where I came from. Keeps me humble."

"Now you've ruined my imaginings of the tortured agent in his lair with cyphers on the desk and villainous plots foiled in the dark of night. But I bet you brood magnificently by that window," she said with a nod to one by his bookshelves.

"You spend a lot of time thinking about me in my flat, Trouble?" His voice dropped lower. "Should I be worried? Or just pleased?"

She ignored the heat crawling up her neck and wandered deeper into the room, running a fingertip over the spines of the books stacked haphazardly on a rickety shelf. Most were political tracts and histories, dense tomes with cracked leather bindings. Nothing to indicate the flat's occupant was anything more than a scholar with middling means.

"Neither. Your predilections don't intere—" The retort faded as she caught sight of a curio on the mantelpiece.

It was a skull. A *human* skull with a jaunty top hat perched on its brow. Sitting there like some macabre conversation piece.

"Friend of yours?" she asked dryly.

Callahan glanced up from shrugging out of his greatcoat. "Freddie Figgs, Mad Freddie to his friends. He always did fancy himself a proper gent."

Of course. Of *course*, he'd display human remains like fashionable baubles. Because why wouldn't this beautiful, infuriating creature flout the most fundamental tenets of sanity and good taste?

"You," she announced, "are a madman. And to think, Wentworth expects me to fake marry you."

"And you, sweetheart, are a menace. And yet, here we both are. It must be kismet." He nodded toward a door across the small sitting room. "Come on, fake wife. Bed's in there."

Isabel followed his gesture, then froze.

The bed.

A narrow, sorry excuse for a bed that couldn't fit two adults unless they slept practically on top of each other. Her throat went dry. Images flashed through her mind – his weight pressing her down, him inside her, kissing her neck—

Callahan, the wretched beast, merely smirked. "Lose your nerve?"

"You should know by now that I never do."

"That's a lie." He stepped into her space, forcing her to tilt her chin up to maintain eye contact. "Do you know, I've been imagining our reunion since the moment you flounced away from me."

"I didn't flounce," she argued. "You kissed me, dumped me with Portia, and then never returned."

His smirk widened into a smile. "That your way of saying you missed me?"

"You have a habit of blundering into my life. It was an expectation."

"That *sounds* like you missed me." He touched her, a gentle swipe of palm down her arm. "You know what I've been thinking about? How to make you pay for avoiding me after our little encounter on the steamer. After I gave such devoted attention to that sweet cunt of yours."

Isabel sputtered. He was unbelievable, honestly. Deranged, half-mad, and too attractive by far. Just the memory of him between her thighs sent heat pooling through her core.

"You shackled me to a bed and tried to force me to apologise," she managed.

"I deserved the apology. You earned the restraints. And just think, if you had given me those two words instead of *losing your nerve*, you little liar, I would have fucked you for days. Instead, you've spent months alone and wanting."

"Who says I've been wanting? Boston is full of handsome men."

"Oh, Trouble," he said with a sigh. "Let's not start this fake marriage with lies. I think we both know I'm the only man who can satisfy you."

She seized his wrist, squeezing hard. "Are we going to be able to pull this off?" she asked softly. "Or will we slaughter each other before the week is out?"

"I imagine you and I will find some measure of agreement. Whether through our mutual performance or the fact that we can't exist in the same room without wanting each other."

"A handful of days, and I'll be strangling you. Mark my words."

"Not if I throttle you first." He tugged his hand out of her grasp. "I'm going to sleep. It's been a damnably long day, and I'm knackered. I'm sure you'd like a rest after the steamer."

He didn't wait for a response, just bent to work at his bootlaces. She shucked her own boots, stripped to her combination, and stretched out on the bed. The mattress dipped as he snuffed out the light and lay beside her.

"Just so you know," Callahan murmured into the darkness, "if you're plotting my murder, strangulation's a bore. Poison's more your style. Tasteless. Effective. One drop in my morning tea and I'd never see it coming."

Isabel bit back a grin. "I've always favoured an ice pick. Clean, elegant. And if you position it properly, nearly painless."

"Christ, Dumont. Are you seducing me with murder tactics?"

"Would it work if I were?"

Their breathing synced in the quiet room. He reached out, knuckles grazing her cheek.

"I missed you," he whispered.

The confession knocked the air from her lungs. Three words that shouldn't have mattered but somehow cracked her open and made her confess what she'd been too much of a coward to say earlier.

"I waited," she admitted. "Every day in Boston, I thought you might show up."

He didn't pull away. Didn't build up walls or go cold. His smile softened, and he tapped her nose. "Next time, don't wait. Just ask for what you want."

Before she could respond, his arm wrapped around her waist, pulling her against him. His heart thumped steadily in a rhythm she could have picked out blindfolded from a thousand others.

17

Basil House was the kind of place Callahan would have robbed in his youth.

It was a towering stone edifice meant to communicate money more than a warm welcome. He counted the windows and guessed there were twenty, maybe thirty rooms. Four visible chimneys. The doorknobs on this place probably cost more than he'd made in a year growing up in Whitechapel.

Gargoyles scowled down at them as he helped Isabel down from the carriage.

"Quite the pile." She scanned the façade with that professional assessment he recognised. "Always wanted to see inside when I was casing these homes. Shame we're here for work rather than pleasure."

"What, not excited about playing with the aristos? Thought you'd be thrilled for the chance now that honest crime doesn't pay you anymore."

Her eyes narrowed. "Do you bill Wentworth separately for the sarcasm?"

"The sarcasm comes free when I spend all night with a woman grinding against my cock and pretending she doesn't notice."

Isabel laughed. "What was it you told me? Next time, don't wait. Ask for what you want."

Then she tapped him on the nose and started for the house.

Infuriating woman.

He gripped his satchel as they climbed the steps, falling into the role of besotted husband. Too easy to play that part. The dossier Wentworth had shoved at him this morning laid out his new identity: James Ashford, an American businessman with more coin than sense. His wife, Lydia Ashford, was an heiress and socialite with scientific interests.

All very respectable. All very false.

The butler who answered Ripon's door had a look that said he'd slid from the womb wearing livery and judging the doctor's technique.

"Mr and Mrs Ashford, I presume?"

"You got it," Callahan replied in his practised New York accent, ignoring Isabel's small jolt of surprise. She didn't have time to read their covers before they left that morning.

The butler's mouth pinched tighter. "Do come in."

Callahan and Isabel followed him into an antechamber that reeked of old money and judgment. Oil paintings stared down from the walls – generations of Ripons with perfect posture and cold eyes. Watching him.

"Banks." A voice echoed from the adjoining room.

The marquess appeared in the doorway. He was younger than Callahan expected, with more muscle than your typical nobleman, short brown hair and brown eyes that assessed rather than merely looked. This wasn't a man who spent his days drinking brandy and reading poetry.

"I'll take our guests from here, Banks," Ripon told the butler. "See to their luggage." He waited until the servant was out of earshot before turning his full attention to them. "So you're Wentworth's people. James and Lydia Ashford sound like names concocted by a third-rate novelist on a deadline."

Isabel grinned. "Isabel Dumont, at your service."

"Save the charm, Miss Dumont." Ripon didn't smile. "Your flirtation might work on your marks, but I'm only tolerating this charade because I owe Wentworth. The bastard always knows exactly which debts to call in. Now, let's dispense with the pleasantries. We've much to discuss and precious little time to do it. Come with me to your rooms."

The marquess led Isabel and Callahan up the stairs, stopping at a second-floor door.

"Here," Ripon announced. "Try not to ruin anything irreplaceable."

The chamber beyond was larger than Callahan's entire damn flat. It was sumptuous, with gilt mirrors, tapestries, and rich fabrics in deep blues and golds. And dominating the far wall, a four-poster bed that could fit half of Whitechapel.

Isabel wandered further in, running her fingers along a marble-topped table. "What's your symposium like?"

Ripon leaned against the doorframe. "Men with too much education and too little practical experience, attempting to impress each other with theories that will never see application. And wives who are simply grateful their hermit husbands have left the house for once."

"Sounds riveting."

"I'd rather swallow broken glass. But my father believed in it, so here we are." He crossed his arms. "Now, perhaps you'll explain why Wentworth insisted I invite a man I've never met to my home. What has this Ramsgate fellow done?"

"Intercepted communications, irregular financial activities," Callahan said. "All pointing to him being involved with an international organisation we've been tracking."

"Criminal?"

"Would we be here if he were running a charity?"

Ripon levelled him with a withering stare. "Let me be abundantly clear. You may look. You may listen. You may even speak to the man. But if I find one drop of blood on my carpets or one piece of furniture where it doesn't belong, I'll personally deliver you to Wentworth with several new holes in your body."

"We'll be discreet," Isabel promised, all sweetness.

Ripon must have been the only man alive immune to that little performance, because he just scowled at her.

"See that you are. The staff knows to accommodate you within reason. Guests arrive tomorrow. Try not to embarrass me."

The door closed behind him.

Callahan exhaled, feeling the emergence of a spectacular headache. "I need a whiskey."

Isabel snorted, still inspecting the priceless baubles around the room. If she stole anything, he'd never hear the end of it from Wentworth. Hell, Ripon would probably shoot them.

"Want to tell me about that fetching accent you put on downstairs?" she asked. "Are we American Ashfords?"

"Unfortunately." Callahan yanked the file from his satchel and spread the papers on the table. Americans. Of all the bloody covers Wentworth could have chosen. "Courier delivered this while you were still drooling on your pillow this morning. Our identities and the schedule. There's a formal opening tomorrow. I figure we mingle, try not to commit any felonies and murder each other in the process. Think we can manage that?"

"I've already managed to endure one night in your bed. I'm sure I'll find the fortitude to withstand a few more."

"So kind of you," he said. "And can you be a fawning newlywed? Or is that too much of a stretch?"

"Please." She slanted him a look. "I once convinced the Archduchess of Austria that I was a long-lost Romanov cousin. I think I can play a besotted bride."

"Of course you did." He shook his head. "Why am I not surprised?"

"Because I'm just that good. Now, I intend to take advantage of these fancy accommodations and get more comfortable."

She reached back and slipped the first tiny button of her bodice free.

Everything inside Callahan stilled. The room. His breath. Time itself. For one disorienting moment, he was back in that Hong Kong hotel room thinking of each button as a piece of armour being peeled away.

They were professionals with a job to do. He meant to tell her as much. Truly. Opened his mouth to say in no uncertain terms that whatever this was between them had to be shelved, boxed up, and shoved into some dusty corner of his psyche.

What emerged instead was, "Do you need help?"

Isabel froze. Her stare locked with his, and she cleared her throat. "Yes, please."

He closed the distance between them. He didn't touch her – not yet – just reached for the fastening behind her neck, listening to her breath snag.

The buttons were tiny, so delicate. He worked them slowly, one after another, revealing the smooth skin of her back. Skin he'd tasted. Skin he'd marked.

By the time he finished, he could hear the shallow, quick rhythm of her breathing.

"There," he said.

She slipped it off, then began unhooking her bustle and front-fastening corset to reveal her thin linen combination. He swallowed, hypnotised by the shift of muscle beneath pale skin as she plucked the pins from her hair until it spilled over her shoulders.

God, he wanted to devour her.

He cleared his throat and turned away, listening to the rustle of fabric as she donned her nightdress. Then, as if she hadn't just reduced him to a speechless idiot, she sprawled on the counterpane and opened the dossier.

"Well?" she said. "Are you going to come over here and review these with me?"

He stripped down to his smalls and settled beside her, trying and failing to find a comfortable position.

She tossed some papers onto his chest. "Take these."

He should say something clever. Something about the mission. The cover identities. Anything to distract himself from the expanse of her thigh left bare by her nightgown and how badly he wanted to push her down onto the mattress.

"Do you ever blink?" Isabel asked.

His gaze snapped to her face. "What?"

"It's like you're attempting to vivisect me with your eyes."

"I'm looking at you." He let his gaze drift deliberately down her body. "That's what normal people call it. *Looking.* Maybe 'observing' if they're feeling fancy. Anyone ever tell you that you have a remarkable gift for killing the mood?"

"What mood is there to ruin? The one where we pretend we aren't imagining all the filthy things we want to do to each other?"

Memories rose – her pulse beneath his fingertips, the slick glide of skin on skin. Isabel twisting a hand in his hair as she urged him *faster, harder, more.*

He was so monumentally fucked. His brain shut down while his body took over, like a drunk falling off a cliff.

"I'm thinking," he said, "that James and Lydia Ashford aren't the hands-off type. He's a scoundrel who somehow convinced this gorgeous woman to marry him. She's clearly fallen for him despite her better judgment. Americans don't have that English reserve. We should consider establishing an easy intimacy so we're comfortable in each other's space. We've been apart for five months."

Isabel, who had been reading the dossier, finally looked up at that. "Should I expect darbies and commands and punishments? Or do you have something else in mind?"

He shifted closer before he could stop himself, sliding a hand under her nightgown to graze her thigh. She was smooth here. Soft.

"I propose a game," he said. "Some competitive espionage to keep things sporting."

The lie tasted good. Made him feel less desperate. As if this was just part of the job and not him dying to get between her legs since Hong Kong.

"Now?" Her breath hitched as his fingers inched higher. "While your hand is up my nightdress?"

"I can do lots of things at once, Spectre." He grazed her pussy and almost groaned. She was wet. Always wet for him. "The rules are simple. Five minutes to review our identities, then we take turns asking questions about our covers. For every correct answer, the asker names a forfeit. A bit of pleasure."

Isabel's thighs fell open. Her nipples hardened beneath the thin fabric of her nightdress, and Callahan wanted to tear the damn thing off with his teeth.

"And incorrect answers?"

He increased the pressure just slightly, circling her entrance. "Then no pleasure for the questioned. What do you say?"

She was already rocking against his hand. Little movements she probably didn't even realise she was making. He'd missed this power – how she tried to pretend she wasn't falling apart when he touched her.

Let her suffer as he had. Every night for five months, with only his hand and the memory of her taste to get him through.

"I accept." Her breathing went shallower as she squirmed. "Are . . . are you going to keep—"

"Oh, this hand is staying right where it is. I never said I'd play fair. Now get to work."

They both reviewed their documents while he gently

stroked between her thighs, never dipping his fingers inside her. Not yet. Just feeling her shiver into his touch, lifting her hips to chase his caress.

She bit her lower lip. Hard. The way she always did when trying not to make noise.

He checked his pocket watch. "Time." He set the papers aside, still stroking her. "Let's see what stuck in that criminal brain of yours. What's Jamie's preferred drink?"

She swallowed before answering. "Whiskey. Single malt. Twenty years aged."

"Good girl."

He slid one finger into her, slow and deep, watching her mouth fall open. A sweet sound left her as he pumped once, twice, teasing.

"Another question. How does he take it?"

"With—" She gasped as he added a second finger. "*God.* With two drops of spring water. Collected by cloistered virgins under the full moon because he's a pretentious arse."

Callahan barked out a laugh. "Now you're taking the piss. Your turn, Mrs Ashford."

"What's Jamie's middle name?"

His mind went blank. All the blood in his body had clearly been redirected south, leaving nothing for his brain.

"Tick tock, darling." Isabel gave a slow roll of her hips, fucking herself on his fingers. "I'd like to climax sometime before the next century."

"Winston." Callahan called up the first pompous moniker that sprang to mind. "Jamie Winston Ashford, named for some great-uncle or other. Pillar of the community, I'm sure."

"Edward, I'm afraid. After his maternal grandfather and

some prized breeding bull or something equally asinine. I'm disappointed, Agent. I expected more from you."

"Hard to remember trivial nonsense while I've got two fingers in your cunt."

"Excuses. I want your mouth."

He pressed against that spot inside her that made her thighs tremble. "Here?"

"No." She arched her neck. "Here. Bite down. I enjoy a little pain with my pleasure."

This woman would be the death of him.

He lowered his head, breathing her in. First, just his lips, testing the flutter of her pulse against his mouth, then his tongue, tasting the salt of her skin. When his teeth finally scraped against her throat, her whole body jerked.

She made a sound – half gasp, half moan – that shot straight to his cock.

He bit down harder, just shy of breaking skin. Marking her.

"My turn," he growled. "Lydia's parents. What are their names?"

"Helena and George," she panted. "Hampshire Granthams. Textile fortune. Moved to America when she was three."

Impressive. But he shouldn't be surprised. This was Isabel. She excelled at everything she did – stealing, lying, making him lose his fucking mind with wanting her.

"Good girl," he murmured again, loving her little shiver at the praise.

"Bite me again," she whispered. A soft cry left her as his teeth sank into another spot. At this rate, every damn person at the symposium would know who she belonged to. "The name of Jamie's prized stallion. What was it?"

Another blank. His brain wasn't working. Not when she kept tightening around his fingers like that.

"Beelzebub."

"Bucephalus. Named for Alexander the Great's legendary charger. Jamie likes to say the beast chose to be reborn as his personal mount."

"Where are you pulling this shite from? It wasn't in the file."

"I'm improvising. Now, my forfeit. Put your mouth on my tits while you fuck me with your fingers." She patted his cheek. "There's a good boy."

Callahan didn't need to be told twice. He yanked down the front of her nightgown and took one of her nipples between his lips. Isabel cried out, arching against him.

"Beautiful," he murmured into her skin. "So bloody perfect."

She squirmed. Her chest rose and fell in quick, shallow breaths that made him want to tear the nightgown off. Ruin her. Mark her. A dark and possessive emotion clawed at him when she responded to his touch.

"I forfeit my question." Her hands twisted in the sheets. "But I'll give you a chance. What's Jamie's favourite thing to brag about at his club?"

"His rare book collection," Callahan said, cupping her breast. The game was just an excuse now, a flimsy pretence to keep touching each other.

Isabel arched into his hand. "And what do you want from me?"

The same thing he'd wanted since the night she held a knife to his throat in New York and looked at him like he was the most fascinating man she'd ever seen.

Callahan released her to drag his smallclothes down, freeing his aching cock. "Suck me, little thief."

There was something innately sensual about the way she slid down his body, curving her back a little as she settled between his thighs. His breath caught as her tongue flicked out, tracing the underside from root to tip. Callahan's hips jerked. A low groan rumbled in his chest.

"Isabel . . ."

She took him fully into her mouth.

"Christ fucking—" His head slammed back against the pillows.

The wet heat of her was exquisite, maddening. Isabel sucked hard and drew away, then sank down again, taking him deeper.

He buried his fingers in her hair, keeping her still as he thrust shallowly.

"Just like that," he rasped. "Take it deep. Let me fuck that gorgeous mouth."

His hips lifted, pushing until he felt the back of her throat. Her fingernails curled into his thigh. Letting him use her. Letting him take. Letting him fuck.

"So perfect," he breathed.

So damn perfect.

She was something out of his darkest fantasies – her lips stretched around him, those green eyes never leaving his face. How many nights had he lain awake wondering exactly this? If she'd take him deep, if she'd let him control the pace, if she'd yield to him. But nothing – not a single fantasy – came close to the reality of watching the most dangerous woman in the country on her knees for him.

There wasn't a hint of submission in her eyes. Just power.

The kind that wrapped around his throat and squeezed while making him beg for more. They both knew who really held power here. She was conquering him. Noting every reaction, every place where his control slipped.

"I need you. Come up here and ride my cock, Mrs Ashford," he commanded.

She gave him one last teasing lick and tugged her nightdress over her head. "So demanding tonight. What's gotten into you, Mr Ashford?"

"Five months is a long time to want something," he said.

She straddled him, not taking him in yet but settling her weight on his thighs. "Yes. I distinctly remember someone not letting me finish."

Lowering herself, she moved her hips in a slow grind. Still teasing him with the maddening friction. He dug his fingers into her hips hard enough to bruise, fighting the urge to flip her onto her stomach and pound into her until she screamed.

"My husband has peculiar tastes, you see." Her lips brushed his ear. "He likes his poor, defenceless wife in chains. Does unspeakable things to her body." Another grind. "Then leaves her aching."

"Sounds like a monster," he managed.

"What would you suggest I do with such a cruel husband? Make him watch while I touch myself? Make him lose his mind?"

"You should stop tormenting him and sit on his cock before he flips you over and takes what he wants."

"One question first."

He groaned. "Of course there is."

She held his gaze, suddenly still. "Have you been with anyone since the steamer? Tell me the truth."

Another lover? He nearly laughed. When she'd infected his every thought since Hong Kong? When even sleep offered no escape?

He leaned in, whispering, "My body is yours."

She went still. An emotion flickered across her face – a crack in Isabel Dumont's perfect mask. Just for a moment, he saw something raw underneath. Something that terrified him more than any knife at his throat ever could.

He'd said too much. Been too honest.

But then she kissed him. Soft. So soft. As if she were asking him a question. *Are you mine? Would you be mine if I asked?*

Yes. Always yes.

Then she lifted up and took his cock inside her.

He muffled a groan. He had memories of how wet she was, how tight, how warm, and none compared to this moment. She rode him slowly with her hands braced on his shoulders, her gaze fixed on him.

As if she needed to see him come apart beneath her.

"Is this what you wanted?" he whispered, sliding his hand to her nape. Kissing her again. "This hard enough for you? Or do you need it deeper?"

"More," she gasped.

Good.

He grasped her hips and rolled her under him. Her surprised gasp cut off when he thrust into her – hard, deep, the way he knew she needed it. She clenched around him, and he moaned.

Memories of Hong Kong couldn't capture this. The beautiful flush of her cheeks, the clutch of her hands, how her nails dug into his shoulders, and the sounds she made when he went harder. Her thigh hooked over his arse, and she canted her hips, fucking him back.

The bed frame knocked against the wall, loud enough that the entire house would know exactly what they were doing.

Let them hear. Let everyone know she was his.

When he looked down at her, a question burned in his throat.

Am I still the only man you've ever wanted?

But maybe the answer was unnecessary. She stared at him like there'd never been anyone else. Like they could be anywhere – this bed, a filthy alley, a crowded ballroom – and she'd still only see him, and it was like time stopped.

His hand closed around her throat, not squeezing, just holding her in place while he fucked her harder. Her nails cut deeper. A tremor went through her that told him she was close.

"Let go," he told her, pounding into her. "Come on, little thief. I want to see it. Let go for me."

She arched against him, head thrown back as she shattered. Beautiful. Wild.

He thrust one last time and spilled inside her, his own release sweeping through him. Dropping his forehead against hers, he let his breathing come down. He gathered her against him. Splayed a palm against her spine and curled the other into her hip.

Mine.

Callahan woke to muffled whimpers.

He lay still, every muscle coiled tight. Then, his sleep-addled brain registered the source of the noise.

Isabel.

She was curled in on herself, her fists clenched. The expression of anguish on her face made Callahan's chest constrict.

"No," she muttered. "Please, I can't—I won't—"

"Isabel," he said, voice low and calming. "Wake up. It's just a dream."

A choked sob escaped her. The sound hit him like a knife between his ribs.

"Trouble," he tried again. "Come on, open those eyes for me."

Her eyes flew open, wild and unseeing. Before Callahan could react, she'd launched herself at him, one hand going for his throat.

He caught her wrist, careful not to grip too tightly. "*Easy*. Easy now. It's just me. You're safe."

Her chest heaved with panicked breaths, then awareness crept into her gaze.

"Ronan?" she whispered, uncertain.

"The one and only." He slid his hand in soothing circles over her back.

Isabel sagged against him. "*Merde*." She rubbed at her eyes. "I'm sorry."

"No harm done. Might requisition some armour, though. For next time."

A small sound escaped her – not quite a laugh, but close enough.

They stayed like that for a long moment, Isabel's breathing gradually slowing.

"Thank you," she said softly.

"What are fake husbands for, if not to rescue their fake wives from nightmares?"

A small smile was her only response, but the haunted look still hadn't left her eyes. Her fingers curled against his skin like she feared he'd disappear if she let go. Vulnerable in a way he'd rarely seen her.

He pressed a kiss to her temple. "Want to talk about it?"

"Not particularly."

"Distract you, then?"

She nodded.

"Did I ever tell you why I was in Athens?" he asked.

Isabel blinked. "I . . . what?"

"Athens. 1870."

"When you were running through the market?"

"I'd been sent to intercept a rogue agent planning to sell secrets to the highest bidder. We had intelligence suggesting he was meeting his contact in one of the markets in the old city."

"Clever," she murmured. "Easy to blend in, lots of potential escape routes."

"Precisely. It took me a week to pinpoint the location of the rendezvous. I spent days strategising my approach and memorising their routines. I failed to account for the possibility that our intelligence might have been compromised."

Isabel leaned forward. "What happened?"

"At least half a dozen armed men came at me from nowhere. One second, I'm watching the exchange; the next, I'm fighting for my damn life. I managed to escape, but not before catching a dagger to the ribs. I was outnumbered, bleeding, and rapidly running out of options. That's when I ran into you."

"You looked like death warmed up," she said, expression softening. "All wild-eyed and covered in blood."

"And you helped me. Why?"

Her gaze dropped to her hands, to the tiny scar across her knuckles. "I liked you."

"You liked me, hm?" He smiled.

"Don't sound so smug. You have a certain charm."

"And?"

"I didn't have anything that was mine back then. Everything was for Favreau. Where I went. What I stole. Who I . . ."

She didn't finish, didn't need to. Callahan's jaw clenched, thinking about Favreau's hands on her.

"But you were different," she continued. "My secret. The one thing he didn't control. I'd get sent to a city, and beneath all the plans and schemes, I'd think maybe you'd find me. Time with you was the only thing I ever stole for myself. I couldn't just leave you there bleeding out in Athens."

An emotion constricted in his chest. "And I couldn't arrest you. Not even when Wentworth was breathing down my neck about it."

They lapsed into comfortable silence, the earlier tension all but dissipated.

"Agent," she said. "Will you—" She shut her mouth. "Never mind."

"Tell me. I promise not to judge."

She swallowed. "I have nightmares every night. Unavoidable. Except for Hong Kong and last night – because I woke up to your arms around me."

He cupped her cheek. "Are you asking your fake husband to hold you?"

He felt the slight tremor that ran through her, the way she leaned almost imperceptibly into his touch. Then a nod. Small. Uncertain. As if she wasn't used to asking for anything, especially comfort. Like she was surrendering. This woman, with all her barbs and thorns, was trusting him with this one thing.

"Come here, fake wife," he said tenderly, gathering her in his arms.

"Just until I fall asleep," she murmured.

"Whatever you need, Trouble."

⊱ 18 ⊰

Isabel stood in front of the mirror. The gown the Home Office had procured was blue silk with delicate Chantilly lace with a neckline that offered a tantalising glimpse of décolletage.

The sort of ensemble that would have men eating out of her palm.

"I don't suppose," she murmured to the maid fussing with the fall of her skirts, "you have any creative ideas for concealing a small arsenal beneath all this? A pistol or two? Perhaps a nice stiletto?"

The girl looked up with wide, startled eyes. "I beg your pardon, ma'am?"

"Nothing, darling. Just idle musings of a deranged mind. I'm sure I'll muddle through."

She dismissed the girl and turned back to her reflection, allowing herself one last assessing glance.

Every part the lethal ornament, ma petite. What fine jewellery you make.

Isabel banished Favreau's memory with a violent shake of her head. Then she drew a deep breath, held it until her lungs burned, and strode into the private sitting room.

Callahan was already waiting, his broad shoulders cutting a fine figure in stark black and white. He glanced up at the soft susurrus of Isabel's skirts.

And went still.

He stared. Drinking her in with a heat that sent sparks skittering across her skin.

"Well?" Her voice emerged huskier than she'd intended. "Will I pass muster? Or shall I go change into sackcloth?"

"You look," he rasped, "like the most dangerous thing in the room. Like a fever dream."

Isabel swallowed hard. "Yours or mine?"

"Everyone's. You'll be the scandal of the symposium. There won't be a man there who won't imagine peeling you out of that dress and seeing if you taste as good as you look."

"Is that what you imagine? How I might taste?"

"You know it is."

How strange, the way the world could tilt on its axis with a few innocuous words.

"Careful, Agent. A woman could get ideas, hearing you say such things." She dragged her stare down. "You clean up well."

"High praise, coming from you."

"Remember," she said, reaching out to straighten his cravat. "You have to play the idiot to perfection while I inhabit the role of a rich socialite. Our aim is to have these illustrious men of science regard you as a malleable fool in desperate need of education, all while fawning over your gracious and obscenely wealthy spouse."

Callahan arched a brow. "This is hardly my first foray into subterfuge."

"Yes, but it's your first performance with me," she said, kissing him on the cheek.

He turned at the last moment, his lips brushing hers. "I'm sure I can keep up."

The symposium's opening ball was full by the time they walked into the ballroom.

The air was thick with expensive perfume, cigars, and fresh flowers. Scientists were gathered in small groups, while rich businessmen and lords mingled among them.

"See anything worth nicking?" Callahan murmured in Isabel's ear.

She slid him a scathing look. "This gown is far too tight for petty theft."

"Apologies. I forgot that the notorious Spectre has standards. Shall I ask what priceless trinkets Lord Ripon keeps in the family vault? Only the best for my fake wife."

"I've turned over a new leaf, haven't I?"

"Truly a loss for criminal society."

Isabel hid a smirk behind her champagne flute. "Shall we mingle?"

They exchanged pleasantries with the other guests. Isabel watched Callahan slip into his vapid persona; Jamie Ashford was a man whose gravest concerns in life seemed to be the precision of his cravat's folds.

"Laying it on a bit thick, aren't we?" she asked.

He flashed a smile. "I'm the very model of noble comportment."

"Indeed," she muttered, silently vowing to flay Wentworth alive for assigning them these particular identities. She was going to stab someone by the night's end, that was certain.

"There's our man." Callahan inclined his head towards a group. "Ramsgate's the one with grey hair and spectacles. Appears to be expounding on . . . gallstones, perhaps? Hard to tell."

Isabel picked out their target easily enough. "Then let's go introduce ourselves."

Tightening her grip on Callahan's arm, she tugged him through the crowd.

". . . a truly fascinating case. You see, the circumstances of the gallbladder's rupture—"

"I beg your pardon," Callahan interrupted. "Did I hear mention of internal organs? How captivating!"

Ramsgate's mouth hung slack, his diatribe curtailed. The other men blinked as though startled out of a daze.

"I—well, yes." The older man peered at Callahan like some curious new species of beetle. "Though I'm not certain—"

"Oh, you must forgive my husband." Isabel bestowed a winning smile on the befuddled assembly. "Jamie does have such a morbid fascination with the gorier realities of science. Why, just the other evening, he bored me absolutely to tears with the riveting particulars of a ruptured spleen."

Callahan released a booming laugh. "Guilty as charged, my sweet! Though, in my defence, the details of that grisly business did make for a cracking good tale. Get it?" He thumped the nearest man on the shoulder, heedless of his wince. "A cracking good tale? On account of the ribs giving way?"

If a feather had dropped at that moment, the sound would have been deafening. The sycophants flanking Ramsgate were doubtless unused to being interrupted by a foppish dandy who wouldn't know an atom from an abacus.

Isabel had to give her partner credit – the man did a fine job of playing the idiot savant.

She widened her smile and interfered before Callahan's performance got out of hand. "You must forgive James his little jokes. An acquired taste, I'm afraid."

"Indeed," Ramsgate managed. "Well, I'm not certain—"

"Oh, how unspeakably rude of me." Isabel offered a gloved hand. "We haven't been properly introduced. I'm Lydia Ashford, and this is my darling husband, James. We're here from New York."

After a moment's hesitation, he reached out to clasp her fingers in a limp, perfunctory grip. "Edmund Ramsgate. A pleasure, Mrs Ashford. And you as well, Mr Ashford."

"I couldn't help but overhear you mention your work." Isabel leaned in, conspiratorial. "My husband and I are always looking for worthy scientific endeavours to support. Financially, of course. It's a particular passion of mine."

A calculated gleam entered Ramsgate's eyes as they swept over the small fortune glittering at her ears and throat. The reaction was subtle, barely there, but Isabel knew that look.

It was almost disappointing how predictable men were beneath their veneer of civility. As transparent as the beggars in the East End.

"Well," Ramsgate demurred, "I wouldn't want to speak out of turn. You have an interest in biochemistry, do you?"

He cut a dubious glance at Callahan, who was staring at the milling throng with the perplexed air of a man who'd stumbled into the wrong study by mistake and couldn't quite determine how to extricate himself.

"I'm sure I can keep up," Isabel assured him, batting her lashes. "And Jamie does so adore hearing me ramble on about my little enthusiasms. Don't you, love?"

"Hm? Oh, rather!" Callahan snapped to attention. "Absorbing stuff. Miasmas and whatnot."

Ramsgate looked mildly appalled, but pushed on, nonetheless. And so began a solid quarter-hour of increasingly esoteric jargon. Callahan had long since progressed from diplomatic boredom to the stare of a man girding his soul for war.

". . . of course, the real challenge is stabilising the compound," Ramsgate was saying. "Ensuring a reliable delivery mechanism . . ."

The prospect of listening to Ramsgate drone on in perpetuity stretched before Isabel like a slow death.

". . . environmental factors can wreak such havoc on more delicate solutions, but I've had some promising results with a tincture derived from the common foxglove—"

Deliverance came from an unexpected quarter when Ramsgate paused to draw breath, and Callahan seized the opening like a drowning man.

"Is it just me," he asked, fanning himself, "or is it deuced warm in here? I'm feeling a touch peaked."

Isabel made a concerned sound. "You do look flushed,

darling. Perhaps a turn on the balcony is in order? A spot of air might set you to rights."

"Capital idea, light of my life." Callahan sketched a bow. "If you'll excuse us, gentlemen? I fear I'm on the verge of a swoon."

As they approached the French doors to the gardens, Isabel heard Ramsgate mutter, "Bit of a milksop, that one."

Callahan shut the doors and leaned against them in exhaustion. "Bloody hell. I think that man actually sucked the soul out of my body. Through my ears."

Isabel rubbed at her temples. "I can't decide if I'm more astonished by his lung capacity or his ability to talk so much while saying nothing."

"He employed some form of circular breathing, I'd wager. Like those chaps who play wind instruments." He shuddered. "I'm not sure how much more of this I can take without running mad. Quicker just to nick his papers."

"They're coded, remember? And we can't arouse suspicion. That means not stealing his scientific effects."

He sighed. "Right."

Isabel's lips twitched. "Poor fake husband."

She found herself all too aware of Callahan's proximity. The solid warmth of him at her side, the faint scent of his soap and tobacco.

"Mm." Callahan tapped his fingers against the wall. "Then I'll keep playing the idiot and hoping he yields something. You keep dangling money in front of his face."

Isabel nodded. Her mind raced ahead, sketching and discarding possibilities, each more unpleasant than the last.

Callahan's hand covered hers. She looked up to find him watching her, something unreadable in his expression.

"You're leagues away," he said softly. "What are you concocting in that devious mind of yours?"

"Just plotting."

"Should I be bracing for explosions? Stabbings? Defenestrations? Threats?"

God, he knew her too well.

"Hush." She turned her hand, twining their fingers together. "I promised Wentworth I'd be on my best behaviour. All worthwhile sacrifices in service to the Crown, remember? That's why I'm trussed up in this dress."

"Naturally." His voice dropped, gone soft. "Though I'd be lying if I said I wasn't itching to strip you out of it, jewels and all."

The space between them seemed to shrink. Isabel couldn't breathe right. Couldn't think straight. There was only the moonlight catching in his dark hair, the hard line of his jaw, the way his eyelashes cast shadows on his cheeks.

Her body burned for him.

"You're a distraction, Agent Callahan." She adjusted her gloves. "We'll try Ramsgate again tomorrow. If nothing else, I could always seduce it out of him. Men tend to talk when I take my clothes off."

His eyes narrowed. "No."

"You don't think I can do it?"

"That's not it." His jaw clenched. "You're not his to touch."

She raised an eyebrow, heart hammering against her ribs. "Whose am I, then?"

"Mine." As if he'd been waiting to say it. The simplest truth in the world. "For the next three days, at least, Mrs Ashford."

Isabel often thought she never wanted to hear the word *mine* from a man. Favreau had said it enough. Had marked her up like property.

But when Ronan said it, a shiver of want went through her. Because to be his wasn't to be owned, it was to be cherished.

My body is yours, he'd whispered last night in the dark, when they'd both been naked and honest. She'd almost confessed then that her body had been his for years. That it would always be his, long after this mission ended. That she'd never stopped wanting him, even when she tried.

"And after the three days, Mr Ashford?" Her voice was a little breathless.

"Don't change the subject." His fingers caught her chin. "Trouble, I'm serious. No seducing. Nothing on your own. No stealing."

"No seducing," she promised. "No stealing."

"*Nothing on your own*," he pointedly finished.

She grinned. God, she loved when he got like this – all protective and commanding.

"Promise."

19

The late afternoon sun dappled the manicured garden. Parasols twirled and coattails flapped in the breeze. The air hummed with a dozen conversations and the clinking of champagne glasses.

Isabel took a slow sip of champagne as she scanned the crowd.

There. Ramsgate was near the rose trellis, hands gesticulating as he spoke. She'd scarcely taken a step when Callahan's fingers clamped around her elbow.

"Why are you swooping in like an overgrown bat?" she hissed out of the corner of her mouth, smiling at a curious matron who glided past.

"You were about to be painfully obvious. Honestly, Trouble, what part of 'we need to blend in' continues to elude you?"

She bristled. "I'm perfectly subtle at all times."

"Says the woman who once burgled the Portuguese crown jewels."

That particular escapade had been the toast of the Continent for a week, the stuff of crowing headlines and scandalous ballroom whispers. It wasn't every day a thief absconded with the gems of a sovereign state while the Queen's Guard made a shambles of the palace, laid low by cascading hysterics and a suspicious swarm of angry bees.

The bees had been her proudest moment. A flash of brilliance, really.

Narrowing her eyes, she asked, "How do you even know about that?"

"I make it my business to know things, Mrs Ashford. Especially where you're concerned. Now smile. We're happy newlyweds, remember?"

"How could I forget?" she muttered. "You've only reminded me a dozen times today."

"Only because you seem determined to scowl at everyone who so much as glances our way. I'm aware you'd rather be elbow-deep in Ramsgate's viscera, but do try to recall that infiltration requires at least a veneer of sociality."

"*Darling*," she cooed, "have I told you what an absolute *joy* it is to be shackled to you in holy matrimony? I can't fathom how I managed a single day without your delightful commentary on my every move!" She lowered her voice. "Now, be a love and go mingle. Preferably far away from me, before all of England thinks I've been surgically grafted to your side. You're meant to be playing the idiot, but men have been known to let things slip around their own. Things they'd never dream of uttering where a woman might overhear."

"Fine. Don't do anything rash," he warned as he departed.

Isabel focused on tracking her prey's circuit through the garden. Ramsgate now stood locked in intent conversation with a taller man, dark heads inclined together. He gestured sharply, and his companion scowled. Were they quarrelling? Or debating some obscure scientific point?

She angled closer, steps slowing, straining to catch the words on the warm breeze.

"I understand your concerns, but . . ." Ramsgate was saying.

The other man's reply was a harsh mutter, too indistinct to parse. But the thunderous cast to his features spoke volumes. Whatever Ramsgate had said, it clearly hadn't pleased him.

As she took another step, a gaggle of matrons descended on Isabel.

"Mrs Ashford, you absolute darling! You must tell us how you met that delicious husband of yours. A love match, was it?"

Oh, this was too perfect an opportunity to pass up. Especially with Callahan looking over, probably summoned by a sixth sense for impending mischief.

"It's the most thrilling story!" She made a dreamy expression. "There I was, minding my business at the Metropolitan Museum, when a dashing stranger came careening around the corner and nearly knocked me clean off my feet!"

The ladies gasped, delicate hands fluttering to throats in scandalised amusement. Across the lawn, Callahan froze mid-step. Good. She had his full attention.

"Turns out, he was fleeing from an angry father. Something about compromising the virtue of the man's daughter, or perhaps his wife." She waved a hand in dismissal. Callahan started walking faster, expression thunderous. "Well, naturally, as soon as he clapped eyes on me, he realised he'd found his one true love. His *saviour* from all his rakish misdeeds! The next thing I knew, he seized me about the waist and . . ." A meaningful pause, a slow grin curving her lips. "We're on the terrace. Alone. In the dark."

The ladies dissolved into a fresh flurry of gasps and fluttered fans.

"Alone . . . with a strange man. But how thrilling!" one of them tittered.

"You wicked girl!" said another. "How positively . . ."

"American?" Isabel supplied, playing up her adopted persona.

"Just so!"

Isabel had to commend Callahan. When he finally reached them, he almost managed to look like a man in love and not someone contemplating murder. The matrons, of course, mistook his fixed smile for one of adoration. Bless their hearts.

Pressing herself to his side, Isabel cooed, "*Darling,* I was just regaling everyone with the riveting story of our first meeting. How you spirited me away in the heat of passion!"

Behind their backs, he gripped her dress hard. "Quite the tale, my *radiant* diamond. Perhaps we should let the ladies catch their breath. I'd hate to overwhelm them with the intensity of our passion. Come, let me introduce you to Professor Ainsworth. He has the most fascinating theories about the mating habits of butterflies."

And with that, he swept her away behind a tree.

"Do me a favour?" he said through clenched teeth. "The next time you feel compelled to add lurid details to our cover story, kindly refrain from sullying my reputation. That story had me out as some kind of rutting beast with the morals of an alley cat. It's a wonder you didn't send the whole garden into fits of apoplexy."

"I was blending," she said, pasting on a bright smile for the benefit of their onlookers. "In case you're unaware, scandalised hens make for far more cooperative witnesses than suspicious dowagers. It's called establishing trust. For intelligence purposes."

"Be that as it may, I'd prefer it if you refrained from casting doubt on my moral character in public."

"Oh? Was it not to your liking?" She fluttered her lashes at him. "And here I thought you'd be flattered to add debauching virgins to your list of fictional accomplishments. Or was it the bit about fleeing angry husbands that stretched credulity? But let's not pretend I was so far from the truth. Our meeting in New York wasn't exactly proper, was it? You cornered me. Pushed me against a wall. Looked like you were going to kiss me."

His eyes flashed. For an instant, she was back on that New York terrace with his body caging hers.

"And as I seem to recall," he said, his voice deceptively soft, "you had a knife at my jugular not a moment later."

"And what a pity. We were having such a nice time until then."

The air between them crackled. They were close – too close. Isabel could see the faint stubble darkening Callahan's jaw, smell the subtle notes of his cologne. She forced herself to take a slow breath.

"Ramsgate," she murmured, dragging them both back to the task at hand. "He was having words with a man earlier. It seemed tense."

Callahan's demeanour shifted, sharpened. She watched the shrewd intellect take over. "You catch what about?" he asked, all business now.

She pressed her lips together. "Not enough before the interruption."

"I'll see if our host is of a mind to gossip."

He steered them towards the marquess, who stood in a group at the far end of the garden.

"Ripon, old boy!" Callahan's voice boomed out as they approached, his manner shifting into that of the affable, slightly dim-witted American. He clapped the marquess on the shoulder. "Wondrous party, simply wondrous. I'd love to talk to you about those delicious canapés!"

Ripon lifted a brow but made no other comment as he detached from his coterie. Isabel had to admire the man's composure – clearly, he'd had other clandestine dealings at social gatherings.

Callahan let the exuberant mask fall away the moment they were out of earshot of the other guests. "I need a name."

If Ripon was thrown by the abrupt shift, he didn't show it. "I'm listening."

Isabel jerked her chin toward the men clustered near the fountain. "The tall one. Dark hair. He and Ramsgate seemed to be in quite a heated discussion earlier before he went storming off."

Ripon scanned the crowd, nodding to a duchess across the lawn. "That would be Viscount Harrington. The man's insufferable. You'd think Queen Victoria herself was visiting, the way he carries on."

"How so?" Callahan asked.

"Demanded the largest suite in the east wing. Had my staff rearranging furniture half the night. Something about needing quiet for his" – Ripon's fingers sketched quotation marks in the air – "important work."

"He's a scientist?" Isabel asked.

"Biochemist." Ripon took a sip of his drink. "As for the argument, I wouldn't trouble yourself. These academic types bicker over comma placement in journals nobody reads."

"Still," Callahan said. "Nothing loosens tongues like a receptive ear attached to a sympathetic nod."

"Tread carefully, Agent. Nervous boffins make for dreadful company. And do please be a bit less irritating with that accent."

With that, Ripon returned to his group of admirers.

"Do you think Harrington knows about Ramsgate's research?" Isabel asked Callahan.

"Maybe," he said, his brow furrowed in thought. "I'll see what I can extract in conversation."

She nodded, an idea taking shape. It was risky, but then again, when had that stopped her? "Then I'm to the withdrawing room," she said, patting his arm. "It's quite warm out here. I need a rest."

Callahan narrowed his eyes, clearly suspicious of her sudden desire for propriety. But he said nothing as she strode away.

As soon as she was out of sight, Isabel slipped inside and went down the corridor, past oils of stern-faced ancestors and tables worth more than most London homes. A footman's voice echoed from somewhere nearby. She froze, counting heartbeats until the sound faded.

Three doors down on the left – that would be Harrington's room, if Ripon's casual mention of the east wing was accurate. She pressed her ear to the wood. No movement inside.

One hairpin. Five seconds. Child's play.

The lock yielded with a muted click, and Isabel eased the door shut behind her. She began to search, carefully replacing everything exactly as she found it. Most of the papers scattered across the desk were indecipherable to her – complex chemical formulae and dense scientific jargon that might as well have been written in a foreign language.

But then, near the bottom of a stack of correspondence, a familiar name caught her eye.

Ramsgate.

She was so engrossed in her discovery that she almost missed the telltale creak of a floorboard outside. Almost.

Isabel's head snapped up. Silently cursing, she folded the letter and tucked it into her bodice. There was no time to return it without risking detection.

The door handle turned. Isabel's mind raced; she could try to claim she'd gotten lost looking for the powder room. Or she could go for a more direct approach – incapacitate whoever was about to walk through that door and escape.

But before she could decide on a course of action, a familiar voice spoke from the doorway.

"Somehow," Callahan drawled, "I had a feeling I'd find you here. For someone who considers herself synonymous with subtlety, you rather tipped your hand today."

❧ 20 ❧

Callahan shut the door behind him and leaned against it, studying his fake wife through narrowed eyes.

Isabel's gaze darted to the window as if calculating her odds of escaping his wrath via a swan dive into the shrubbery.

"Don't even think about it," he warned. "I'd haul you back before you made it halfway down the lattice."

"I haven't the faintest idea what you mean."

"Of course not. You were only admiring the fucking vista, weren't you? Enjoying the view of the gardens and whatnot."

He shoved off the door and walked towards her. Isabel held her ground, but tension thrummed through her, the slightest hitch in her breathing as he invaded her space.

She deserved to squirm.

"Tell me," he continued, "did my instructions not to do anything on your own simply fall out of your pretty head? Or are you congenitally incapable of following orders?"

"I just—"

"Just couldn't resist a locked door, is that it? Just had to go poking around in some posh git's unattended correspondence like an addled magpie?"

She snorted. "I was taking a turn about the house and happened to find myself outside Harrington's rooms. Nothing untoward about that, is there?"

Such a liar. Such an absolute bloody menace. Isabel Dumont was many things, but innocent had never been one of them.

Callahan caught her chin between his fingers. "Let me make this simple for you. Sass me all you want. Swindle your way through life. Hell, stab me again if it makes you feel better about how badly you want me to throw you down and fuck you raw. But you do *not*. Get. To lie. To me. Are we quite understood?"

"I thought lies were part of our arrangement, *Mr Ashford*," she said, not backing down an inch.

"Is that the only currency you think we trade in, *Mrs Ashford*?"

A savage craving rose in him, the kind of need that revealed the animal in his skin that wanted to bite her until she submitted. Until she confessed what they both knew.

"This is a fake marriage, remember?"

"You want to know what I think?" he asked. "I think you've spent so long lying that the truth feels foreign."

Her pulse jumped under his thumb. Fast. Nervous. Excited.

"Our marriage may be fake, Isabel, but the way you look at me isn't. Your body gives you away every time." He watched her pupils dilate, heard the small catch in her throat. "Some nights, I lie awake thinking about all the ways

I could shut that smart mouth of yours. Maybe I should fuck it into submission."

Those green eyes flashed. For a moment, neither of them moved. Neither of them spoke. The distant strains of violins from the garden filled the silence.

Then she lunged.

Her mouth crashed against his. The kiss was wild and starving – more war than surrender. Like she was trying to prove something. She bit and sucked and conquered. Fighting him for control, but he was bigger, stronger, and just as desperate. Growling, he angled Isabel's head to deepen the kiss, sweeping his tongue along hers.

She bit his lip hard, and the copper taste of blood flooded his mouth. Callahan groaned. If anyone walked in right now, they'd see the Ashfords about to fuck like they were fighting. They'd see her pressed against him like she was trying to climb inside his skin.

And Callahan wouldn't stop. *Couldn't* stop. Not when she made that little sound in the back of her throat – half whimper, half demand.

Let someone see him claim her. He'd spent long enough denying himself when it came to Isabel Dumont. He wanted to drown in her, to map the terrain of her body until she was seared into his memory. Until she was all he could taste, all he could feel, the only prayer on his lips.

"Reckless," he growled against her throat. "Impulsive. Infuriating woman."

"Overbearing." She clawed her nails down his back. "Autocratic. Insufferable man."

Callahan twisted his fingers in her hair. "Do you have

any idea what happens to overconfident little thieves who get caught trespassing? The consequences when they push too far and provoke the worst in the men charged with minding them?"

Isabel strained against his hold, breath coming faster. But Callahan kept her pinned in place, his next words whispered in her ear.

"They get punished."

He spun her around and bent her over the desk. Gripping her skirts in his fist, he yanked them up, baring her silk stockings and undergarments.

She stiffened, craning her head to glare at him. "If you lay a single untoward finger on me, you uncivilised reprobate, I'll—"

"Quiet," he ordered. "This is a lesson in what happens to naughty girls who don't do as they're told."

She squirmed. "What if Harrington comes in?"

"Then he'll get a fine demonstration of how I deal with my troublesome fake wife." He grazed his teeth over her racing pulse. "You've no idea how long I've imagined having you bent over for me. So here's what's going to happen now, *Mrs Ashford*. I'm going to discipline you for your reckless behaviour. Then I'm going to fuck you until you can't remember why we were fighting. How does that sound?"

"You're twisted."

"And you're wet." He yanked her undergarments down her thighs. "Spread your legs."

She didn't move.

"Now, Mrs Ashford."

Isabel released a stuttering breath but obeyed with a stern look over her shoulder. Even positioned for punishment, she radiated the command of a queen.

This woman would break a better man than him.

Good thing he wasn't better.

"There's my girl," he purred, smoothing his palm over the curve of her backside. "Tap the desk three times if my attentions become unwanted."

Straightening, Callahan shrugged off his jacket and laid it over a nearby chair. Then he rolled up his shirtsleeves. "Now, where were we?"

The first crack of his hand against her right arse cheek rang out.

Slap.

Isabel jolted forward. "*Fuck.*"

"Language," he said, trailing fingertips down her spine. Taking his time. "How many do you think it will take for you to act like a proper wife, Mrs Ashford? Five strikes on this pretty arse? Ten? How many before the lesson sinks in?"

"However many my *darling* fake husband deems sufficient," she demurred.

"Hmm. Such good behaviour already. One might conclude you've a taste for this manner of correction."

She didn't answer. Didn't need to.

"Six should do it," he decided. "But only if this arse is red when we're done."

He waited until her fingers curled against the desktop, savouring the anticipation. Then he brought his hand down again in a stinging slap.

"Two," he said. "Keep count. Lose track of or omit a number, and we start over."

The third blow landed harder, a red handprint blooming on her pale skin.

"Three," she gasped out.

"*Very* good, sweetheart."

He rubbed at the spot, waiting for her to relax. Isabel pressed back into his palm. The movement was unconscious, instinctive – a wordless plea for more.

"Submission looks exquisite on you. You should wear it more often."

He felt her shiver at the praise before his hand came down.

Slap.

"Four." She clutched the table hard. "Are you enjoying this, Mr Ashford? How depraved."

"Depraved, am I? Because I think you like being bent over, Mrs Ashford." He leaned in until his lips brushed her ear. "Is it the risk that excites you? Knowing someone could walk in and see me owning you?"

Without warning, he slid two fingers inside her.

"Oh, *God*." Her head dropped forwards.

"There's my answer. So I suppose that makes you just as *depraved* as I am."

Slap.

"Five," she moaned. "Harder, Mr Ashford. Punish me."

Callahan let out a laugh. "That mouth of yours is going to get you into trouble one of these days."

Isabel met his gaze over her shoulder. "Promise?"

Slap.

"Six," Isabel managed, the word coming out on a shaky exhale.

"Time to occupy that mouth, Mrs Ashford." He eased his

fingers out of her and raised them to her lips, painting them with the evidence of her desire. "Suck. I want you to taste your depravity."

Isabel parted her lips and took his fingers deep in her mouth.

Christ God, he was so hard, it hurt.

"That's it," he crooned. "See how beautifully you submit when properly handled?"

Pulling free from her mouth, he sank his fingers inside her once more.

Isabel shuddered. "I don't think you put your back into that punishment, Mr Ashford."

Something dark and possessive flared in his chest. Even now, she challenged him.

"Count out another six," he growled, bringing his hand down hard across her arse. The mark bloomed red instantly.

Slap. Slap. His handprint was a deeper red now.

"Eight. Nine."

"Tell me why you're being punished."

She panted. "I infiltrated Harrington's chambers. Without you."

"And?"

Slap!

"I risked exposing us both by being caught."

His hand fell once more. Isabel pushed her backside into him, grinding against his hard cock.

"Eleven."

"And what have we extracted from today's session in discipline, my sweet fake wife?"

"No covert reconnaissance without consulting you first."

"There's my clever girl." He delivered his last spank

with a light nip to her jaw. Then he unfastened his trousers and nudged his cock against her. "I promised you a proper fucking, and I am, as ever, a man of my word. Ask nicely."

"Please fuck me, Mr Ashford," she moaned.

"Hold on tight, little thief."

He thrust hard into her.

For a moment, Callahan pressed his forehead between Isabel's shoulder blades, overwhelmed by the sensation of her, hot and tight and perfect.

"God," he breathed. "You feel so good."

He set a punishing pace. Each thrust was a confession, an absolution, a claiming. Isabel used the desk as leverage to back into him with every movement. Taking what he gave. Letting herself be claimed.

"Is this what you wanted?" Callahan growled, one hand fisted in her hair while the other gripped her hip hard enough to bruise. "To be fucked over Harrington's desk?"

"It wasn't in my plan," Isabel gasped, "but I can't say I'm disappointed about this turn of events."

"No, you're not, are you? Because the charming *Mrs Ashford* is a deviant, isn't she? I'll bet my darling fake wife would love it if people saw her being fucked and used. Wouldn't she?"

Her fingernails curled into the table. "God, the mouth on you."

"You made me this way, Trouble," he whispered, low and dark. "Every time I see you, I want to put you on your knees and keep you there."

Because that was the truth, wasn't it? He wanted to keep her. On her knees, bent over, fucking her, fighting with her. Any way he could get her.

Callahan's hands roamed Isabel's body, kissing every part he could reach, loving the way she arched into his touch. His other hand snaked around to where they were joined, rubbing firmly.

"Yes," she whispered. "Right there."

"That's it." He rubbed her faster. "Come, Isabel."

With a cry that Callahan muffled with his hand, Isabel climaxed as he fucked her harder. *Harder.* Giving one last brutal thrust, he spilled his release with a strangled groan.

Callahan slumped forward, pressing his forehead between Isabel's shoulder blades as he struggled to catch his breath.

"You're all right?" he whispered. "Was it too much?"

"I think you've broken me in the best possible way."

A breathless chuckle as he withdrew from her. "Then I've accomplished my aim." He righted his clothing and ran a hand through his hair.

"Arrogance is unbecoming on you." Isabel bent to snatch up her undergarments, sliding them on with a wince. "Don't let it go to your head."

Callahan looked around at the scattered papers and journals in Harrington's room. "Find anything useful before I disrupted you?"

"Possibly." She retrieved a piece of paper stuffed between her breasts. "This is a letter from Ramsgate dated two months ago. I didn't manage to read much of it before you bent me over like an overbearing scoundrel."

Callahan took the missive from her and scanned the contents.

"Well?" Isabel demanded as she rearranged Harrington's effects just as she'd found them. "Don't leave me in suspense."

"Harrington expressed reluctance to answer Ramsgate's questions." He glanced up at her. "Nothing else jumped out at you?"

"Nothing of merit, no."

"Then we'll focus our efforts on Harrington tomorrow. See if we can't determine what Ramsgate asked him for."

⤳ 21 ⤳

Isabel slipped from the sheets and dressed, careful not to disturb Callahan.

The door hinges creaked as she eased into the corridor. She'd never been still for long. With Favreau, there had always been another job. Before that, in childhood, her hours had been circumscribed by lessons and the distant, unyielding figure of her father.

Even in Boston, she had a routine. Breakfast, briefings with Vale, afternoon tea, dinner, a walk. At night, she always watched the stars and listened to the distant noise of the city.

She learned that staying still was when the thoughts crept in. And with the thoughts came memories. She had darker ones than most, a lifetime of cruelties and hunger and grasping hands. The blades that cut her open.

Memories like hers thrived when the world went quiet.

Earlier, she'd used Ronan. When a nightmare threatened her peace, she'd pushed him onto his back and he'd sleepily watched her as she rode him. Two hours later, she woke him again, and he'd pleasured her with his tongue.

Waking him a third time was tantamount to weakness, and that wasn't acceptable.

So she moved. Her wandering feet took her down the servants' staircase. She'd long ago internalised the most forgettable routes in any house. The better to avoid detection.

Isabel cut through the kitchen, deserted at this late hour. She appropriated a jug of ale from a cupboard, then continued her restless patrol, skirting the perimeter of the room until she spied the door she was seeking: the one that led to the gardens.

The air was rich with the scent of rain-damp leaves as Isabel scaled the ivy lattice on the house's rear façade. Three floors up, she swung over a stone balustrade and sat, setting the jug of ale between her thighs.

She allowed her eyes to drift closed. The gleam of Favreau's smile rose from her memories, the whisper of his blade at her stomach, the caustic burn of his spend inside her.

You make a magnificent canvas, ma belle. Don't you like the pain?

No.

Not that kind of pain.

Not with him.

Isabel forced air into her lungs. Let those memories stay locked in their iron boxes, chained and muzzled. For now, there was only the dome of stars above and the answering vault of the city, a thousand pinprick windows glowing gold.

The lattice creaked. A booted tread came from behind

her, scarcely louder than a cat's. Isabel stiffened, every sense surging to high alert.

She slid a palm over her knife. Her mind cycled rapidly through pressure points and soft targets – throat, liver, kidneys—

"Trouble. You're slipping."

Callahan. Of bloody *course*.

"Am I?" she asked dryly.

He sat beside her. Not for the first time, she was struck by his beauty. Dark hair mussed from sleep, feet bare in unlaced boots, his linen shirt gaping to reveal the strong column of his throat.

Yes, Ronan Callahan was devastating.

She took a swig from the jug before holding it out. Callahan accepted the offering, his knuckles brushing hers. The fleeting contact sent a shiver through her.

"For the most notorious thief on the Continent," Callahan said, pausing to swallow a mouthful of ale, "your situational awareness leaves something to be desired. Letting yourself be snuck up on? It's begging for a knife between the ribs."

"The only one who swoops in to menace me at inopportune moments is you."

He slanted her a look. "If I'd wanted to menace you, you'd have my blade at your throat. Instead, we're having an almost civilised conversation."

"Is that your way of saying you've no intention of finishing me off?"

"I'm becoming accustomed to you warming my bed. It'd be a shame to see such a pretty head parted from your shoulders." He knocked his knee against hers. "Makes for a messy coverlet."

"Such concern for your linens." She clucked her tongue. "And here I thought you cared."

"Oh, I care." The sudden heat in his gaze sent a flutter low in her belly. "I care very much about keeping you in one piece so I can take you apart myself."

She watched him take another long pull from the jug.

"So," he said, setting the ale aside, "want to tell me why you're restless tonight?"

"Maybe I just fancied a nightcap under the stars. I'm not angling to die of exposure, if that's your concern."

"Good. Death by freezing lacks a certain flair. An opium haze, a poisoned kiss . . . there's an elegance there."

"This from the gentleman with a human skull on his mantelpiece."

"Everyone needs a hobby."

Isabel felt her mouth curve despite herself.

They lapsed into a companionable quiet, passing the jug between them. The distant clatter of carriage wheels and the hollow clop of hooves against cobblestones drifted up from the streets below.

"I never watched the stars in Paris," Isabel said quietly, apropos of nothing. She kept her gaze fixed on the distant glimmer of the Thames. "I was always busy. Always working or distracted. But in Boston . . . in Boston, I'd climb out onto the roof of Portia's townhouse and just look. For hours, sometimes."

She could feel the weight of his stare, heavy as a touch.

"It was like I could breathe again, out there above the city. Like I could finally think. I'd trace the constellations with the tip of my finger . . ." She mimed the motion, her hand outstretched. "And pretend I could touch them. That if I reached out far enough, I could scoop up a handful of stars and tuck them away inside my ribcage. A little piece of light, just for me."

Callahan's exhale was soft. "Did it help? Soothe you, I mean?"

"Sometimes. Mostly, it just made me realise how small I was. How inconsequential. When your choices are steal or starve, lie or die, you learn to live with so little. Existing in a cage becomes your entire world. When you know what it is to want – truly want, with an intensity that consumes you – it's terrifying to imagine being satisfied."

His fingertips grazed her cheek. "Why are you really out here, sweetheart?"

"I met Favreau seven years ago today."

Isabel's gaze dropped to her hands. Those memories whispered from their little box at the back of her mind, all the things she buried deep that liked to sink their claws in during dreams.

"I was a virgin before that," she said quietly. "Did you know? I mentioned in my briefings sent to Wentworth."

A soft exhale left him. "No. I didn't read them. They felt too . . ." He cleared his throat. "Personal."

"Well, I described Louis Favreau to Vale physically, but didn't mention that he's quite beautiful. Blond, tall, blue eyes. To a half-starved girl of sixteen, he looked like an angel. That's what I called him when he caught me attempting to pick his pocket. *Un ange*. And for those first few weeks, he was. He bought me food and clothes and looked at me like I was the only person in the world. Do you have any idea what it's like to be someone's sole focus? To be taken care of when you have nothing?"

Callahan's expression was gentle. Not pity, just understanding. He shook his head.

"When a man starts to hurt you," she said quietly, "you do anything to get the good back. Even if he holds you down and you realise it's not safe to say no."

Callahan slid his fingers into hers, holding tightly. "It won't be like this forever. The nightmares. The restlessness. I know it doesn't seem that way now."

"Do you whisper that to all the battered creatures who warm your bed? Am I just another bird with broken wings for you to soothe?"

She expected him to recoil. To take the excuse she offered to retreat into banter or brittle silence. But he remained still.

"You know you aren't."

But she was broken. She didn't even think she deserved this man, let alone his kindness. Parts of her still wanted to push him away. Save him from cutting himself on her jagged edges. She was built to break men.

"What if I used you again?" she asked. "Wanted you to hold me down and fuck me until it hurt? Would you do it? Would it get you hard to hurt me?"

She watched his throat work as he swallowed. Imagined sinking her teeth there. To stake her claim in the same primal language he'd used to write his possession across her skin.

"I get hard from you." Stark. Unvarnished. "From the way you look at me when I'm buried inside you like you can't decide if you want to claw my heart out or swallow it whole. I'll fuck you however you want me to, Isabel."

She glanced down at their entwined hands, the way his fingers engulfed hers. There was a terrible sort of symbolism in that – the notion that he could enfold all her broken pieces, swallow up the fractured sprawl of her until she disappeared entirely. Until Isabel Dumont was nothing more than a memory, a whisper of smoke on the wind.

"I think Favreau broke something in me," she confessed, the words tearing themselves free.

"Do you?" Callahan's voice sharpened.

"I thought when I was free of him, I'd never want a man's hands on me like that again. That I'd want . . . softness. Gentleness."

"Isabel . . ."

"I like it when you bruise me and cuff me, and I surrender. What does that say about me? That I can only find pleasure in the echoes of my own violation? Ronan, I think he *broke me*—"

"No." Callahan gripped her shoulders. "You're not broken. What that twisted fuck did to you wasn't about desire. It was about power. What we do together? That's about trust." His palm cradled her jaw, breath ghosting across her parted lips. "Little thief. Would you feel safe enough to say no with me?"

"Yes," she breathed. Immediate. Unwavering.

"There's the difference." He stroked his thumb along her cheekbone, unbearably tender. "Safety. The certainty that I'll never take more than you're willing to give. The fact that you crave pain doesn't make you broken. It's all right to want it, sweetheart. It's pain you choose."

It was too much. The steady conviction in his gaze, the absolution of his touch.

"I'm so desperately sorry for Hong Kong," she whispered, her eyes stinging. "I should have told you on the steamer when you asked—"

"Isabel, you don't owe me any explanations. What's done is—"

"I was pregnant."

The confession dropped between them like a stone into a pond, the ripples of it radiating out.

Callahan's breath left him in a sharp exhale. "What?"

Isabel curled in on herself, shoulders hunching. Her gaze skittered away to fix on some distant point over his shoulder, unable to look at him.

"I was carrying Favreau's child. He would have done anything to keep me with him, and a pregnancy was a vulnerability. A *baby* was a vulnerability. That's why I was desperate to escape in Hong Kong. I couldn't let him find out or risk starting to show."

He reached for her, stroking her hair. No demand in his touch, just . . . comfort. Soothing her.

"What happened after that?"

"There are ways for women to get rid of a pregnancy, and I couldn't keep it. I didn't want to. But I need you to know why I couldn't let you close back then. Why I had to burn every bridge and disappear the way I did. I would rather you be angry with me than see you dead."

Callahan dragged her closer and held on tight. She turned her face into his shoulder, her eyes wet.

"The things we do to survive mark us," he murmured into her hair. "But we endure in the only ways we can. We adapt and overcome because the alternative is to let the world grind us to dust. I forgave you for Hong Kong a long time ago."

She leaned in, pressing her lips to his in a gentle kiss. A tentative exploration of new territory. It was achingly gentle, this careful mapping of scars. A hushed dialogue of breath and touch and understanding.

When they parted, Isabel rested her forehead against Callahan's. "Thank you."

"Always."

⤫ **22** ⤫

Callahan stood at the edges of the crowd, nursing a glass of champagne.

Isabel was speaking with Harrington. She'd woken up that morning more determined to finish this mission than ever. Maybe because of everything she told him last night about her and Favreau.

Pregnant. She'd been pregnant in Hong Kong.

He'd held her when she finally settled in to sleep, considering this piece of information that reframed her actions. She'd been terrified in that gaming hell; he'd recognised that much. But now he felt foolish for not understanding that she had what amounted to a ticking clock in her mind.

Stop talking like you know me, she'd said then.

And he thought he had. Because he'd followed her aliases and heists, but he didn't truly understand the woman herself or what she went back to after every time they met.

It made him want to put a fist through a wall.

He downed his champagne, focusing on the other guests.

To his left, a cluster of men were engaged in animated discussions about the latest advancements in steam engine technology.

"I tell you, gentlemen, the future lies in compressed air!" declared an older gent. "Mark my words, in a decade, we'll have engines running on nothing but the air we breathe!"

His companion scoffed. "Nonsense, Higgins. It's all about hydraulics, my good man. Water power is the way forward. Why, I've been working on a design that could revolutionise—"

Callahan's focus drifted to another group nearby. This one seemed to be embroiled in a heated debate about the merits of various preservation techniques for biological specimens.

"Formaldehyde is all well and good for soft tissues," a woman with an impressive plume of feathers in her hat was saying, "but for delicate structures like insect wings, nothing beats an ethanol solution."

A dour-faced man with a monocle nodded. "Quite right, quite right. Though I've had some success with glycerine for plants. Keeps the colours remarkably vivid, you know."

Christ, was there no end to the prattle?

"You look like you're moments from tossing someone out the window."

He turned to watch Isabel approach. She was resplendent in a gown of deep emerald silk that made her eyes shine like cut gems. Everything in him softened. What he wouldn't give to have her alone right now.

"Trouble," he murmured. "I see you've decided to save me from the tedium at last."

Her lips twitched. "Poor Callahan. Subjected to the horrors of intellectually stimulating discourse. However will you survive the trauma?"

Callahan opened his mouth to assure her that his continued well-being amid the symposium from hell was very much in question, when some sod took that opportunity to interrupt.

"I say, old chap, you wouldn't happen to know the proposed ideal ratio of a copper-zinc alloy for the plating process, would you? I have it on good authority that 1.1 recurring is the golden mean, but can't for the life of me recall whether that refers to tensile strength or conductivity."

Callahan turned slowly. He fixed the interloper with a gaze that had quelled charging brigands. The man's babbling cut off, and he swallowed audibly.

"Ah. I see you're otherwise engaged. Terribly rude of me to intrude. I'll just . . . go and . . . that is to say— Right! Cheerio!"

The man departed with such haste that he nearly bumped into a servant bearing a tray of champagne.

"Making friends, I see." Isabel's voice shook with laughter.

"I don't have friends here," Callahan said, clamping his fingers around her elbow. "I have you."

With that, he tugged Isabel across the room and into a shadowed alcove. The velvet drapes swished shut, concealing them from view.

Callahan crowded her against the wall, slanting his mouth over hers in a kiss that was all heat and hunger. He still couldn't get enough. He pressed his thigh between hers, gratified by the hitch in her breath. The way her eyes went soft and hazy with want.

"Well," she breathed, "hello to you, too."

"How's your arse today, little thief?"

"Sore," she said, even as her hips met his in a slow grind.

He chuckled. "Good. I want you to feel the ache of me for days. Every time you sit, every time you move. A reminder of what I can do to this beautiful body."

She snorted. "Degenerate."

"You like it. Now, tell me: any luck extracting intelligence from our esteemed Viscount Harrington? Or was he too busy staring at your tits to string two words together?"

She made a face. "I might as well be a decorative piece of furniture. He considers my intellect roughly on par with a concussed badger."

"So you didn't manage to extract anything relevant? Nothing about his work or what Ramsgate wanted from him?"

"He's proving a surprisingly tough nut, loath as I am to admit it," she said. Her lips pursed in irritation. "While I excel at subterfuge, you may protest my usual methods of extracting information."

"Rob the blighter blind?"

"Getting him drunk and seducing him while lending a sympathetic ear. Ale and climaxes are truth serums to the over-indulged and under-cautious, and I excel at telling men exactly what they want to hear."

Callahan's hand tightened on her waist. "*Isabel*—"

"I was strictly professional with Harrington," she reassured him. "Not even a hint of flirtation. My fake husband is the jealous sort, you see."

"Yes, he is. He's very jealous, and he doesn't share." He

dipped his head, lips ghosting over her neck. "I have an idea. One that removes the viscount from the influence of polite society. Men speak more freely over drink and cards. I'll invite him out tonight."

"And what am I meant to do in the meantime?"

"Keep an eye on Ramsgate. Be your charming self. Dazzle the masses with your wit and beauty. Perhaps liberate a few possessions for old times' sake."

She heaved a sigh. "Fine. Go on, then. Work your masculine wiles on Viscount Harrington. I'm sure he'll be helpless to resist your charm."

"Your faith in me is truly touching, Mrs Ashford," he said, dipping his fingers beneath the neckline of her gown to graze the swell of her breasts.

She gave a soft groan. "You need to go before we scandalise the symposium, Mr Ashford."

"What's the concern, little thief? That I'll fuck you behind this curtain where everyone can hear?" he asked, his teeth scraping over her pulse point. "Or that you don't think you can be quiet if I do?"

"*Ronan.*"

"Saying my name in that breathy voice of yours isn't helping the situation."

She put a hand on his chest. "Business first. Go deal with Harrington."

With a groan of regret, he stepped away, putting distance between them before he succumbed to the temptation to hike her skirts up and take her there against the wall.

"Fine. Be right back."

He departed the alcove, scanning the milling aristos

until he spotted the viscount, who was locked in conversation with three other men. Callahan pasted on his most vacuous grin and ambled over.

"I say, what's the topic of the hour?"

Harrington turned. "Ah, Ashford. I'm afraid it's all rather more specialised than garden parties and shooting weekends."

Translation: *don't strain your liquor-addled brain.*

Callahan only smiled wider. "Oh, I do enjoy expanding my horizons. The wonders of science and all that. Though" – he leaned in, lowering his voice – "I'll confess, all this technical talk leaves me parched. I don't suppose you fine gentlemen might fancy an excursion to more, ah . . . stimulating environs this evening?"

He caught the glimmer of interest in Harrington's expression. "Did you have something particular in mind?"

Callahan shrugged. "Whatever passes for a den of revelry in these parts. Strong spirits, pretty company, a few hands of cards to pass the hours. You know, gentlemanly pursuits."

The viscount clapped him on the shoulder. "Splendid idea, Ashford! There's an establishment I frequent nearby. Crimson Veil. You'll be our guest, of course."

Ah, there we go.

After a few more meaningless pleasantries, Callahan made his escape and rejoined Isabel in the alcove.

"Well?" she asked.

"He took the bait. We'll be going to the Crimson Veil."

"Nothing risky, Agent. And I had better not smell a doxy on you when you return."

Grinning, he skimmed his knuckles along the back of her hand. Callahan heard her breath catch.

"If you're a *very* good girl while I'm away," he said, watching her pupils dilate, "I'll lay you out on the bed and bury my tongue in your pussy."

A ragged groan escaped her. Callahan grinned, slow and filthy.

"And if *you're* good, Mr Ashford," she replied. "I may let you play with one of my knives."

"Tease."

"Boor."

The clashing scents of perfume and tobacco assaulted Callahan's nostrils as he entered the Crimson Veil. He tipped his hat to the doorman, and the brute barely spared him a glance before waving him through.

Callahan's gaze swept the main floor, taking in the groups of men clustered around gaming tables with doxies sprawled on their laps. The club was decadent. Everything was gilded and gleaming, the sort of place that made his skin itch. Thick cigar smoke hung in a haze. Murmurs of conversation and feminine laughter threaded through the air.

It took only a moment to locate his quarry.

Viscount Harrington held court near the back of the room. Cut crystal tumblers of amber liquid and a scatter of playing cards littered the polished surface before him.

"Harrington, old boy!" Callahan called, his voice loud and jovial, like a man deep in his cups. He swayed slightly as he wove through the crowd.

The viscount glanced up at his approach. "Ashford. I was beginning to think you'd reconsidered."

"Perish the thought!" Callahan collapsed into the empty chair at the table. "Whiskey, neat," he said to a passing server. "None of that watered-down piss."

Harrington's moustache twitched in what might have been amusement. "Making allowances for your American tastes, I see."

The other men eyed him with curiosity. Callahan could practically hear the thoughts churning. Who was this brash American? How deep were his pockets? And most importantly, could they fleece him at cards?

Callahan let none of his unease show. "Gentlemen," he nodded to the assembled company. "A pleasure. I trust you'll go easy on a simple Yank like myself at the tables?"

As cards were dealt and banter flowed, Callahan kept a surreptitious eye on Harrington. He bided his time, laughing at jests, commiserating over the follies of women and youth as he waited for Harrington's tongue to loosen enough.

Then, a flash of blonde hair snagged his attention. His gaze cut over, his breath stuttering to a halt.

Isabel.

Gone were the fine silks she donned as Lydia Ashford. In their place, she wore the gauzy garment of the Veil's courtesans. Her blonde curls tumbled loose and messy over her bare shoulders.

She looked ready to be fucked.

For a dizzying moment, Callahan forgot how to breathe. Forgot his own name. Forgot everything except the visceral punch of pure want that seized him.

This was what madness felt like. Chains of duty, logic, morality – it all shattered. Left nothing but greedy, grasping hunger. It reared up inside him, demanding he go to her, tear that dress off, and stake his claim.

Men would see her.

Men would see her messy, tumbled hair.

Men other than him would want to have her.

He watched as she leaned close to another woman – a brunette. They whispered together, heads inclined. Then they both glanced over. Straight at Harrington.

She wouldn't dare—

But apparently, she would. The two women linked arms and walked over.

"Well, now," Harrington purred with interest. "To what do we owe the honour of such fine company?"

The brunette draped herself over the viscount's chair. "Forgive the intrusion, gentlemen, but Emerald and I couldn't help noticing how lonely you all looked."

Emerald.

Brilliant. Another alias for the collection.

Isabel, meanwhile, had circled to Callahan's side of the table. He avoided looking at her, keeping his gaze fixed ahead.

Please, he found himself thinking. *Please, for the love of all that's holy, walk away.*

But fortune had evidently decided to well and truly fuck him tonight because the next thing he knew, Isabel had perched herself on his lap, positioned so that her face was hidden from the table at large. Callahan went still at the feel of her. Her weight settled across his thighs, dressed like sin incarnate. Like all his filthiest fantasies come to life, except for the part where they were surrounded by a bunch of inbred toffs and he couldn't actually do anything about the growing problem in his trousers.

She looped her arms around Callahan's neck. "Hello there, handsome. Fancy meeting you here."

"What the fu—" Callahan began, but Isabel slapped a palm over his mouth.

"Relax," she whispered, her voice pitched for his ears alone. "I coached Lily on what to ask. Just follow my lead. I'm here to help."

Help. Right.

Because having her plastered against him like a human blanket was absolutely fucking helpful.

He pried her hand off. "I thought I told you to stay behind and let me handle this."

"Yes, I seem to recall you saying something to that effect. Right before I nodded and agreed and proceeded to ignore you. I was bored."

"Bored?"

She smiled. "And maybe I missed you."

Missed—

She ground down with a roll of her hips. Callahan hissed, fingers sinking into her waist. "Behave. Or I swear on all that's holy, I'll bend you over this card table in front of everyone and spank that pert arse."

Isabel's grin widened. *"Promise?"*

"Well, aren't you lucky, Ashford," one of the other men – Callahan thought his name might be Fitzwilliam or Farnsworth or some other ridiculous appellation – said with a leer. "Quite the armful you've got there. What would Mrs Ashford think?"

Callahan glared up at Isabel. "I reckon Mrs Ashford

understands that I'm a man of insatiable appetites. Must be my natural charm and magnetism."

Isabel grinned.

And then she was moving against him in a slow grind that had him seeing stars. Callahan bit down hard on the inside of his cheek, fighting to keep still. To let her set the pace, even as every instinct screamed to grab hold and thrust up against her.

But that wasn't the game. Not here and now. So he let her ride him in a maddening tease.

Meanwhile, the brunette – Lily, Isabel had called her – had perched herself on Harrington's knee. She toyed with the lapel of his jacket, batting her eyelashes. "Tell me, my lord. Is it true what they say about men of science? That your minds are always working?"

"Quite true," the viscount said. "The life of an intellectual is one of constant grappling with life's mysteries and the boundaries of propriety."

Lily widened her eyes. "Propriety? However do you mean?" She leaned closer, the pale swells of her breasts threatening to spill free of her dress. "Surely a great man like yourself wouldn't shrink from advancement?"

Harrington's gaze was glued to her décolletage. "Depends on the advancement."

As Lily worked her magic on Harrington, Isabel continued her performance for the benefit of the other men at the table.

"You're so tense, darling," she purred. "Why don't you relax? Let me take care of you."

Callahan's hands came up to grip her hips, partly to keep her from falling and partly to keep himself from doing something stupid, like grinding her against his erect cock.

"Sweetheart," he growled, low enough that only she could hear, "if you don't stop squirming, things are going to get uncomfortable fast."

Isabel's only response was to nip at his earlobe, drawing a strangled sound from his throat. The little hellcat was enjoying this far too much.

"I've heard such terrible rumours of brilliant men like yourself being led astray," Lily was saying. "Tempted into paths of darkness in the name of progress. But I'm sure *you* wouldn't fall prey, would you?"

"Of course not. But I've been corresponding with a colleague who . . ." Harrington trailed off, shaking his head. "But I shouldn't speak of such things. It's not proper conversation."

Lily pouted. "But now you've piqued my curiosity. I promise I can keep a secret." She leaned in, whispering something in Harrington's ear that made his eyes go wide and his cheeks flush.

Callahan strained to hear, but Isabel chose that moment to nip his jaw. "Having fun?"

"Oh, absolutely," he replied through gritted teeth. "Nothing I love more than having my fake wife grinding on my lap while I try to eavesdrop on a scientis—*Jesus Christ.*"

Isabel had placed her hand right on his cock. He gripped her waist, fingers digging in.

"Behave," he hissed.

She had the audacity to smirk at him. "Make me."

Before Callahan could formulate a scathing response, Harrington's voice rose, drawing his attention back.

". . . asked me questions about a combination of chemicals that I find deeply concerning," he was saying, his words slightly slurred. Lily had been plying him with whiskey, and it seemed to have the desired effect. "If my suspicions are correct, the potential applications could be dangerous."

Lily gasped, her eyes wide. "How dreadful! But surely you wouldn't allow such dangerous research to continue?"

"I've voiced my concerns, of course. But he's—" Harrington made a noise. "Never mind. I'm sure you don't want to hear me prattle on when we could be doing something much more interesting."

"We should go," Callahan muttered. "Before he sobers up enough to recognise you. He's sounding reluctant to continue."

He stood, lifting Isabel with him. She kept her face turned away from Harrington, burying it in Callahan's neck as if overcome with passion. "If you'll excuse us, gentlemen," he said with a rakish grin. "Duty calls."

But as they moved to leave, Harrington's hand shot out, grabbing a generous handful of Isabel's backside. She stiffened, a small sound of surprise escaping her.

"Now, now, Ashford," the man slurred, glassy-eyed with drink and lust. "No need for selfishness. Surely you wouldn't mind sharing?"

A chorus of agreement from the other men. Scarlet bled into the edges of Callahan's vision.

But Isabel pivoted, hiding her face behind a fall of hair, and stroked a finger down Harrington's cheek. "You naughty boy. I'm flattered. Truly. Alas, my hands are quite full."

"I'll occupy you," Lily cooed to Harrington. "Perhaps we could find a private spot?"

Before the bastard could reply, Callahan swept Isabel up and strode for the nearest empty room. He shouldered the door open, slamming it behind them.

The moment they were alone, he set her down and rounded on her. "What in the nine hells was that?"

One arched brow. Utterly unruffled. "That was called improvising. You're welcome, by the by."

He raked fingers through his hair. "You could have been recognised! Hell, you nearly were! If he'd gotten a clear look at your face—"

She scoffed. "Please. Half the men out there couldn't see past my tits if they tried. Including you." She smoothed her skirts. "Besides. We have a better idea of what Harrington was so hostile to Ramsgate about. Dangerous science, ethical violations. He might have been working on a chemical weapon for Favreau and sought the expertise of a colleague to perfect his work."

"Ethical violations? That's what you took from that?"

"Among other things. What part of me doing my job are you struggling with? Is this because you heard precisely nothing out there? Is that it? You're too easily distracted, Agent."

Callahan's control snapped. In two swift strides, he had her pinned to the wall. "It was a little difficult for me to concentrate with you grinding on my cock, Isabel."

Her eyes flashed. "Is it that I was grinding on you or that I was doing it where other men could see, and you're a selfish, greedy fake husband who wants me all to yourself?"

Rational thought vanished, and he crushed his mouth to

234

hers. She met him with equal ferocity, hands twisting in his hair to drag him closer.

He lost himself in the slick friction of her mouth, her tongue stroking his. His hands slid down to her thighs, shoving at the fabric until he found skin. A growl rumbled up from his chest as he hitched her leg over his hip, fitting their bodies together. The hard ridge of his cock nestled against her core, only a few thin layers between them.

She tipped her head back with a moan as his fingers traced higher, skating over smooth thighs. Up and up until he reached the slit in her undergarments. A choked whimper caught in her throat. He needed to touch her, taste her, take her apart until she shattered—

A shrill scream cleaved the air.

Isabel froze. "What in damnation?"

Callahan's lust-drugged mind struggled to parse what had just happened.

Another cry, panicked. Coming from down the hall.

He pushed away from Isabel and seized her hand, hauling her out of the room. They burst into the chamber at the end of the passage to find Lily still screaming, and—

Harrington.

The viscount lay on the floor in a pool of blood.

23

Callahan bit out a curse. "Well, this complicates things."
Isabel slanted him a withering glare. "Your penchant for stating the obvious never fails to astound."

Already, alarm was beginning to spread through the club. Murder, it seemed, was the only thing scandalous enough to disrupt the Veil's debauchery.

Isabel turned to Lily, whose screams had faded into hiccuping sobs. "Tell me what happened."

Lily's gaze snapped to her. "I—I don't know, miss. One moment, his lordship was whispering in my ear, making free with his hands, you know." A shaky swallow. "And the next . . ."

"The killer," Callahan pressed, losing his American accent. "Which way did he go?"

"Out the back." A choked sound, halfway between a sob and retch.

"What did he look like?"

Lily shook her head. "Didn't get a proper look, did I? Tall bloke. Broad in the shoulders. Wearing a long, dark coat."

Isabel gave Lily's shoulder a quick squeeze, then turned to Callahan. "I'm going after him."

Callahan opened his mouth to argue, but Isabel was already moving towards the rear entrance.

"*Isabel*. Wait—"

She whirled on him. "Our lead was just murdered for a reason. I want to find the murderer and question him. At knifepoint."

Callahan made a frustrated sound. "And naturally, you've elected yourself for the task."

"I can handle the Syndicate's bully boys. Fetch Wentworth and make sure he's apprised of the situation. We've a dead nob to contend with now, and if word gets out to the symposium, Ramsgate will bolt. We'll need the Office's resources to contain this mess." Every instinct screamed against splitting up, but the rational, calculating part of her knew one of them had to manage the scene. "Don't worry, I'll only engage if I have a clean shot at death or capture."

Callahan looked like he wanted to argue, but he stepped back.

"One hour, Trouble. Whether you catch the bastard or not, get that pretty arse back to Basil House, or I'm coming after you."

"See you in an hour, then."

She slipped out the rear entrance, emerging into a narrow alleyway. The night air was cool and damp, the cobblestones slick.

And there, disappearing into the gloom – a tall, broad-shouldered silhouette in a dark coat.

Isabel ran after him.

One hand hiked up her skirts, the other seeking the blade strapped to her thigh. She took a corner hard. Another turn, another. Blood roared in her ears. One more corner and—

She skidded to a halt when the alley terminated into a brick wall. She pivoted. Nothing. No sound, no movement. Just the harsh rasp of her breathing and the distant clatter of carriage wheels.

"Come out, you bastard. I know you're here."

A mocking chuckle came from the shadows to her left. She knew that laugh.

Favreau.

"Still so spirited. It's part of your charm."

"So you're fond of telling me."

She gripped the blade hard as he stepped out of the dark.

Even now, the sight of him struck like a blow behind her ribs. Silver-blond hair, winter-pale eyes, a mouth made for cruelty. To think she once found that smile charming. There was no warmth in this man, only the pitiless cold of a winter midnight.

Animal instinct screamed at her to flee. To make herself small and unobtrusive. After everything, he still reached deep, hooked talons into the most fragile parts of her and *pulled*.

"You must be wondering why I've summoned you to London." His tone was conversational, almost pleasant.

She glared at him. "You didn't *summon* me anywhere."

A smug smile tugged at the corners of his mouth. "Is that what you think? That you being here is happenstance? That the intelligence the Office so deftly snared, the trail of intrigue you've followed to this very moment, is anything but a lure?"

Stupid. Stupid, stupid, stupid.

She tasted copper on her tongue. She'd bitten her cheek. "Ramsgate? His research—"

"Oh, his research is genuine. He served as bait, you see. A novel little puzzle meant to whet the Home Office's appetite and draw out their latest asset. And here you stand. Did you think you could flee so easily? That there wouldn't be a reckoning?" He moved towards her, slow and relentless. "You know better, Isabel. You know *me* better."

"Is this where you take me by force? Send your men after me like you did five months ago?"

"No. I've sacrificed enough loyal soldiers on the altar of your spite. You'll return to me of your own free will. Kneel at my feet and beg for the privilege."

Isabel swallowed against the sudden tightness in her throat. "The only one of us who will kneel is you. You don't own me, you arrogant prick."

"Don't I? Have you forgotten so quickly, *mon cœur*?" He lifted a hand and trailed his fingers down her cheek. She just managed not to flinch. "The things I taught you? The way I made you *sing*? No matter how far you run or how desperately you try to carve me out, my marks are all over you. You're mine."

No. No, no, no.

Nausea churned in her belly. She wanted to cringe from that touch, from the scouring memory of a hundred other touches. His hands on her, that low, rumbling laughter as she lay still beneath him, the knife gliding over her skin—

"Is that why Harrington had to die? Because he touched what you consider yours?"

A muscle jumped in Favreau's jaw. "Harrington knew

too much about the particulars of Ramsgate's project. Disposing of him was good business." His gaze flicked back to her face. "The fact that he dared lay a finger on my most prized possession expedited matters."

Then his hand lashed out, catching her wrist.

Her dagger clattered to the cobblestones. His palm cracked across her cheek, snapping her head to the side. Pain bloomed, sharp and bright.

"I indulge you." Favreau's voice caressed her ear, a dark croon. "Your rebellions, your flights of childish pique. The delusions of freedom. But my patience has limits, Isabel."

She spat in his face.

He dashed away the gob of saliva, his mouth pursed in distaste. "So wilful, *mon cœur*. Why do you make me hurt you?"

In a blink, Favreau slammed her to the ground. He was on her in an instant, knees bracketing her hips, palm splayed between her breasts. Keeping her pinned. He tugged at her bodice and *yanked*. Tearing fabric, baring skin.

Reaching into his coat, he withdrew a small knife. Isabel knew that blade. Knew the edge of it, the cruel bite. It had mapped her in searing strokes a hundred times before.

And now it pressed into the hollow of her throat.

"A more permanent reminder is in order," Favreau mused. "A declaration of ownership." He trailed the blade along her neck. "I should carve my initials here, I think." A considering tap between her breasts. "So the next time that filthy Irish dog touches what's mine, he's reminded who you belong to."

She couldn't move, couldn't breathe. "Don't. Favreau, *don't*."

He went still. She could feel the slow rise and fall of his chest.

"It pains me to repeat myself, but you know the rules. Only two phrases should fall from your lips in moments such as this. 'Yes' and 'please', Isabel."

Then he started cutting.

A choked sound escaped her throat. Favreau tightened his grip, bruising fingerprints into her arms. Holding her still. She remembered this ritual all too well, knew what struggling would do. So she lay very, very still.

And she let him carve.

Callahan's voice rose from her memories, calming. *We endure in the only ways we can, Trouble. We adapt and overcome because the alternative is to let the world grind us to dust.*

She wasn't in her body. It was all right because she was outside of it. There were only ocean waves. Isabel had long since memorised the cadence of different seas, the way the waves struck a particular rhythm unique to each place. Each wave was a breath. A reminder.

Alive alive alive.

And she went into that drowning deep in her mind that he couldn't touch. It was soft there. It was quiet. The waves surrounded her, and she floated above her body.

And she was all right. He didn't touch her here.

Not even when he finished, and she saw what he'd carved.

The two ugly letters.

L. F.

Louis Favreau.

A shudder went through her, violent enough to clack

her teeth together. He gentled her through it, the hand on her nape almost a caress now.

"Shh, *shh*. It's done, *chérie*. No more confusion. No more doubt." His mouth brushed her temple, tender now. Gentle in the way he used to be before he ever showed her ugliness. "You know where you belong. With me. Beneath me."

His fingers flexed on her neck, a warning. A noose, tightening by degrees.

"Surrender, and I'll be merciful." His lips pressed to hers. Tasting her. "I'll even let your Irishman live."

Everything stopped. Her heart, her lungs, the frantic whirl of her thoughts. In that silence, the only sound was his rasping breaths as he kissed her again.

The world shattered. She felt it like a fissure opening up in her chest.

Ronan.

It was the cruellest cut. Threatening the one thing she'd carved out in the wretched landscape of her life.

"You know what I'll do," he said, very soft. Almost gentle. "The ruin I'll make of him if you refuse me. Is that what you want? Because I promise you, I'll draw it out until you'll beg me for the mercy of a clean kill. I'll make it hurt, Isabel."

She wanted to be strong, to snarl. To be stone. Steel. A creature of jagged edges and frost, like him.

But she wasn't, was she? Not really. Not where it counted.

"End this." His nails sank into her flesh. "Offer yourself for his worthless life, and I may spare him."

"No." Her voice shook.

"You'll change your mind. But I'm feeling generous, so

I'll allow you a reprieve for tonight. Savour your freedom while you're able and consider my offer." He kissed her forehead. "*À bientôt, ma petite.*"

Then he was gone, leaving her bleeding and alone.

✥ 24 ✥

"Lily," Callahan called, careful not to startle the poor woman who just witnessed a gristly murder. "A word."

She approached him warily. The strain of the evening was etched into her face. Her hands trembled before she clasped them in front of her.

"Yes, sir?" Her voice shook.

"I need you to listen, pet. Can you do that?"

The tiniest dip of her chin was his only answer.

"Good girl. I want this place locked up tight as a drum, you hear? No one in or out. And that room" – he jerked his head towards the door where Harrington's corpse was cooling – "is to stay exactly as it is. I don't care if the Second Coming of Christ manifests in there, not a single thing gets touched. The coppers'll be here soon. You tell them that verbatim. Understand?"

Lily nodded, some panic in her eyes receding in the face of clear instructions. "Is there anything else you need, sir?"

"Send someone to Basil House. A fast runner who can keep their mouth shut. Tell them to fetch the Marquess of Ripon. Say it's urgent business regarding one of his guests." Callahan withdrew a handful of coins from his pocket, pressing them into Lily's hand. "For your trouble. And your discretion. Might want to grab yourself a tot of gin, settle your nerves."

She curled her fingers around the coins. "Consider it done, sir."

Callahan turned to go, then paused. He glanced back at Lily, taking in how she seemed to hold herself together through sheer force of will. "You likely won't see me again tonight, but I'm sending round a man named Mattias Wentworth. Tell the girls he's safe to let through. He'll have his lads take care of that body for you, quick and clean. No one the wiser, come morning."

Relief flickered over Lily's face. "Thank you, sir."

With a final nod, Callahan strode out into the night. He quickened his pace, hunched against the chill. The sooner he got to Wentworth, the sooner they could start damage control.

And the sooner he could get back to Isabel.

Callahan's boots echoed in the foyer of the Home Office. Even at this late hour, a few gas lamps burned, and staff crossed his path. There was always someone here who never slept.

Which included Wentworth.

He took the stairs two at a time. When he reached the

office, the spymaster was bent over his desk, working late as usual. He didn't startle at Callahan's abrupt entrance, merely glanced up with a raised brow.

"We have a problem," Callahan said without preamble.

At that, Wentworth straightened. He was already reaching for his coat. "I assume this is more pressing than whatever sent you off in your evening kit?"

"Right. It's a bloodstained, body-shaped problem currently growing cold on the floor of a whorehouse, to be precise."

Wentworth pinched the bridge of his nose. "Fuck. Tell me."

"One of Ripon's guests was murdered tonight. Viscount Harrington. A gent with particular scientific inclinations, as it happens. Specifically, an interest in Ramsgate's work."

"What do we know?"

Callahan fell into step beside the spymaster as they strode from the office. "It was a professional job. Quick and clean. Harrington was dead before he hit the floor, his throat slit. The killer slipped in and out again while the viscount was intimate with a doxy. Poor thing saw it happen."

"And Harrington? Did you glean anything from him before he bled out?"

"He let slip that Ramsgate was mucking about with some chemical combination the viscount considered 'concerning'. Isabel believes it might be a weapon."

"We need to contain this. Keep it quiet so Ramsgate doesn't know the Syndicate is cleaning up loose ends."

"Already ahead of you. I've got the staff at the Crimson Veil sitting tight, and I sent for Ripon."

"Good thinking. Your cover. It's secure?"

"As secure as it can be, given the circumstances. Why? Having doubts about my ability to play the bumbling American?"

"I have doubts about everything, Callahan. It's why I'm still alive." Wentworth hailed a hack and turned to Callahan before getting inside. "I'll go and run interference with Ripon and have a few of my men keep eyes on the house to make sure Ramsgate doesn't leave, just to be safe."

Callahan nodded. The urge to return to Isabel was a physical ache in his chest. "I'd best be getting back. Wouldn't do for Mr Ashford to be absent."

Callahan was relieved to see light spilling from beneath the bathing chamber's door when he returned to Basil House. A muted sloshing came from within – the shift of water in a bath.

Thank God. She was safe.

"Isabel? Did you find our killer?"

"He ran off. I'll just be a minute." Her voice sounded wrong – thready and distant.

Unease prickled Callahan's nape. He shucked his coat, setting it over the chair.

"Wentworth is keeping word of tonight's unpleasantness at the Crimson Veil contained for now. One of his men is watching the house to keep Ramsgate secure. We'll need to search the room before the symposium concludes."

He paused, waiting for her response. But there was only the rasp of his own breath.

"Isabel?"

"Right. Tomorrow." The words were hollow. As if some

vital spark had gone out of her. "One day left to accomplish our mission. I haven't forgotten."

To anyone else, the words might have seemed ordinary. Unremarkable. But Callahan knew that voice – all its shades and permutations.

Every instinct clamoured a warning.

He closed the distance to the washroom, pushed through the door, and went utterly still.

There was blood in the bathwater.

Isabel sat huddled in the tub, knees hugged tight to her chest. Blonde hair clung to her face and throat in damp tendrils, water droplets glistening against her skin.

She looked impossibly young. Unbearably fragile in a way someone so fierce had no right to be.

"Isabel," he said. Tentative. As if the slightest misstep might shatter her into pieces too small to gather. "What happened?"

Gently, gently. The way you'd coax a wild thing closer. Isabel Dumont had endured a lifetime's worth of cruelties and careless brutalities by men who sought to break her. He would not add to it now.

For a long, airless moment, she said nothing. Callahan barely breathed.

Then, so quietly he almost missed it: "It was Favreau." Three words. Toneless. Devoid of inflection. "He knew Wentworth was intercepting intelligence on Ramsgate. He planted them deliberately to draw me to London."

He didn't give a damn about that. She was bleeding.

"Let me see."

Their gazes locked. The armour of the Spectre fell away

to reveal the shattered woman beneath. Slowly, she leaned back.

And Callahan saw it – jagged letters carved between her breasts.

L.F.

The ugly scrawl of possession. Of ownership.

He sucked in a breath. "*Christ fucking God.*"

"He gave me all of them. Every scar." Distant, detached. Almost cold. Her fingers skimmed over the silvered slashes – the violence etched into her flesh. "Favreau liked to cut me. Liked to see me bleed while he—" A sharp, hitching inhale. "While he—"

"Stop." Callahan gentled his voice. "You don't need to say it. I know."

He sank to his knees beside the tub. This close, he could count every bruise, every scrape. The delicate fan of her lashes against too-pale cheeks, the purple smudges exhaustion had thumbed beneath her eyes.

And Callahan opened his arms.

"Come here," he murmured.

She leaned into him without protest. It terrified him, this sudden malleability. As if Favreau had reached into her chest and scooped out all her spark and fire.

"I have you," he told her. "I have you."

Her fingers dug into his shoulders. A shudder rippled through her. "In the alleyway . . . it felt like before. Before I left him in Hong Kong. I felt like that woman again. Letting him—Letting him—"

"Shhh." Callahan tightened his hold. "He hurt you, Isabel. He tortured you."

"I was so scared."

"Isabel. Look at me."

He tipped her face up to his. Her eyes were wide and dark.

"I have you," he murmured. "Let me take care of you."

She gripped his wrist. "You've a talent with a blade, don't you?"

"Little thief, you—"

"Carve over them," she said, her breath coming fast. "Reshape the letters into yours. Put your name on me. *Please.*"

Fuck. Fuck, fuck.

"Sweetheart, after what Favreau just did—"

"Pain I choose, remember? That's the difference. The only man's name I want to wear on my skin is yours." She made a soft noise. "It doesn't have to mean anything. I'm not asking for promises or—"

"It means something," he said softly. "To me." Sighing, he reached for his ankle and slid his blade out of the sheath. "Tell me if you need me to stop."

Callahan held her stare as he palmed his knife. Patient. Waiting for permission.

"I trust you." A whisper.

Oh, his heart. She was killing him.

"Deep breath, love."

And he began to cut into her.

When Callahan was a lad, Whelan used him for wet work. He had a pretty face and a body good for selling, sure, but he was also strong, fast, and good with a knife.

And he never flinched when he mutilated people.

That takes a certain talent, Whelan claimed. Many men could kill and make it brutal, but most didn't have the talent for the small agonies that made someone cry and yield. They didn't have a talent for *carving*.

Carving, Callahan learned, was a more precise art. It took patience. A strong stomach. Steady hands. Things most lads don't have. And that's because when Callahan did Whelan's dirty work, he wasn't present. His mind left. It took with it all the complicated emotions like empathy and humanity and tucked them away in favour of survival, because a carving done well meant an entire month of food in his belly. That was how well his expertise paid.

He refused to tuck away those emotions now; he didn't go to that quiet place in his body.

Callahan wouldn't leave her. He would stay present. Because she needed both his steady hands and his care.

She needed *him*.

Each cut of the dagger was a prayer. A silent litany spilled out in blood, consecrated by pain and the sweet sting of a hurt that healed. With each delicate, deliberate stroke, Callahan unmade Favreau's brutality. In its place, he planted his own claim – the initials he wanted her to wear not as a brand but as a promise.

They flowed like calligraphy, elegant. This, of all things, deserved to be done well. To be made lovely, even in its savagery.

He splashed away the blood, wiping the canvas clean so he could perfect his masterpiece. Each scar became a story, written in steady strokes.

I love you, his hands said.

I love you, his heart said.

And the years he'd endured under Whelan finally yielded something he could be proud of.

R.

L.

C.

"The L," Isabel said with a soft sort of wonder, the emotions too tangled to pick apart. "What does it stand for?"

"Liam."

"Ronan Liam Callahan." Her accent wrapped around the syllables like a caress, nestling them close to her heart. "Your mother must have loved you very much to give you a name that beautiful."

"She did." A pang, soft and bittersweet, behind his breastbone. "More than anything in the world. And I loved her just the same."

"What happened to her?"

Callahan exhaled slowly. "She fell ill when I was small. Lingered for a time, but in the end . . ." He shook his head. "There was no one else after that. No family to speak of except the lads I ran with."

He could paint his history in shades of abandonment, of the aching absence of a boy left behind. A hard-won survival in the streets. A kingdom of stray dogs fighting for scraps. His life before he'd crawled his way up with Nick Thorne, when he'd let his knuckles and knives do his talking, carving out his place in a city that didn't care for lost Irish boys.

Isabel squeezed her eyes shut. "Mine was ill, too. And after – there was only Emma. She was the reason I—" She broke off, jaw working. "The things I let Favreau do . . . the things I did for him . . ."

Callahan set the knife aside. "You don't need to explain. Not to me."

He understood better than most the unholy bargains struck for love, the pieces of yourself you carved away to keep another whole. Because that's what this was. His knife cut into the woman who held his battered heart in her bloodstained hands. He loved her. Viciously, tenderly.

Hopelessly.

Isabel kept studying the labyrinth of wounds and scars, old and new. At the initials etched so carefully between her breasts.

"Thank you," she breathed. "You have a master's hand."

"I wanted it to be beautiful. Wanted you to look at it and feel . . ." He fumbled, the words tangling. "Feel cherished."

A beat. Their eyes met and something passed between them, bright and aching. Too raw, too fragile to be given voice. Her fingers fluttered at the edges of the fresh cuts, tracing them with reverence.

"I do," she whispered. "I do."

Callahan's heart stumbled, lurching against his ribs. He cleared his throat. Looked away before she could see too much.

"You should rest now. Let me tend these, and then sleep."

He rose, pulling Isabel gently up. He dried her off, scrubbed away the last traces of blood, and carried her to the bed. From the depths of his valise, he withdrew a tin of salve and bandages. The tools of his trade, though he usually employed them in the aftermath of violence rather than tenderness.

"This will sting," he warned as he unscrewed the lid.

The ghost of a smile. "I've had worse."

Callahan's fingers gentled as he smoothed the ointment over her skin. "I know," he said simply.

Once the salve was applied, he wound strips of linen over her injuries. Isabel held still, only the flutter of her lashes betraying any discomfort. When it was done, he tied off the last bandage and sat back.

"Isabel." Callahan's voice fractured around the shape of her name. "May I kiss you?"

"You're asking tonight?" she said in surprise.

He skimmed his thumbs over her cheeks. "I think tonight you deserve to be asked."

Some emotion flickered over Isabel's face. Complicated. Wanting.

She swallowed. "Kiss me."

He leaned in, brushing his lips over hers. A whisper, the barest graze of skin. And again. Soft. Coaxing. Asking permission with each tentative foray. No heat, no scorching urgency. Just connection, a tether of touch. His lips moved against hers, almost hesitant – a supplicant before an altar.

An unspoken language, a solace that a man like him had always fumbled to give voice to. He was a creature of sharp lines meant for dealing death. But for her . . . for her he could be gentle. Soft in all the ways that mattered. He painted his devotion into her with touch, with taste. A wordless confession too fragile yet for the hard edges of speech.

Long moments later, Callahan forced himself to retreat. To lay his brow against hers as they traded air.

"Would you like to sleep now?"

A slight nod.

"And would you like me to hold you? While you rest?"

A stuttering inhale. "I'd like that very much," she whispered. "Ronan Liam."

❧ 25 ❧

Isabel surfaced from the depths of slumber, the last tendrils of a half-remembered nightmare still clinging to her.

Callahan slept on, his breaths deep and even. For a long moment, Isabel simply lay there, savouring every point of contact between her body and his – the heavy arm slung low across her abdomen, his thigh pressed to hers.

I love you, she wanted to tell him.

Her fingers drifted to the fresh bandages beneath her nightgown, tracing the phantom ache of newly carved letters.

R.L.C.

She loved them. Before he'd put the bandage into place, she'd marvelled at the careful way he shaped each letter. As if he intended to erase the memory of Favreau's violence with his care.

"I can hear you thinking," Callahan mumbled, the words gravelly with sleep. "It's criminal at this hour."

A reluctant smile tugged at one corner of Isabel's mouth. "Someone's surly before he's had his tea."

The arm at her waist tightened, hauling her back against him. "I'll give you surly." He kissed her cheeks, her eyelids, her neck. "How are you feeling? Any pain this morning?"

Yes, she wanted to say. *I feel too raw.*

Favreau would never stop hunting her. But Isabel was fast and clever and desperate, and desperation had always served her well. She could survive. She could—

"Isabel. Stay with me."

But memories rose, phantom bruises blooming over her skin. Fingers digging deep, pain sparking along her nerve endings.

Ma belle. Ma petite sauvage.

"*Isabel.* Come back to me."

Slowly, she turned her head, pressing her lips to the centre of his palm. She wanted to crawl into his lap and lose herself in him. Let him fuck her until she shook apart. Callahan made her want impossible things.

"I'm fine," she said.

"Liar."

"We have work to do."

Callahan sighed. "That we do."

With a last, lingering squeeze, he released her and rolled to his feet.

By unspoken accord, there were no indulgent touches or heated glances as they made themselves presentable, just the efficient choreography of two professionals with a mission to complete.

Isabel fixed a sunny smile on her face as they descended for breakfast, channelling Lydia Ashford with practised ease.

Callahan bantered with their fellow symposium attendees,

Jamie Ashford's boyish charm and flirtatious grins in place. But Isabel could feel the coiled tension thrumming through him. She sensed it in the way his fingers flexed against her back as they circulated the room.

It was almost a relief when she overheard a snippet from a cluster of men by the buffet.

". . . still abed. Someone ought to check on the poor fellow."

"What's this?" She drifted closer, allowing curiosity to soften her features. "Is someone unwell?"

The oldest of the three men turned towards her. "Mr Ramsgate hasn't come down yet. Most unlike him to miss the morning sessions."

"Nothing serious, I hope?"

"Brandy's likely the culprit. Biochemists and their delicate constitutions and all."

"How dreadful."

Her attention slid to Callahan, who was chatting with a group of women by the buffet. Their eyes met briefly, and he gave an almost imperceptible nod.

She turned back to her conversation, making appropriately vapid comments about the weather while tracking Callahan's exit from the corner of her eye.

Five minutes. Ten. Fifteen.

When his fingers finally closed around her elbow, Isabel nearly jumped. The subtle pressure of his grip told her everything she needed to know.

"Excuse me," she murmured to her companions. "My husband requires my attention."

Callahan's face was a mask as he steered her through the crowd.

"What is it?" she whispered once they were out of earshot. "Is he ill?"

"Come with me."

Three words, and the bottom dropped out of her stomach.

He led her up the stairs and down a long corridor, stopping at a door halfway down. Without a word, he pushed it open.

The smell hit her first. Metallic. Thick. Familiar.

Ramsgate lay sprawled across the bed, the white sheets beneath him seeped in blood. The spatter on the walls told the story of a violent end.

"Favreau?" she asked, her voice steady. Her hands didn't even tremble. "Did he follow me back?"

Callahan shook his head, his face grim. "Wentworth had men watching. No one came or went after we returned." He moved closer to the bed, studying the body with professional detachment. "This happened earlier. Probably right after the symposium adjourned yesterday evening and before Favreau moved on to Harrington at the club. It seems he was busy tying up loose ends last night."

"He got what he wanted – me back in London. Ramsgate served his purpose."

An icy feeling spread through her chest. If Favreau already had what he needed from Ramsgate, then the weapon was finished. Ready.

Her attention caught on a small leather-bound notebook clutched in the man's fingers. She tugged it free, her breath catching as she flipped through pages covered in cramped writing and intricate diagrams. Something cold settled in her stomach.

"This one isn't coded," she said. "Which means Favreau

left it here on purpose. One date matches Harrington's letter."

"We need to get this to Wentworth," Callahan said. "Let's find Ripon."

The marquess was in the breakfast room with a cluster of scientists. When he saw Isabel and Callahan, he immediately paused the conversation. "Gentlemen, I'm afraid you must excuse me. Urgent matters, you understand."

He didn't wait for their response; he just steered Isabel and Callahan down the hall and into an empty sitting room.

"What now?" Ripon demanded, dropping all pretense of aristocratic niceties.

Callahan didn't soften the blow. "You've got a corpse upstairs."

"Bloody buggering fuck, not another dead guest." Ripon's shoulders slumped as he dragged a hand down his face. "Who is it this time?"

"Ramsgate," Isabel supplied.

"Right. Of course."

"We think he's been dead since last night," Callahan added. "Looks like Favreau spent the evening ridding himself of unneeded complications."

"Christ. This keeps getting better and better, doesn't it?"

"We're leaving to brief Wentworth now. I assumed you'd want to be a part of that particular conversation," Isabel said.

"Oh, yes, wouldn't miss it for the world," the marquess said. "Just let me go and inform my staff that if they value their positions, they'll forget they ever clapped eyes on Ramsgate's rooms. I'll meet you out front directly."

He strode off, already barking orders.

Callahan turned to Isabel. "This is all going rather spectacularly to shite, isn't it?"

"You expected anything else?"

"Hope springs eternal." He offered her his arm. "Shall we?"

Wentworth looked up from behind his desk as they filed in. He took in their dour expressions and heaved a gusty sigh.

"Don't tell me," he drawled. "You're about to ruin what was shaping up to be an altogether pleasant morning after last night's mess."

Callahan snorted. "Fine, I won't tell you. Drink?"

"Make it a double."

As Callahan busied himself at the sideboard, Isabel fished Ramsgate's journal from the folds of her skirts and passed it to Wentworth.

"What fresh hell is this?" he asked.

"We need someone who can parse that scientific gibberish," Callahan said, handing round the drinks. The whiskey burned a welcome trail down Isabel's throat. "Ramsgate is . . . no longer available for clarification."

Wentworth blew out a short, sharp breath through his nostrils. "Marvellous." He stood and walked to the door. Yanking it open, he stuck his head out into the hallway beyond and called out to some unseen underling, "Fetch me Jones, will you? Soonest. And send some lads round to Ripon's mansion. I need a bit of sprucing up. The discreet sort. Unseen. *Again*."

Isabel rather pitied the poor sod on the receiving end of that directive. Few things were more stomach-churning than a good, old-fashioned "sprucing up" in this line of work. Blood was damnably hard to get out of upholstery.

Minutes later, a man slipped into the room. He was tall and thin, with dark hair and a severe set to his brow. Not handsome, exactly. But interesting. His shoulders were rigid, his posture too perfect. Military training, perhaps?

"Gentlemen, Miss Dumont – this is Alaric Jones," Wentworth said. "Expert in all manner of mysterious substances and attendant buggery. If anyone can parse Ramsgate's scribblings, it's him. Alaric, I need you to read this scientific blatherskite for me, if you would."

He passed over the notebook. Alaric bent his head to study it, the furrow between his brows deepening.

"Well?" Callahan prompted. "What exactly are we dealing with?"

"An organophosphate, by the looks of it." Alaric's voice was lightly accented. German, perhaps. "Attacks the nervous system on contact. Asphyxiation would follow swiftly after."

"And how quickly does it kill?" Wentworth asked what they were all thinking.

"Five minutes. Maybe less." Jones closed the notebook. "It depends on how it's delivered. Inhaled is quickest. Skin contact, slightly slower. I've only seen research like this in . . ." He hesitated. "Places where morals are flexible."

Their gazes settled on Isabel. Of course. Who better to comment on the movements of a madman than the woman who'd once been his most prized possession?

She took a steadying breath. "The symposium's closing ball is tomorrow. And no one knows Ramsgate is dead yet. Favreau wants me. He'll make his move there and threaten me openly. He wants me to feel trapped, to see returning to him as my only choice. This entire situation – Ramsgate, the weapon, all of it – was orchestrated to bring me back to London. Back to him."

"Are you suggesting we use my guests as bait, Miss Dumont?" Ripon asked.

"I'm the bait," she replied. "Your guests are potential collateral damage."

"That's a cold way of looking at things."

"I spent seven years at Favreau's side. I watched him torture men for sport. I helped him destabilise governments." Her nails dug crescents into her palms. "Cold is all I know. But I'll go with him willingly if I see no other option."

"No." Callahan caught Isabel's elbow. "We're not dangling you in front of Favreau."

"I'm not asking for your permission, Agent." The formality was a shield between them, something to keep her from falling apart. She faced Ripon again. "The ball preparations need to continue as planned. No one can suspect anything's wrong."

26

Isabel fumbled with the buttons at the small of her back. Each one was a battle she was ill-equipped to win after the long day behind her.

The door swung open, and Callahan entered the room wearing his evening attire. No man had a right to look that beautiful while she stood there still half-dressed and frustrated. She took her time looking at him. The width of his shoulders, the perfect fit across his chest, the way his hands hung relaxed at his sides. Everything about him was precise. Deadly.

"Don't just stand there," she said, turning to show him her back. "Make yourself useful."

He closed the distance between them without a word. His fingers were warm against her skin as they worked each button. When he reached the middle of her back, he paused.

"Here . . ." His touch lingered over the bandages he'd re-wrapped that morning. "Does it pain you?"

"No more than the rest."

She'd had worse. She'd survived worse.

Callahan's arms slid around her waist from behind, drawing her against his chest. She stiffened instinctively, braced for ... something.

But he only held her more firmly and rested his chin on her shoulder.

"Nervous?"

"Cautious," she corrected. Nervous was what normal women felt before balls. Cautious was what kept you alive when someone wanted to carve into you. "There's a difference."

"Is there? Given what happened with Favreau—"

"Don't." She made her face blank, wiped away every trace of emotion like she'd been taught. Like she'd taught herself. "We have work to do. Nothing else signifies. My feelings are irrelevant."

Callahan said nothing. His palm glided over her shoulder. Those fingers grazed down, down, catching on the edge of her bodice. He pushed the fabric aside, exposing the bandage covering his initials carved into her skin.

"Your feelings are never irrelevant," Callahan said softly. "Not to me."

Something broke inside her chest. It felt like hunger, like thirst – like wanting something so badly it made you stupid. She'd spent years running from this feeling, this need to belong to someone who might throw her away. It was the oldest hurt, this wanting.

She'd built her walls so high, and somehow he kept finding ways over them, under them, through them. The gravity between them terrified her. It was like standing at the precipice of a cliff with the wind at her back.

She could see the bottom. Could see exactly how far she'd fall if she let herself love this man.

How much it would destroy her when it all went wrong.

"There are perhaps a dozen highly trained operatives in this building," he continued. "All of them are dedicated to keeping you safe. More to the point, I would cut down a hundred men before I let them lay a finger on you."

Isabel squeezed her eyes shut, allowing herself a final, selfish instant of weakness. She let herself imagine, just for a moment, what it might feel like to let his hands peel away the thorns and armour. To be held and cherished and remade into some soft new shape.

But armour was all she had. Without it, there would be nothing left.

She stepped away, the air between them suddenly too thin.

"Shall we go?" She tugged her bodice back into place, hiding the bandages. Hiding his mark on her. "Wouldn't want to keep our adoring public waiting."

Something flickered across his features. Regret, perhaps. Or resignation. But he merely inclined his head.

"After you, Mrs Ashford."

Candlelight bathed the parquet in an amber glow. Liveried footmen wove through the crowd with trays of champagne and tiny savouries. The air was thick with the mingled scents of flowers, tobacco and spirits, and too many bodies crushed together.

"Shall we dance?" Callahan murmured. "It would give us a better view of the room."

She didn't answer, just let him lead her to the floor. Callahan's arm slid around her, drawing her in close. They moved in circles. *One-two-three, one-two-three.* Isabel kept her eyes on the crowd, scanning every face. Favreau could be anywhere. Watching. Waiting.

"You look like I'm torturing you," Callahan chided. "This is supposed to be a loving marriage, remember? Pretend I've just paid you a compliment."

"Like this?" She bared her teeth in what felt more like a grimace.

"Maybe don't look like you're about to bite me." He paused. "Unless that's on offer later."

"I thought I was supposed to be the proper Mrs Ashford."

"You're supposed to be besotted with your husband. Not plotting his murder on the dance floor."

She let him spin her, using the movement to scan another section of the room. "I'm choosing to be selective with my wit tonight. Saving it for worthier targets."

"How judicious of you. And here I thought scandalising these fine people was your favourite pastime."

"I've found I prefer more intimate audiences these days."

Something dark and hungry flashed in his eyes. His fingers dug into her waist, just hard enough to make her breath catch. Isabel almost missed the flash of emerald green that caught her eye across the room.

She frowned. Lady Camberley stood surrounded by a cluster of admirers, a small crystal vial in her gloved hand.

"What's happening over there?" She nodded toward the group.

Callahan glanced over his shoulder. "Ripon said

something about a perfume demonstration. A new type of bottle. The idle rich and their silly baubles."

Lady Camberley pressed something on the vial. A fine mist sprayed across her neck and chest.

Aerosolised. Asphyxiation in minutes.

Isabel's grip tightened on Callahan. "*Ronan*. The perfume—"

The woman clawed at her throat and collapsed to the floor. Then another. Someone shrieked as a third guest dropped, gasping for air. Isabel's stomach lurched. She'd seen death before, but this was different. This was a slaughter. Bodies hit the floor while the orchestra kept playing, oblivious to the chaos for three more seconds before the music died. Champagne glasses shattered. Women screamed. Men shouted.

But she barely heard any of it.

Because Favreau was here. He wouldn't miss his moment of theatre, his chance to see her squirm. To watch her realise how completely he controlled the situation.

Men in dark suits materialised from the crowd – Wentworth's agents, moving to control the chaos and usher out the other guests.

"Trouble, look at me," Callahan commanded. "Wentworth's men will handle the civilians. We need to find Favreau."

His eyes were steady. Grounding. But she didn't have time to let him anchor her.

"Remember what I told you about how he looks. Like an angel. Blond hair. Blue eyes. You'll know him when you see him."

Before Callahan could stop her, she shoved into the throng. The ballroom had descended into chaos – ladies screaming, gentlemen shouting orders, staff cowering. Isabel shoved past them all. The crush of bodies made it hard to move.

Isabel fought her way outside the ballroom and into the corridor. Trying to think. Where would he go? Where would he wait for her?

Something caught her peripheral vision – a flash of movement at the end of the hall.

She didn't get three steps before a hand shot out from a doorway and jerked her inside a bedroom. She reached for her blade, but Favreau was faster.

Her knife clattered to the floor as her back hit the door.

"*Ma petite*." Favreau loomed over her, ice-blue eyes alight with hunger. "Have you reconsidered your choices now that you see the consequences? There's so much innocent blood on your hands, Isabel. And for what? For your precious freedom? For your Irishman?"

"Get off me," she hissed, twisting to break his hold.

But he knew all her moves. He'd created them, refined them, beaten them into her over the years. His hand tightened until her bones ground together.

"You've forgotten who made you," he hissed. "Who trained you."

"Go to hell."

He wrenched her arm behind her back.

"Let me be perfectly clear," he snarled. "You will come to me by eight tomorrow morning. The plain brick house in Spital Square. Alone. No tearful farewells to your Irishman.

No warnings. Just you, returning home where you belong. If you don't, I'm using Ramsgate's weapon on more people. How many have to die, Isabel?"

"This place is full of agents," she gasped. "You won't make it out alive."

His laugh was soft against her ear. "My men have this place surrounded. One signal from me, and your precious Callahan's brains paint these walls. I wonder – would you recognise him without that handsome face? Would you still want him then?"

The image made her knees weak. Ronan's blood, his eyes empty, his mouth slack. She couldn't breathe.

"Eight o'clock," Favreau whispered, kissing her on the lips. "Or I'll keep killing until you come. Don't disappoint me."

Then he crossed to the window and disappeared into the darkness beyond. Isabel slumped against the door, her legs barely holding her weight.

One. Two. Three. Inhale.

Four. Five. Exhale.

That was all she allowed herself – five breaths to feel the fear. Five seconds to be human.

Isabel swiped her hand across her mouth, adjusted her dress, brushed her hair back from her face, and checked the hall.

Clear.

Then she straightened and stepped into the ballroom.

Wentworth's men had taken control, barking orders as they cordoned off sections of the room. Medics knelt beside bodies on the floor. Isabel counted six victims – six people who wouldn't be dying if she'd just gone with Favreau months ago.

She scanned the room for Ronan, blinking hard against the burning in her eyes.

The moment he spotted her, Callahan strode towards her.

"Jesus, Trouble." His grey eyes raked over her as if searching for any signs of harm. "You disappeared on me. Did you find him?"

The lie rose to her lips, easy as breathing. "No. It was absolute chaos. I got swept up."

Ronan's eyes narrowed. He looked like he wanted to say more, but Wentworth appeared at his shoulder.

"Callahan," the other man said, his voice low. "Get Miss Dumont to the safe house immediately. I've had clothes and necessities delivered. A carriage is waiting at the servants' entrance." He glanced around the room. "This is a bloody disaster, and I need you both gone before anyone thinks to start asking questions."

Ronan's expression hardened. "Sir, with respect, there are wounded. I should—"

"No longer your concern. You have your orders. Be quick about it. I'll expect your report in the morning."

The safe house was exactly as she remembered it from five months ago – the same worn furniture, the same faded drapes, even the same chip on the mantelpiece.

Isabel watched Ronan move through his security routine. Lock the door. Check the windows. Test the back exit. She'd seen him do this before, but tonight it made her throat ache.

Tomorrow morning, she'd be gone.

He kept stealing glances at her between tasks. Not subtle ones, either. Long, searching looks that made her skin heat.

He was worried about her. The realisation twisted something in her chest. The same man who'd carved his name where Favreau had tried to claim her. The man who'd wrapped her wounds and held her when the nightmares came. He could break her if she let him. Ruin her.

"You're looking at me like you're about to bolt," Ronan said suddenly, straightening from where he'd been checking under a table. His voice was rough. "Don't. Please."

Isabel swallowed hard.

Tell him.

If she told him about Favreau's threat, he'd put himself between them. He'd die trying to protect her, and she couldn't bear it.

The yearning swelled beneath her ribs. She crossed the space between them in three quick strides and pulled his mouth down to hers.

Take me, undo me, break me.

If this was destruction, she wanted all of it.

∂ 27 ∂

The world went sideways the instant Isabel's mouth collided with his.

Callahan's mind emptied of everything but her – the heat of her skin against his palms, the glide of her tongue, the soft noises she breathed into him. Just Isabel, wild and urgent in his arms.

"Not that I'm complaining, but what brought this on?" he whispered.

Isabel's gaze skittered away. Vulnerability sat strangely on her. "I needed a moment. To feel . . . real."

Ah, Christ.

Callahan's heart cracked against his ribs. He knew the ugly, serrated pieces of her history that still had teeth. Some scars never stopped hurting.

He curled his fingers around her hips, guiding her to the bed. "Let me make you feel real, then."

They removed each other's clothes, shaking hands interspersed with fleeting touches – relearning all the secret places that made the other gasp and shiver.

Of all the times they'd come together, it had never been quite like this. Reverent. Aching. A meeting of broken edges, trying to make something whole.

When she was finally bared to him, Callahan took a moment just to look at her.

"Beautiful," he murmured, trailing fingers over the hollow of her throat, the arch of her collarbones, the lush swell of her breasts. "So damn beautiful."

He followed the path forged by his hands with lips and tongue and the barest graze of teeth, worshipping her. Mapping the tracery of silvered scars and the fresh bandage over her sternum. Silent vows breathed into pebbled flesh.

His. Only his.

Always.

By the time he settled between the cradle of her thighs, she was trembling. Callahan caught her gaze and held it as he lowered his head and put his mouth on her.

"Yes," she gasped. "*Yes.*"

He focused on wringing more of those sweet noises from her, licking into her in slow, deliberate strokes. She was hot and slick against his tongue, hands twisting in his hair. It was too much and not enough. He sealed his lips around her clitoris and sucked, fingers thrusting into her.

She cried out as she climaxed, arching off the bed. Callahan worked her through it until she was shaking and so unbearably lovely he could hardly stand it.

Surging up her body, he claimed her mouth in a hard, hungry kiss, letting her taste herself. She curled her legs around his hips, and he groaned.

"Inside me," she mumbled. "Please, Ronan—"

Hearing his name on her lips nearly undid him. Callahan reached between them to position his cock. He paused, the air between them electric. Waiting.

"Look at me, Trouble."

Their eyes met. Slowly, achingly, he pressed forward.

They both moaned. Callahan forced himself to go slow, to savour her. Gritting his teeth against the urge to simply *take*. But then Isabel rolled her hips, and—

He broke.

Braced above her on his elbows, Callahan started to move, each thrust measured. Deliberate. She rose to meet him, fingers clawing at his back, his arse, urging him harder. Deeper. He obliged, picking up the pace until the rhythmic creak of the bed filled the room.

When her second peak hit, she gasped out his name.

"That's it," he coaxed. He thrust hard into her, seeking his own completion. "Let go for me, sweetheart."

With a harsh groan, Callahan buried his face in her neck and let his own release crash through him. His thoughts blanked, every cell in his body singing with pleasure so acute it bordered on pain.

Long, lazy minutes passed as their breathing slowed. Callahan had just enough presence of mind to roll to his side, bringing Isabel with him so she was tucked against his chest. If he concentrated, he fancied he could make out the slow, steady thrum of her pulse, an echo of his own, a Morse code tapped out into the chambers of his heart.

Here, it said. *Still here.*

Her fingertips tracing his face jolted him out of his reverie, light as moth's wings as she mapped his cheekbones, the ridge of his brow, his jaw. There was an aching sort of tenderness in her touch. Something uncomfortably close to memorisation. As if she thought this was the last time she might ever be permitted to learn him this way.

Before Callahan could second-guess the impulse, he turned his head to press a kiss into the palm cradling his cheek.

"I love you," he murmured.

Three small syllables he'd bitten back a thousand times.

A beat of silence, nothing but the harsh rasp of his breathing. The naked vulnerability laid out between them like an offering. Callahan briefly considered snatching them back, shoving this dangerous truth back into the locked box inside his chest where it had taken up residence years ago, sprouting insidious roots in Hong Kong, Athens, New York. Every heated glance and breath, every slide of skin and shared secret.

Finally, Isabel loosed a trembling exhale. Her smile was a fragile, bittersweet thing, and when she leaned up to brush her lips over his, it felt like goodbye.

"I love you too, Mr Ashford," she whispered against his mouth.

Something plummeted in Callahan's chest, even as he reached up to tangle a hand in her hair, keeping her close. Because that wasn't his name. Not the one he wanted to hear from her, in the intimacy of tangled sheets and languid caresses.

It was a door closing. Like she was rebuilding her walls brick by brick, mortaring the cracks with that false name.

And he was letting her.

Because in the end, loving her and losing her hurt less

than never having her at all. So he memorised her weight in his arms, the rise and fall of her ribs beneath his splayed palm, and told himself it was enough.

He willed his breathing to even out, feigning the deep, slow rhythms of sleep until Isabel's breaths became soft and regular, her body going slack in repose.

Only then did he reach out, let his fingertips hover above the constellation of freckles dusting her shoulder but never making contact.

It was the only concession he'd allow himself, the bittersweet ache of this not-quite-touch in the witching hours. The agony and the ecstasy of *almost, nearly, just short of.*

Just for a little while longer.

The scant inches between them might as well have been a chasm, and Callahan let himself drift, let the exhaustion of the last few days drag him down into the waiting dark.

He never felt her leave.

Callahan woke to silence.

He reached out, seeking Isabel's warmth, but his searching fingers met only cool sheets.

"Isabel?"

Silence. A silence with teeth.

Already knowing what he would find, or rather, what he wouldn't, Callahan made a swift circuit of the flat. Each room yielded the same result: nothing. As if she'd never been there at all.

A glance at the window confirmed it was still early, the sky heavy with the promise of rain. Wherever she'd gone, she'd likely managed a head start of several hours. More than enough time to vanish into the city's underbelly.

He dressed quickly and yanked open the door, consumed by the imperative need to act, to move. He hailed a passing hack.

"Whitehall," he barked.

The ride passed in a blur of streets. Callahan leaped down, tossing a few coins to the jarvey over his shoulder.

He ignored the startled squawk of the clerk at the reception desk as he strode past to Wentworth's office. Callahan rapped his knuckles against the wood and shoved inside.

The spymaster's eyebrows climbed as he took in Callahan's dishevelled state. "Agent. I was scheduled to visit the safe house this afternoon to brief you on Ripon's. To what do I owe the pleasure at this obscene hour?"

"She's gone. Isabel slipped out sometime in the night."

Wentworth's expression shuttered. "You believe her departure was coerced." It wasn't a question.

"She'd never go to that bastard willingly. Not after—" He broke off as he mastered himself. "I think she saw him last night. And I think he made clear, on no uncertain terms, that he would hurt more people if she didn't return. And I think Isabel went as some noble sacrifice—"

"Forgive me for saying, but Miss Dumont doesn't strike me as the type to submit herself as a *noble sacrifice*. Let's not be delusional."

"Then she went to kill Favreau," he snapped. "The result is the same. She's with that bastard, and God knows what's happening to her right now."

For a moment, the spymaster simply watched him.

Callahan fought the urge to fidget under that penetrating stare.

"You know," Wentworth said, "when I assigned Miss Dumont as your partner, I did so with some reservations. And not just because I found out my agent threw caution to the wind and fucked a wanted criminal."

Callahan blinked, thrown by the non sequitur. "Sir?"

"Her history is chequered, to put it mildly. Clawing her way to the top of Favreau's empire breeds a certain moral flexibility." He paused, letting the implication hang. "But she came to us in the end. Turned her coat, offered up Favreau's secrets in exchange for her sister's safety and her own freedom. It was enough to make me wonder if perhaps there wasn't some shred of decency, after all."

"You can't honestly believe—"

Wentworth silenced him with a look. "I believe Miss Dumont will act in the manner she feels best ensures her continued survival. An alliance with Her Majesty's government is simply a temporary condition of that survival. How can you be sure she hasn't leveraged your personal investment to facilitate her return to Favreau? She has proximity to power in the Syndicate. Power she lacks here."

The question hovered between them. And Callahan – who had grown up hard, who'd clawed his way out of the rookeries with nothing but gutter-cunning, whose first lessons had been in hunger and cruelty – flinched.

Because hidden under duty and purpose, he was still that grubby orphan with quick fingers and scars all over his body. Still half-convinced the noose would drop any day, that the gilt and polish of his new life was little more than the thinnest veneer over the festering rot beneath.

Rationally, he knew Wentworth was wrong. Knew it with the same fierce, unshakable certainty that the sun would rise in the east. But some small, twisted part of himself – the part that had always whispered he'd never be good enough, never be clean enough to deserve softness, or kindness, or love – shuddered in old fears. Ones that festered since Hong Kong.

After all, what was the Spectre but an actress? A performer?

Ale and climaxes are truth serums to the over-indulged and under-cautious, and I excel at telling men exactly what they want to hear.

But—no. She couldn't fake what happened after Favreau murdered Harrington. Couldn't *fake* begging Callahan to carve his initials into her.

The only man's name I want to wear on my skin is yours.

"No," he said with certainty now. "She wouldn't do that."

"Is that so?" Wentworth's gaze sharpened. "I know what the woman means to you, Agent. More than is strictly wise for men in our profession. It's little wonder she saw an opportunity to exploit that connection for her own gain. Love is a liability in our line of work. It makes you weak. Clouds your judgment. Causes you to overlook things you shouldn't."

"I know who and what Isabel Dumont is, Wentworth." He'd traced the fucking scars on her body. "If you trust my judgment, then know that I wouldn't lay my life down for this woman if I weren't certain, with every bone in my body, that she loved me back."

Wentworth rubbed his eyes and sighed. "Fine. My men

are searching for Favreau as we speak, and when they find him and Spectre, I'll use my not-inconsiderable clout to re-release her into your custody. I just hope she doesn't destroy you."

∽ 28 ∾

The building loomed before her. No windows broke the expanse of soot-darkened brick, just a door set flush with the pitted wall.

The portal to her own personal hell.

She'd memorised the address Favreau had given her. He always did love his games. His pageantry. All part and parcel of the monster's modus operandi – wound them up and watch them dance.

Until she'd gnawed off her own limbs to escape.

This time, she wouldn't be fleeing. She wouldn't be submitting. This time, she would be biding her time, and she wasn't going to leave until Favreau was dead.

Her fingers trembled as she pushed at the door. There were about a dozen of Favreau's men sitting on the furniture scattered throughout the bottom antechamber of the building. A few were sitting and playing chess, and a few others were drinking.

"Lads," she said with a smile. "I assume you're here to greet me."

Wordlessly, one of them came forwards to pat her down, divesting her of every single knife she had hidden on her person. So much for this being an easy kill.

Then he jerked his chin to the stairs. "He's waiting for you. Fifth-floor flat."

She turned and climbed to the top flat. The door was already ajar, the monster confident in the return of his prized pet. The interior was a jarring contrast to its plain external walls, full of gilt furniture and paintings pilfered across the finest private galleries. Favreau had a taste for opulence; his boltholes from London to Greece were furnished to his exacting standards.

He was sitting in the bedchamber, sprawled in a throne-like armchair by the fireplace, idly swirling a snifter of brandy. His sleeves were pushed up to his elbows. A fallen angel in repose.

God, she hated him.

"Welcome home, *ma chérie*. Temporary accommodations, you understand, until I can secure our travel."

"And where might we be headed? Paris? Oslo?"

"So inquisitive. Some things never change." He sighed and set the glass aside with a muted clink, the known precursor to violence. "Regrettably, I'm afraid the specifics of our destination must remain a surprise. You know how I adore my little mysteries."

Isabel gave a slow perusal of their surroundings. "Well. You always did have a way with interior decorating. So garish and overwrought. We're in London, darling, not Versailles."

The blow caught her off guard. A bright starburst of pain exploded across her cheek. She staggered back a step, but his hand lashed out to seize her jaw. Fingers digging in.

"Still so spirited. So very brave, even now. But I was remiss, wasn't I, in our time apart? I let you forget your place. An oversight I intend to remedy."

She held herself pliant in his grip, willing stone into her limbs, into the frantic thrum of her heart.

Deny him his pleasure. Conceal your fear. Give no ground. Wait.

Wait.

"By all means," she bit out, "remind me. Refresh my memory."

Calculation and something darker flared behind his eyes, stripping away the last veneer of civility.

"You delight in provocation. In begging me for correction."

"What can I say? I live to please."

Favreau released her, as if her insolence was beneath his notice. "You will please me, one way or another. I'll have you obedient, *ma petite sauvage*." He rang the bell pull on the wall, and one of his underlings came to the door. "I think our hellion could use a little rest. She'll need her strength for my plans. Use a double column tie with multiple constrictor knots, or she'll pry it loose." A measured look at her. "She's good at that."

He was the one who taught her how, after all.

The thug took her arm, pulling her none-too-gently towards the bed. He shoved her onto the mattress and wrenched her arms back to bind her wrists. She focused on her breathing as he threaded the free end through the slats of the headboard and began knotting it.

Breathe. Just another obstacle. We'll get out, and then we'll be ready.

And Louis Favreau will die bleeding.

Only when she was trussed to his satisfaction did the brute depart. Abandoning her to Favreau's nonexistent mercies.

The mattress dipped as he settled beside her. One hand drifted up, fingertips dragging over her cheek. Over the fluttering pulse at her throat, pausing to press into the divot between her collarbones. An anatomist mapping the terrain of her body, contemplating how best to carve her open.

"Now then," he said, "your future. Let us discuss it."

"By all means, don't keep me in suspense."

"Still so impertinent. So convinced of your own cleverness."

He lowered himself on top of her. She couldn't breathe. Blackness crept into the edges of her vision. Pressure banded her chest and her throat, the roaring surge of her blood deafening in her skull. The cadence of ocean waves crept in.

"Did you miss me, *mon cœur*? Did you ache for my hands on you at night? For the sting of my blade?" His lips grazed her cheek. "You know what I want. How long will you suffer for your pride before you bend?"

Bend. Break. The distinction seemed academic.

"Never took you for the pining sort," she said. "We were apart for a year, and there are plenty of women desperate enough for a warm bed. I should've thought you'd fill the vacancy quickly."

"Oh, I kept myself well-amused," he conceded. "But none of them were you. They couldn't match your fire, your resolve. All of them ended up screaming under my knife. It was disappointing, Isabel." A sigh, almost wistful. "So why content myself with pale imitations, hm? With anything less?"

A laugh clawed out of her. "How sweet. I didn't know you cared."

He cupped her throat. "I care very much. I care that you thought you could abandon me. That you sullied this body with another man's touch." His fingers skimmed downwards. "Did he make you feel adored? Did he whisper endearments while he fucked you? Did he promise you were special? Cherished? And you believed him, didn't you? Let yourself imagine he could save you."

His hand drifted lower, unbuttoning her dress and unfastening her front lacing corset to bare her breasts.

"Go to hell," she hissed.

"Hell is my life without you in it, my love."

Then his mouth was on hers. Devouring. Vicious and violating. She gagged, trapped there as he pillaged her mouth.

He wrenched back, breath ragged.

"I want to see my marks," he said, tearing away her bandage. "I want to perfect it—"

He went still. A tremor chased up his arm where he gripped her, some animal tension coiling beneath his skin. Surprise and fury reflected in his beautiful features as he took in Ronan's beautifully carved initials.

"What," he said, precise and terribly cold, "the fuck is this?"

Vicious satisfaction lanced through her. She bared her teeth in a savage grin.

"What's the matter, Louis?" The words were knives, honed to draw blood. "Don't like seeing another man's claim on your belongings? I begged him for it, you know. And he obliged. Beautiful work, isn't it?"

A truth chosen for maximum hurt and to grind salt in the wounds. To carve away his smug superiority and leave him wild and bleeding.

No escape now. Just his body looming over her, caging her beneath him. His eyes incandescent with fury.

"You think you're so clever. But it changes nothing." A shift of muscle, his free hand delving into a pocket. He extracted his dagger. "I'll just have to remind you of your place, won't I?"

He paused, studying her through narrowed eyes, searching for some tell. Some flinch or fracture.

Isabel breathed through the panic. She'd endure this. Endure him. Outlast his rage and emerge on the other side. She had before.

He caressed the blade down her torso, tracing idle patterns. Teasing. Torturing. Intimately familiar with how to unmake her. How to inject the maximum of malice into the lightest touch.

"I'll peel his marks from you until not a single letter remains. Until all that's left . . ." His dagger traced the elegant swoop of an R, the curve of the L. ". . . is me."

"Louis," she whispered, almost tenderly. "You have to know that this time will be different. Tie me up, make me bleed. But this time, we end with you dead at my feet."

Then she bent forwards and sank her teeth into his bottom lip. Blood flooded her mouth. She gulped it down and bit harder, until he jerked away with a curse.

His chest heaved as he stared down at her. Without a word, he raised a hand and wiped the blood from his mouth. Then he smiled.

"Yes," he said. Reverent. Trembling with a perverse sort of joy. "There it is. That wildness is why I had to have you. That's why no other woman satisfies me."

Favreau pushed off her. He hid his knife, adjusted his cuffs and smoothed his shirt. Donning civilisation like a mask, the monster subsumed beneath a veneer of cool refinement.

"I have a few minor arrangements to make before our departure. Should you get it into your head to try something foolish that involves a knife anywhere on my body, it won't end well for you. I'll have your agent taken apart, and you'll stay strapped to my bed until you submit. Cling to that, hm? During the lonely hours ahead."

And then he left the room, pulling the door shut behind him.

Isabel counted breaths. Heartbeats.

She shifted, the movement sending bright sparks of pain lancing up her arms as the knotwork constricted. Already she could feel the trickle of blood, the sticky damp of torn flesh.

But now was not the time for weakness. Now was the time to wait. She had plans to make, a weapon to find. No matter what happened to her, Favreau's life ended tonight.

Now was the time to put the monster's lessons to good use.

Isabel got to work on the ropes.

⅋ 29 ⅋

Callahan hadn't slept more than two hours. The safe house bed felt too big, too empty. And every minute Isabel spent with Favreau made his hands shake.

He trudged through Whitechapel. The rain had stopped, and puddles reflected the lamplight as he approached the Brimstone's back entrance. Brock and Clive, Nick's guards, huddled against the brick wall, sharing a pipe.

Brock pushed off the wall. "Well, fuck me. Look who decided to grace us with his presence. Thought you'd found yourself better company up in Whitehall."

"Missed you too, Brock." He nodded at the door. "Nicky in?"

"Aye. In his office."

Callahan moved to pass, but Brock's hand gripped his arm. "He's busy. Important folk waiting."

He looked down at the hand, then up at Brock's face. He didn't blink. Didn't speak. Just stared until something in his expression made Brock shift uncomfortably.

The other man released him with a grunt. "Your funeral."

"Keep up the good work," Callahan muttered, shoving past. "Standing around. Looking pretty. Very difficult."

Inside, men in expensive suits slumped at gaming tables and women in various states of undress collected empty glasses. Tuesday night at the Brimstone. Business as usual. He made for the grand staircase at the rear, climbing until he stood before the imposing oak door of Nick's office. He rapped his knuckles.

"Enter."

Nick Thorne's office was nothing like the rest of the Brimstone. No gilt mirrors or red velvet, just dark wood walls, worn leather chairs, and a cosy fire. Callahan liked it better. It reminded him of who Nick had been before he'd become king of his little empire.

The other man didn't look up right away. Just kept scribbling in his ledger like Callahan might disappear if he ignored him long enough.

"Must be serious," he finally said, setting down his pen. "Five months of silence, and now you stumble in looking half-dead. Last I heard, you were hunting some Russian bastard after Montgomery's wife. How did that turn out?"

"The Russian is enjoying a dirt nap, and Lady Montgomery is safe with her husband."

"Nothing like a good rescue story." He cocked his head. "So, what catastrophe brings you to my doorstep this time? Pirates? Traitors? The fucking Queen herself get kidnapped?"

Callahan opened his mouth to reply, but before he could get a word out, the office door swung open, and Lady Alexandra Grey swept in with a ledger tucked beneath one arm.

"Nick, have you seen the accounts from last Thursday? I wanted to check the numbers from the—" She broke off when she noticed Callahan. "_Mr Callahan?_ What the devil are you doing here?"

He blinked. Of all the people he'd expected to see in the Brimstone at this hour – or _any_ hour, really – Alexandra bloody Grey was not one of them.

"I might ask you the same," he said, recovering quickly. "Is your brother aware that you're paying calls to gaming hells?"

Alexandra propped a hand on her hip. "_This_ gaming hell belongs to my reprobate husband. A fact of which James is well aware, I assure you." Her glance flicked between them, and Callahan could all but hear the gears turning. "You two know each other."

And you and your bastard husband reconciled? he didn't say. Christ, this was shite timing.

He resisted the urge to squirm like a grubby urchin caught with a stolen apple. He'd faced down murderers, thieves, and corrupt politicians without breaking a sweat, but somehow, she made him feel about two inches tall and covered in coal dust.

"Our paths may have crossed," he hedged. "On occasion. You know how it is in our line of work. All sorts of interesting people in dark alleys and smoky back rooms."

Alexandra gave him a look that suggested she was seriously considering filleting him with the nearest sharp object. "Mmm. And for how long, exactly, have your . . . _paths_ been crossing? Do enlighten me."

Callahan shot Thorne a desperate look. _Save me, you bastard._

But the traitor just sat back in his chair with a faint smile. He was enjoying this, the prick. Probably mentally composing poetry about Callahan's impending demise at the hands of his vengeful wife.

Right. Coward's way out it was, then. He'd faced worse odds. Probably. At some point. In the distant past.

Callahan cleared his throat, doing his best impression of a man who wasn't about to be eviscerated. "A few years, give or take."

"A few decades, more like," Thorne put in, the sod. "We go back to our misspent youth, Ronan and I. Don't we, bruv? Back before he decided chasing the straight and narrow was more his style than picking pockets."

Thanks for nothing, you treacherous wanker.

He braced for the explosion. What he got instead was a calm, accessing sort of look, her head cocked to the side.

"I see." Her voice was soft. Too soft. Like the silence before thunder. "And when Nicholas and I were married – five years ago now, wasn't it? – you were aware of this fact, Mr Callahan?"

He looked at the door, calculating how many steps it would take to reach it.

Too many.

His mind scrambled for an explanation that wouldn't end with him taking an impromptu swim in the Thames. Somehow, this calm interrogation was a thousand times worse than her railing at him. He'd have preferred shouting. Shouting, he could handle.

"Yes."

"Yes," she repeated.

Nick's smile widened.

"Who do you think kept things running in the East End while I was busy courting your fortune in the country?" the bastard tossed in. "Callahan made a fine substitute. Knew which palms to grease, which throats to squeeze."

Alexandra whirled on Callahan. "You helped Nick steal my money and never said anything?"

"I didn't even know you back then," Callahan protested, holding up his hands in a placating gesture. He had a sudden, visceral memory of facing down a bear during a mission in Russia. This felt more dangerous. "You were the Earl of Kent's sister, far removed from London, and certainly not the thorn in my backside you are now. I was just doing a favour for an old friend. You understand how it is. One minute, you're sharing a pint; the next, you're making plans with your mate to fleece an unsuspecting noblewoman. These things happen."

This time, Alexandra rounded on Thorne. "Did you put him up to it? Planting himself in my path, playing helpful citizen so he could report my movements back to you?"

Nick's brows shot up. "No. Actually, I nearly broke his teeth when I found out he was spending time with you. Thought he was trying to steal you away for himself."

"Nick didn't put me up to anything." Callahan could feel a headache building behind his eyes. "He didn't even know we were in contact until a few months ago. The likelihood of you both reconciling seemed a distant possibility at best. About as likely as the Queen taking up juggling or Parliament accomplishing something useful."

Alexandra's lips twitched, but she schooled her features back into a stern frown. "I haven't forgiven you, Mr

Callahan. I ought to have you horsewhipped. Or something worse. I haven't decided yet."

"I'll accept the punishment for eternity, I'm sure."

"We'll discuss your betrayal later. There will be consequences. Lengthy, uncomfortable ones." She took in his appearance. "You look like you're about to vibrate out of your skin."

Callahan ran a hand through his hair, acutely aware of how he looked. Like something the cat dragged in, chewed up, and then regurgitated onto the carpet.

"I need to find two people in the East End. First one's a man. Tall. Blond hair, blue eyes. Speaks with a local accent to outsiders, but French to his inner circle." His throat tightened. "Second is Isabel Dumont."

Nick looked exasperated. "The Frenchie? Again?" He reached for the whiskey decanter, poured a glass, and slid it across his desk. "If she's been warming another man's bed, there are less destructive ways to handle it. Drink. Fuck someone else. Move on."

"She didn't leave me for another man. She disappeared to protect me. Favreau has her."

"Louis Favreau? Syndicate leader?" Nick's playful demeanour vanished. "Damn."

But Alexandra grinned. "Mr Callahan, are you suggesting you and Emma's sister are involved? How delicious. Do tell me more. Spare no detail, no matter how sordid."

"Do you ever feel tempted to gag her?" he asked Thorne. "Or is that just me?"

Nick ignored that. "Alex, get O'Sullivan," he ordered, all business now. "We'll need everyone. Check with your contacts in the brothels – see if any Syndicate men have been talking after they've had their fun. But keep it quiet. This one will take a delicate hand. And possibly a few well-placed bribes. Maybe a kidnapping or two. You know, the usual."

"I'm aware of the protocol," she said. "I was there when Syndicate assassins came for Isabel and Emma five months ago. Cracked one's skull with a fireplace poker before helping to smuggle them away to a steamer. It was all very exciting. Much more interesting than garden parties, I must say."

Nick muttered something that sounded like "bloodthirsty little savage" under his breath, but wisely refrained from further comment.

Alexandra returned her attention to Callahan, her earlier amusement fading into genuine concern. "Is Emma in any danger? Should I send word to James?"

"No." The tension in his shoulders eased slightly. At least one of the Dumont sisters was safe. "She's protected as the Countess of Kent. Isabel cut all ties with her. She won't reach out until Favreau is in the ground."

The lady exhaled and nodded. "All right. I'll go see if the doxies have heard anything."

As soon as she was gone, Thorne's attention shifted back to Callahan. "I wasn't aware your missing Frenchie got herself caught up in the Syndicate. Give me something to work with, or I'll just start arming every man I've got."

Callahan winced. "Isabel Dumont's alias was Spectre."

"Well, bugger me." Thorne gave a low whistle. "You always did have particular tastes. What is it about women who could slit your throat that gets you so riled up? The danger? The thrill?"

"Says the man who married a woman capable of taking down trained assassins with a fireplace poker. I'd say we're about even when it comes to dangerously competent women."

Thorne chuckled. "Fair enough. But are you certain she's not playing you? Running back to Favreau now that she got what she needed? I'm not trying to be cruel. But we need to consider it."

"Would you go back to Whelan? Ever?" Callahan asked quietly. "For any reason that didn't involve Alexandra's life hanging in the balance?"

The answering silence was heavy with shared history. Nick had been the one to get them out of that nightmare. He'd taken the East End from Whelan and drove out his enforcers. They'd both spilled blood over it.

Thorne's expression softened. "Understood. But when we do find her, keep her close, yeah? I don't fancy tearing apart the East End every few months because you can't hold on to your woman."

"I'll do my best. Though I warn you, she's slippery. Makes eels look stationary by comparison."

"All the best ones are," Thorne said sagely. "That's how you know they're worth the trouble."

❧ 30 ❧

There was a rhythm to pain. A meter. A cadence.

Isabel knew this with the same visceral certainty as her own name. The ropes bit into her wrists with each shallow breath, keeping time like a metronome. Flay and soothe. Flay and soothe. Bright sparks of agony, followed by a duller throbbing that settled under her skin.

She let her head fall back against the headboard. The sensation grounded her. Reminded her that she was still here. Still breathing.

In. Out. In. Out.

With each careful exhale, she forced down the fear, the revulsion, the phantom echo of Favreau's hands on her. She took those feelings and locked them away in that dark place inside herself where she kept such things. Where she hid all the bits of herself she could not afford to feel.

Tears were a luxury, and luxuries were for the weak. Isabel had long since carved weakness from herself, learning young that it was a thing that got you caught. Got you killed.

Breathe. Feel the air in your lungs, your ribs expand with it. This is real. You are real.

Time became an endless stretch of shallow breaths and hurt – the pain in her shoulders, her arms, her wrists. She let it wash over her in waves. Let it carry her out of herself.

Favreau would return.

He would come, and there would be more agony. He would smile that slow, knowing smile, and it would be just like it had been before.

No. Never again.

She would not break.

Isabel shook off the daze with a shudder. She couldn't drift now. She needed the clarity that had saved her in impossible situations.

Desperation had been her constant companion since she was old enough to grasp its shape. She knew how to take that gnawing dread and spin it into something that could cut. Panic was an indulgence. Icy logic, ruthless calculation – that was a weapon.

And right now, she needed a weapon.

She dragged her fingers over the whorls and ridges of the headboard at her back. Favreau had undoubtedly paid a fortune to a master woodworker to whittle a tree into submission.

There.

Her thumbnail snagged on a splinter marring the grain. Some flaw in the wood or a slip of the carving knife. She traced that little imperfection again, no wider than a shilling. It wasn't too sharp, but it was enough.

And so Isabel began to saw at the ropes.

The angle wrenched at her shoulders and spine with every movement, but she welcomed it. Used it as fuel.

Flay, soothe. Flay, soothe.

The rope was thicker than she'd like – something meant to lash down cargo – and the fibres were rough against her skin as she moved back and forth, back and forth. Let the hurt flow through and over and out of her. Down in the vault of her mind it went.

She might have been sawing at the ropes for hours or days. All that remained was the need to be free. The determination that had seen her through the fetid alleys of Paris, the gilded drawing rooms of Vienna and St Petersburg, and the thousand hurts.

Isabel imagined the blood on her hands was Favreau's.

She sawed and sawed and *sawed* until—

The rope snapped.

An exhale shuddered out of her. For a moment, she collapsed against the headboard.

Just a minute, she told herself.

Just a minute to let the relief wash through her. Then she straightened, carefully removed the ropes from her bleeding wrists, rolled her aching shoulders, and stood.

The floorboards creaked under Isabel's boots as she crept to the door. She tilted her head, straining for some indication of what lay on the other side.

Two male voices. Of course, Favreau wouldn't leave her alone.

Isabel cracked the door just enough to glimpse the hallway beyond. Two men stood with their backs to her, shoulders slumped against opposite walls. Big, armed, and bored.

Perfect.

She recognised their type immediately: hired muscle with small brains. She'd outmanoeuvred dozens just like them over the years. The tricky part would be keeping them quiet once she made her move.

If anyone downstairs heard the commotion . . .

No. When Favreau returned, she wanted him all to herself.

"Hate this sodding job," the taller one complained, scratching at his beard. "Don't see why we're playing nursemaid to the boss's bit of muslin. Not like she's going anywhere."

His companion rolled his eyes. "Pierce, I'll pay you a sovereign to shut your gob for five minutes."

"All I'm saying is—"

"No one cares what you're saying. You don't get paid to flap your gums."

Isabel's estimation of the chatty one dropped another notch. Not enough sense to take that opportunity to shut his fool mouth. No, he wanted to grouse, wanted to spread his discontent far and wide.

Idiot.

She retreated into the room, scanning for a weapon. The place was mostly bare, but her gaze landed on a pale green vase with a wide, heavy base perched on the dresser. Expensive and beautiful.

And soon to be bloody.

She hefted it in her hands and tested its weight. Not ideal, but it would do. Isabel pictured exactly how she'd swing it – right at the junction where the chatty one's skull met his spine. The sort of impact that would either kill him or incapacitate him in seconds.

She returned to the door with the vase clutched against her chest and her body humming with anticipation.

"She's pretty, though," Pierce was saying, lowering his voice. "You think the boss would mind if we had a peek? Just a quick look up her skirts?"

Time's up.

Isabel exploded through the doorway. The guard's eyes widened before the vase connected with his skull. The wet crack of porcelain against bone sent a familiar thrill down her spine. His knees buckled.

One down.

"What the fu—" The second guard's hand scrambled for his weapon.

Her elbow slammed into his throat, crushing his windpipe. He choked, eyes bulging, and she followed with a swift kick between his legs.

"Look at me," she whispered.

He raised his head, pain clouding his features. Isabel brought her knee up hard, feeling the satisfying crunch of his nose shattering. She grabbed his head between her palms and gave a quick, brutal twist.

Crack. She snapped his neck.

Isabel stood over the bodies, heart hammering against her ribs, breath coming in shallow bursts. Not from exertion. From something darker that lived in the hollow spaces between her ribs.

"That's for calling me muslin," she murmured, nudging the first guard with her toe. "And for thinking I was someone you could touch."

She searched their pockets and took the sharpest knife she could, then hid another at her waist.

Killing was the easy part. Cleaning up was always messier.

Isabel grasped the first guard by his ankles and pulled. Her muscles screamed in protest as she dragged him towards a small storage room off the hallway. The second body was worse. Halfway to the room, she had to stop and lean against the wall to catch her breath.

"Should have killed you closer to the door," she told the corpse.

Once the bodies were stowed, Isabel dabbed at the blood spatters on the wall with her sleeve, smearing them into rust-coloured streaks. Not perfect, but it would have to do. Her hands wouldn't stop shaking now that the killing was done. They always did this – steady during, trembling after.

She retreated to the bedroom and perched on the edge of the bed, arranging herself carefully. Legs crossed at the ankle. Hands folded in her lap, hiding the knife beneath her fingers.

The picture of submission.

The shaking in her hands subsided and the throbbing in her wrists faded to a dull ache. She imagined Favreau's expression when he realised what she'd done. Imagined his blood spilling across the floorboards. He'd made her prey once. Never again.

The doorknob turned. Isabel tightened her grip on the knife.

And the monster with the angelic face stepped inside.

"Hello, my love. Did you miss me?"

ॐ 31 ॐ

Callahan and Thorne met Wentworth outside a derelict gin house. His fingers itched for a cigarette. For his knife. For something to do besides think about Isabel with that monster.

"Tell me you found something," he said to Wentworth, not bothering with a greeting.

"Maybe." The spymaster adjusted his collar against the evening chill. "Had a sighting of a bloke matching Favreau's description about an hour ago. One of my lads is following up. I was just about to meet him."

Callahan's teeth ground together so hard his jaw ached. Every second that passed was another second Isabel was—

No. He couldn't think it.

Thorne's gaze met his, a question in the slight tilt of his head. *You steady?*

No, he wasn't holding shite together. But Isabel needed him functioning, not broken. So he pushed it down, locked it away – that raw terror of what might be happening to the woman he loved while he stood there, useless.

"Let's go," he muttered.

The three men started off, weaving through Whitechapel's warrens. Eyes followed their progress. Hard men who'd kill for a few coins slipped into the shadows as Thorne passed. They knew better. In this part of London, Thorne wasn't just a man – he was the law, the executioner, the king of this kingdom. Even the most hardened cutthroats understood to lower their eyes when he passed.

But Callahan barely registered, was too lost in the memories rising like floodwater. Isabel's face swam up from the depths. The night they'd met in New York when she'd pinned him with the dagger.

What fun would it be if you caught me so easily? I'd be so disappointed if we never danced again.

He'd felt it then – that pull. That certainty that he wanted her.

Callahan wanted to marry that woman.

"You're doing it again," Thorne said, interrupting his thoughts. He squeezed Callahan's shoulder. "That brooding shite won't help. We'll find her."

Callahan exhaled shakily. "You didn't see what he did to her, Nicky."

As much as he tried to shove the images away, they clawed to the surface like they always did when he closed his eyes. Isabel's bare skin, mapped with thin white scars from that bastard's blade. The way she'd trembled the other night in the bathtub, water tinged pink around her, Favreau's initials carved into her chest. Still fresh. Still bleeding.

"Wherever she is," Wentworth said, "I'm sure Miss Dumont isn't waiting to be rescued. If your instincts about her are correct, I won't be taking Favreau alive tonight."

"My worry isn't that she went without a plan. It's that she wants him dead more than she wants to live."

And I'll be left with nothing but ashes.

Footsteps splashed through puddles behind them. Callahan turned, reaching for his pistol, but it was only Alexandra, her cheeks flushed as she emerged from the fog.

"Hi, sweetheart." Thorne tugged his wife into his arms. "Where's O'Sullivan?"

"In Spitalfields following a lead. But listen, there's news—"

"What is it?" Wentworth asked, all business.

"One of my girls – Tilly down at the Hen and Fox – she came to me not half an hour ago. Said there were men drinking in the back room who were speaking French with each other. She overheard them talking about an old house near Spital Square and a delivery that needed special handling."

Callahan's pulse thundered in his ears. *Delivery.*

He didn't want to ask, but he had to know. "Did they say anything else? About her condition, or—"

"Easy, lad," Thorne said quietly. "Let her finish."

Alexandra hesitated. "The rest was too muffled for Tilly to catch. But she said she went by the place after they left. There were more men inside. At least a score, maybe double that. And they were armed."

Callahan knew this was coming. Favreau wasn't stupid. The bastard would have Isabel surrounded and protected like the treasure he believed she was. Getting to her wouldn't just be difficult – it would be a bloodbath.

Unless . . .

"We need to split them up," he said, the idea forming as

he spoke. "Draw some out. Create enough chaos for me to slip inside to get her."

Wentworth's eyebrow lifted. "And which of you gentlemen will be handling this distraction? I don't recall assassin-baiting among your listed talents."

The corner of Thorne's mouth curved upward – that same dangerous smile Callahan had seen right before bar fights and knife brawls when they were younger. The smile that meant someone was about to bleed.

"I might know a thing or two about causing trouble," Thorne said, turning to Alexandra. "What do you think, love? Ready to raise some hell tonight?"

She looked delighted. "With you? Always."

"Keep talking like that," he said, kissing her knuckles, "and we might never make it to the diversion."

Wentworth cleared his throat. "Much as I hate to interrupt whatever elaborate mating ritual you two are performing, perhaps we could return to the business of finding Favreau and rescuing Miss Dumont? What did you have in mind for this diversion?"

"How do you feel about small, contained explosions?" Alexandra asked, all but vibrating with excitement. "I have some concoctions that should do the trick nicely. The girls at the Hen have been experimenting with black powder and—"

"I don't want details," Wentworth cut in, lifting a hand. "Plausible deniability. Just . . . try not to destroy an entire neighbourhood. Her Majesty takes a dim view of urban renewal through fire."

"When do we move?" Callahan asked.

Wentworth checked his pocket watch. "One hour. That gives Lady Alexandra and Thorne time to position themselves." His eyes moved between the couple. "Sufficient?"

Thorne's fingers found Alexandra's, squeezing once. Some silent conversation passed between them that Callahan couldn't read.

"More than enough," Thorne said. "I'll gather my men. We'll be ready."

Callahan thought of Isabel's face. Her scars. The way she'd held onto him after Favreau hurt her.

"Tell them to bring weapons," he said. "If Favreau's touched her, I'm going to cut his heart out while he watches. And then I'll make him eat it before he dies."

⤜ 32 ⤛

"What an obedient little pet you are," Favreau said. "Waiting for me just as I left you."

Isabel's throat tightened as she forced herself to look at him, not through him or past him like she wanted.

Right. At. Him.

Her fingernails bit into her palms, holding back every memory of his knife tracing her skin, his voice whispering all those vile promises. Paris felt like another lifetime.

Another woman with her name and face, but not her strength.

"Not a pet," she said. "Not yours. Not anymore."

The knife was warm in her palm. She raised it slowly, deliberately, so he'd understand what was coming for him.

Favreau's lips twitched. The bastard was enjoying this.

"And what exactly do you think you're going to do with that little knife, *ma chérie*?" His voice dripped with condescension. "There are twenty men in this building who would cut you down without blinking if I gave the order."

"Two of them are already dead. That leaves eighteen."

He laughed. "Oh, Isabel. The only way this ends is with you kneeling at my feet as you were meant to be. You're mine."

Something snapped inside her.

She launched herself at Favreau, knife slashing. His dodge wasn't quick enough. The blade caught his cheek, opening a shallow cut.

Favreau's fingers rose to dab at the wound, his eyes lit up with a perverse sort of glee. "There she is. My feral girl. Vicious and cruel and hungry."

"I was hungry because you starved me." Memories flashed – days spent huddled during his punishments, her stomach cramping with hunger, waiting for the scraps he threw her way. "I was cruel because it's all you taught me."

"And you took to my lessons beautifully once I owned you."

She lunged. The knife slashed across Favreau's chest, tearing through his shirt. He grunted in surprise and stumbled. She'd never managed to catch him off guard before.

"You can collar me," she snarled, "but you'll never *own* me."

Isabel didn't give him time to recover. She drove him back, each strike calculated. She didn't need to kill him yet – just hurt him. Mark him. Every slice was for a different memory: the broken wrist when she hadn't stolen something fast enough, the cigarette burns when she'd refused to smile, the nights he'd watched her sleep.

And Favreau was *laughing*.

Goading her, taunting her, his words lost in the roar of blood in her ears. But Isabel was beyond hearing. There was only the savage song humming in her veins. The violence. The promise of retribution.

Favreau's shoulders hit the wall, and the blade slipped beneath his ribs. Not deep enough to kill him, not yet, but enough to make him feel it. Let him experience the agony she had. Let him *drown* in it.

"Remember when you did this to me?" she whispered, twisting the knife until he gasped. "You said pain was the best teacher."

"I remember everything, my Isabel. You're magnificent."

"*Shut up.*" She pressed the knife harder.

His hand shot out, catching her wrist and yanking her. They crashed into the bedside table. A lamp smashed to the floor. Favreau used his weight to force her back onto the mattress, and when her spine hit the edge, she was that girl again – trapped under him, helpless.

"There's no escape. Wherever you run, I'll find you." His fingers found her throat and squeezed. "I'll always find you. Even in death."

The walls of the room seemed to close in. All she could feel was the press of his body against hers. It was too much, too familiar, threatening to drag her down into the black. Her mind began to fragment, old memories clawing up from where she buried them.

And then, as if in answer to a prayer—

An explosion outside shattered the silence.

Favreau's head jerked toward the noise, his grip slackening just enough.

Just enough.

Isabel drove her knee up between his legs. He made a strangled sound, doubling over. She didn't hesitate – she rolled out from under him and brought her elbow down between his shoulder blades.

"That's for every innocent you destroyed," she snarled. "Every life you stole."

Another blast rocked the building, closer this time. Shouts echoed in the corridor – men's voices calling out in French and English. Something was burning; she smelled the smoke.

Favreau pushed himself up. Blood trickled from the corner of his mouth, but his eyes – God, his eyes followed her with the same possessive gleam they always had.

"You need me," he said. Almost tender. "Who are you without me, hmm? I made you extraordinary. You don't have it in you to kill me. You never did."

A third explosion rattled the windows, and dust rained from the ceiling.

"She might not have it in her," a voice growled from the doorway. "But I fucking do."

Callahan.

He stood there like something from her dreams – tall, dark, holding a pistol pointed at Favreau. His face was bloodied, his shirt torn at the shoulder, but his hand was steady.

His eyes found hers across the room, and for a moment, nothing else existed. Not Favreau. Not the explosions. Just them.

Then Favreau's hand fisted in Isabel's hair, yanking her against his chest. A blade kissed her throat.

"Lower the pistol, Agent," Favreau hissed, his breath hot against her ear. "My hand might twitch. And that would be . . ." The knife dragged lightly over her jaw. "Such a waste of a beautiful face."

Callahan's aim never wavered. "Let. Her. Go."

"Or what?" Lips brushed Isabel's temple. Mocking. "You'll shoot? Risk killing her to get to me? I've watched you with her, Agent. You won't endanger her life."

Isabel watched Callahan – the fury, the tension in his shoulders. But beneath it all, she saw him calculating. Measuring angles. Considering options. Trying to find a way to take the shot without harming her.

But Favreau needed to die, no matter what it cost her.

A strange peace washed over Isabel then. The animal panic ebbed, replaced by a crystal clarity she'd felt before she jumped from a roof or scaled an impossible wall. Isabel's fingers found the second blade hidden at her waist – the one she'd taken from the guard outside. Her stare held Callahan's, willing him to understand everything she couldn't say.

I'm sorry.

I love you.

Then she swung back her hand and plunged the knife into Favreau's eye.

He screamed, dropping his dagger. He clawed at the weapon protruding from his socket as he stumbled backwards.

And Callahan fired.

Isabel didn't flinch. She couldn't look away as the bullet punched a perfect hole between Favreau's brows, his remaining eye widening in shock.

Then Louis Favreau, the monster who had haunted Isabel's steps for so long, collapsed. The sound his body made hitting the floor was the sweetest thing she'd heard in years.

The pistol slipped from Callahan's fingers. He closed the distance between them, hauling her into his arms. She breathed him in, solid and warm and *real*.

"Jesus Christ," he muttered into her hair. "Next time, fucking warn me before you stab someone in the eye."

"What was that outside?" she asked, her voice muffled against his chest. "Sounded like the building was coming down."

"Lady Alexandra's diversion. Apparently, she's been experimenting with volatile compounds in her spare time. Aristos and their boredom."

His fingers traced her jawline, tilting her face up to his. The tenderness in his touch made her chest ache. He studied her, hunting for injuries, for trauma, for something broken.

"You're bleeding," he said, his thumb brushing her neck where Favreau's blade had grazed her.

"It's nothing. I had everything under control before you came barging in."

"Right. My mistake. I should have let you handle the eighteen armed men and the bastard with a knife to your throat."

"I'm glad you're learning."

"You need that cut looked at. And maybe a drink."

"Or six," she muttered.

She glanced at Favreau's body. In death, with the blade sticking out of his eye socket and the bullet hole in his forehead, he looked smaller somehow. Less the towering monster of her nightmares and more just . . .

A man. Flesh and blood and bone, fragile as anything.

"I always thought it would be me," she said softly. "In the end. That I'd be the one to kill him."

"Does it bother you that it wasn't?"

She considered it for a moment – all the times she'd imagined this exact scene. "No. I think . . . I'm glad you were here. That I didn't have to face him alone at the end."

His expression softened. "Let's go, sweetheart."

But Isabel couldn't move. Something clutched at her heart, squeezed until she couldn't breathe. All the things she'd never dared say, all the vulnerability she'd buried – it rose up, impossible to contain another second.

"I love you."

The words burst out of her, graceless and artless and raw as an open wound. Isabel didn't try to take them back or soften them with excuses or explanations. Just let them stand, naked and terrifying.

Callahan went very still. "Say it again."

Isabel fisted her hand in his shirt, tugging him down until she could feel his breath against her lips.

"I love you." She said it against his mouth. "I've loved you for so long, I don't remember what it was like before."

His hands came up to frame her face. When he kissed her, it wasn't gentle. It was hungry and urgent and *necessary*. She opened for him with a sigh. Lost herself in the slide of his lips. In their shared breathing. It was a claiming, taking everything she offered and demanding more.

When they finally broke apart, they were both panting. He dropped his brow to rest against hers.

"I have loved you," he said, each word deliberate and rough, "since you first tried to cut my throat."

Isabel laughed.

☙ 33 ❧

The thing about ghosts was that they never really left you. Even with their bones salted and burned, their spirits consigned to the aether, some small, gibbering part of you still expected to find them lurking around the corner. Waiting. Watching with hungry eyes.

Louis Favreau was dead – a fact Isabel had witnessed firsthand.

And yet.

Three days. Seventy-two hours since that confrontation, and Isabel still found herself tensing at unexpected sounds, still jolted awake in the night, the ghost of Favreau's fingers wrapped around her throat. He'd left his marks on her.

Wherever you run, I'll find you. I'll always find you. Even in death.

And it killed her to admit he'd been right. He was there in every shadow and noise, spreading through her like a poison. Like a hidden knife waiting to slice her open when she least expected it.

She shook off the thoughts as she mounted the steps of the British Museum. This wasn't a heist. She wasn't casing the place or planning which treasures to steal; she was here to see Emma.

Simple. Normal.

So why did her heart pound as if she were about to steal from someone?

Her sister waited by a marble bust, looking every inch the countess she now was. Her pale blonde hair caught what little light filtered through the high windows. Too perfect. Too far removed from the girl who'd once shared a pallet with Isabel in the worst parts of Paris.

Emma turned at Isabel's approach and smiled. "There you are. I was beginning to fear you'd been embroiled in some new nefarious plot."

"Just traffic," Isabel said with a laugh. "Nothing so exciting."

"Shame. You know how I love a thrilling tale."

The easy banter soothed some of the jagged edges of Isabel's nerves. She'd missed it.

Emma tilted her head. "Are you going to stand there all day, or will you give me a proper hello?"

She hesitated, torn between the desperate urge to fling herself into her sister's arms and the certainty that she couldn't be seen embracing the Countess of Kent. That phantom itch between her shoulder blades persisted – the skin-crawling conviction of being watched.

"I can't." She hated the pain that flashed across Emma's face. "Favreau might be dead, but I won't risk anyone connecting us if they find out who I am." She swallowed, the words sticking in her throat. "Emma and Isabel Dumont are dead. The Countess of Kent is a stranger to me, here to admire the art. Nothing more."

Emma flinched. "I understand," she said, but the hurt lingered in her expression. She smoothed her skirts. "How are you? Really?"

Isabel didn't know how to answer. She'd spent so long running from Favreau and sleeping with one eye open. Now he was gone, and she should have felt relieved. Free.

Instead, she was . . . hollow. As though someone had scooped out everything inside her and left nothing behind. There was only a void where her rage and fear had burned. Without Favreau, she felt off-kilter.

"It's like I've been holding my breath for years," she said. "And now I can breathe, but it's like I've forgotten how."

"Oh, Isabel. He was your monster for so long, it's only natural to feel a bit lost."

Tears blurred her vision. Her attention caught on a nearby statue – a woman with her arms gone, yet there was a stubbornness to the set of her jaw. A quiet strength.

"Do you know what I find oddly comforting about these old relics?" Emma asked, following Isabel's stare. "Despite everything, they endure. Fragmented and imperfect, but there's so much beauty in the tenacity of their existence. Those statues have survived deluges and disasters. All the things that tried to destroy them." Her gaze found Isabel's. "Just like you. The parts he tried to break don't make you less."

That hit like a punch to the sternum. An ache in her chest spreading until it encompassed her heart – a thing still so fragile.

"I don't know how to be me without him," she whispered.

"You were Isabel before him. And you're still Isabel." Emma reached for her and stopped halfway. Even that small restraint hurt. "I know we need to be careful. I know you can't visit. But I think it bears saying plainly: I've missed you more than I have breath in my body to tell."

"I've missed you, too. Painfully. Every day."

Emma fished a handkerchief from her reticule. "Look at us," she said, blotting at her damp eyes, "weeping like a pair of tragic widows. We'll have tongues wagging among the exhibits at this rate." Something over Isabel's shoulder snared Emma's attention. "Well, now. It appears we have a shadow."

Isabel looked. And there, at the far end of the gallery, stood Callahan. His hands were in his pockets, hair pushed back as if he'd been running his fingers through it. When their eyes met, his went soft and tender.

He told her a thousand secrets with that look.

The air was suddenly too thick to breathe. In that instant, there was no one else in the world. Only him and her and the electric thrum of connection.

"He lights you up, even from across the room," Emma said. "I know this can't be easy for you. Letting someone close after Favreau. Trusting him not to break you all over again. But Mr Callahan's eyes put the sun itself to shame when they're on you. Like he's witnessing a miracle."

"I love him," Isabel whispered. "I love him so much, and it terrifies me. I'm afraid that if I look away, he'll disappear. Or see everything I am and decide I'm not worth it."

"The heart's a resilient beast, but even it needs a spell to heal. Give yourself time to let yourself be loved the way you've always deserved by someone who knows every shattered piece of you. Like these statues: we all find beauty in broken things."

"I'll try."

"That's all anyone can ask." Emma squeezed her arm. "In the meantime, I ought to dash. James will be wondering where I am. If you can't visit me, send letters. Go through official channels if you must, but *write*. You'll be an aunt by Michaelmas."

Isabel's lips parted. "You mean you're—"

Emma smiled. "Not showing yet, but yes."

"I—" She dabbed at a traitorous tear that threatened to fall. "Tell me everything. When I write."

"Of course," Emma said, features softening. "I love you, Izzy. Please take care of yourself."

Isabel watched her sister melt into the crowd, then dragged her gaze back to Callahan. He hadn't moved.

She inclined her head. *Come here*, that gesture said. *Come and let me look at you properly.*

He came, closing the distance between them until he stood near enough to touch.

"Have you taken to following me again, Agent?"

The formal address sat strangely on her tongue. Ironic, that. As if something in the bedrock of the world hadn't shifted when she'd stood over Favreau's cooling corpse. As if the man watching her now wasn't at least half the reason her moorings had been cut so cleanly away.

Callahan's lips twitched. "You know me, Trouble. I've always been enamoured of shiny things behind glass."

"And here I thought time might have cured you of your criminal predilections."

"Oh, I remain a man of questionable morals," Callahan said, his voice dropping to that low rumble that made her skin tingle. "In fact, right now, I'm thinking about dragging you behind that exhibit and reminding myself how you taste."

Heat rose in Isabel's cheeks. She glanced around to see if anyone had heard. A woman in a high-necked gown gave them a suspicious look.

"Behave," she hissed. "This is a place of academic inquiry, not a den of iniquity. Did you want something specific, or are you just here to torment me?"

He stepped closer. Close enough that she could smell him – whiskey and soap and *him*. "When a woman tells a man she loves him and then vanishes for three days, it raises questions." Another step. "I had to see you. Make sure you hadn't run off to Paris or wherever the hell you go when you're avoiding things that scare you."

Isabel fought the urge to back up. "Don't be ridiculous. I'm not scared."

No, she was terrified. There was a difference.

"Trouble. I know exactly what's happening in that head of yours. You want to bolt like a scared rabbit." His thumb brushed her wrist, finding her racing pulse. "But you also want to kiss me until neither of us can breathe. Which is it going to be?"

Isabel went still.

He was right. Some wild, panicked part of her was calculating escape routes. The nearest exit. The crowd she could lose herself in. How quickly she could disappear into London's maze of streets.

"Running's the only thing that's kept me breathing."

"I know, love." His fingers slid between hers. "And you've protected yourself so well. But you don't have to be alone anymore."

She thought of Favreau's eyes going glassy. The pool of blood spreading beneath him. She'd spent the last three days afraid she'd imagined it. Afraid to settle, to let herself be happy.

"What if I went?" Her voice was barely a breath. "What would you do? Would you let me?"

Callahan's expression was so tender it cracked her heart wide open. "Yes. And then I'd follow you to the ends of the earth, because where you go, I go. But I'd love it very much if you came home with me." He dipped his head, his lips skimming her cheek. "Let me show you all the reasons to stay, little thief."

Heat unfurled low in Isabel's belly. She could picture it – his flat, his bed, his body over hers. Under hers. His hands everywhere.

"You make it sound so simple," she whispered.

"Simple? No. Worth it? Absolutely." His breath was hot against her skin. "My flat, sweetheart. Come on. Let me worship you."

"Ronan," she said, swallowing hard. "People are staring."

His mouth stayed where it was. "I don't care. Say it, Isabel. Say you'll come home with me."

She studied him. The freckle at the corner of his mouth. The stubble darkening his jaw. This man had seen the darkest parts of her – the thief, the liar, the killer – and still looked at her like she was something precious.

And there was a hunger in his eyes that matched her own.

"Take me home, Ronan."

34

The gas lamps flickered in the hall as Callahan and Isabel walked to Wentworth's office.

He shot a sidelong glance at her. They'd lost themselves in each other for fourteen days. For the first time, it was only them. No missions. No Favreau. Just him and Isabel tangled in bedsheets and each other. He could still feel her thighs around his hips, still taste her.

His gaze dropped to her mouth, recalling how she'd bitten his shoulder that morning to keep from screaming. His skin still stung from it.

"You're staring very intently," she murmured. "What are you thinking about?"

"Just remembering this morning."

She glanced at him then, a slow smile spreading. "Which part?"

"The part that left teeth marks on my shoulder."

A fetching little blush spread across her cheeks. "Behave. Wentworth is many things, but I doubt 'voyeur' ranks high on the list."

"Pity. The man could use more excitement in his life."

When they entered Wentworth's office, the spymaster looked like he'd been dragged behind a carriage. Dark circles shadowed his eyes, and his usually impeccable appearance had slipped – hair dishevelled, jacket slightly rumpled. The man was clearly running on nothing but spite and black tea. Callahan knew the aftermath at Ripon's had been a nightmare of paperwork and panicked aristocrats. Then, of course, were the explosions in Whitechapel that had to be blamed on Favreau. Word had it that Wentworth personally had to assure Her Majesty that the danger had passed, Favreau was dead, and any surviving Syndicate men were being hunted down.

"Callahan, Miss Dumont. How kind of you to pry yourselves off each other long enough to grace me with your presence. Sit down. And for God's sake, please refrain from fornicating in my presence."

Callahan smirked as he and Isabel sat in the plush leather chairs in front of the desk. "Do you ever actually leave this place, Wentworth, or do you sleep in here and subsist on whispers and the occasional cup of tea?"

Wentworth speared him with a chilly look. "Some of us don't have the luxury of disappearing for a fortnight to fuck our problems away. If I weren't here at all hours, you lot would beat down my house door. A man must have some place that remains sacrosanct."

"Ah, I've missed this. It's been ages since you last summoned me for a proper bollocking. I was beginning to think you'd found a new favourite."

"Careful what you wish for. I'll not have your cheek

today." Wentworth laced his fingers together. "To business. With Favreau dead, every power-hungry bastard with half a brain is competing to replace him. We need someone to gather intelligence, and unfortunately for me, that someone is you two."

"You want us to infiltrate the network?" Isabel asked.

"Vienna, to be specific." Wentworth reached for a folder and slid it across the desk. "We've reports of activity there – the remaining dregs of the Syndicate scrambling to shore up alliances and resources. You'll be travelling as wealthy Russian nobles settling in for the season. Send me every scrap of information you can unearth." He gestured between them. "I assume you two can manage to act married for a few months without strangling each other?"

Married.

The word reverberated through Callahan. What he and Isabel had was messy. Hard. But it was theirs, and he'd bleed to keep it. When she looked at him, he felt seen for the first time in his miserable life, and he wanted something that would last. Something he could hold on to.

Something real.

"What if I didn't have to pretend?"

Isabel's head whipped toward him. "Pardon?"

He shifted in the chair to face her, catching her hands between his. "No more playacting. No more lies. Just you and me, building something honest beneath the aliases. I love you, Isabel." He pressed a kiss to one palm, then the other. "I want the name behind your alias to be mine." Another kiss to her fingers. "And if you tell me you don't want this, I'll never speak of it again. We'll go to Vienna and play our parts so well that no one will suspect a thing. But say yes, and it can be real. Be my wife. Let me spend every day trying to deserve you."

His mouth found hers, and time stopped. Callahan kept the kiss gentle, waiting for her to respond and give him an answer. But Isabel didn't move. Didn't reply. Then, to Callahan's horror, her shoulders hitched. Once, twice. Then he tasted salt on his tongue.

Tears.

She was *crying*, and it felt like being gutted.

He tore free. "I've bollocksed this up completely, haven't I? You don't have to let me down easy, Trouble. Just say the word, and we'll—"

Isabel shot to her feet. Before Callahan could react, she was in his lap, pressing her mouth to his forehead, his cheeks, his jaw – frantic little kisses that left him dizzy.

"Yes," she breathed. "Yes, you silly man. I'll marry you."

The word bounced around inside his skull. *Yes. Yes. Yes.* One word. Three letters. The scaffolding that his entire world suddenly hinged on.

He couldn't breathe. Couldn't think past the heat of her body against his. The scent of her filling his lungs. His fingers wound into her hair, gripping harder than he meant to, but she didn't seem to mind. Not with the way she pressed closer, kissing him deep and messy.

Then he laughed, half-incredulous, half-delirious with joy. "Yeah?" he asked, needing to hear it again.

Isabel's smile was radiant. "*Yes.*"

A sharp, deliberate cough shattered the moment. Callahan dragged his lips from hers to see Wentworth watching them with the long-suffering expression of a man who'd seen far too much in his years of service.

"As heartwarming as this display is," the spymaster said, "I feel obligated to remind you both that this is, in fact, still my office. Do please get out before you fuck on my desk."

Callahan cleared his throat, still unable to suppress the stupid little grin on his face. He gently lifted Isabel and set her back in her chair.

"Apologies, sir. You'll have to forgive a man's enthusiasm."

"I'm not in the habit of begrudging my agents their moments of satisfaction. I'll have the paperwork drawn up tonight." At Callahan's blank look, Wentworth made a noise of exasperation. "For the *wedding*, man. Surely you didn't think I'd dispatch you to Vienna unwed? Far better to have the deed done soonest. Less chance of one of you changing your mind."

EPILOGUE

VIENNA, 1873

Six months later

Callahan tugged at his cuffs, resetting the lines of his evening kit. This was exactly the kind of gathering where the remnants of the Syndicate would slither out of the woodwork.

And it was exactly the kind of gathering where Isabel shone brightest.

Callahan's wife stood amid a cluster of admirers, her laugh carrying over the orchestra. For six months, they'd been Maria Mikhailovna and Alexei Pavlovich Volkov, Russian nobility with money no one questioned too closely. Tonight, she wore blue silk that plunged low in the back, leaving her shoulders bare. Her hair was swept up with a curl resting on her neck to hide the mark he'd left earlier. The loop of a scar was barely visible below her necklace. To the casual observer, it might have looked like the remnant of some childhood misadventure.

But Callahan knew the shape of those scars intimately. After all, he'd been the one to carve them.

R.L.C.

Imagining all the marks under her dress made something hot and possessive twist in him. Sometimes, he thought about leaving them where everyone could see. Somewhere that couldn't be concealed with jewels or high collars. But he also liked knowing that beneath the prim façade, his wife was covered in proof that she was well-fucked.

And only he got to see it.

She felt his gaze – she always did – and her eyes met his across the room. Six months married, and that look still hit him harder than any punch he'd taken in the East End. The wanting was a physical thing clawing in his skin.

He crossed the ballroom towards her. As he approached, the strains of conversation drifted to his ears over the swell of music.

". . . cannot imagine how you manage it, Mrs Volkova," a brunette with too much jewellery was saying, leaning into Isabel's space. "My husband barely notices I exist. Yet yours watches you as if he's starving. What's your secret?"

An impish dimple flashed in her cheek. "A wife ought to have some mystique, don't you agree? If I told you, I'd have to kill you."

The women tittered, delighted by what they assumed was playful banter.

They had no idea.

That was a warning – his wife showing her teeth. It shouldn't arouse him, the knowledge of her casual deadliness. But he was a sick, twisted bastard, and it only made him want her more.

"I'm afraid I must steal my wife for a moment," he said as he wrapped an arm around Isabel's waist. "You ladies won't begrudge me a dance with the most beautiful woman in the room, would you?"

He brought his lips to her knuckles as his eyes promised darker, filthier things. A chorus of sighs and fluttered fans answered him as he led Isabel away.

"Come to rescue me?" she asked.

"We both know I was rescuing them from you," he said, dragging her into a waltz. "You looked about thirty seconds from stabbing Lady Lavinia with a cocktail fork. Don't think I didn't notice."

"Did you see how she pawed at you during the last quadrille? Shameless."

Ronan pulled her closer than propriety allowed, sliding his palm lower on her back than he should. "There it is. That jealousy. Makes me want to bend you over right now. Let everyone see exactly who you belong to."

"Behave yourself, Mr Volkov. We have a job. Our mark could walk in any minute."

"He's not here yet. And that dress is making me lose my mind."

"*Ronan.*"

He should be used to this by now. This hunger. The way she dismantled him with nothing but a look. But it was worse since he put that ring on her finger. Sharper. Deeper. Because he knew she was his.

He leaned in, lips brushing her ear. "Remember what you promised me? If I behaved?"

Isabel's fingers tightened on his arm. "You've been so very patient. I suppose I should reward you."

Her hand brushed against his cock, hidden by their bodies

as they turned. So fast he almost thought he'd imagined it. *Almost.*

The woman was a menace.

The waltz ended, and Ronan pulled Isabel against him. "Meet me in the alcove," he whispered. "Five minutes."

He walked away before he yielded to the impulse to haul her over his shoulder and carry her out of the ballroom like some savage claiming his prize.

Ronan nodded at a passing diplomat. He made small talk with some German baron whose name he couldn't remember. The next five minutes were the longest of his life as he mingled and exchanged pleasantries. But all the while, his gaze kept straying to the gold curtain cordoning off a secluded alcove. At last, he gave his excuses and disappeared beyond the heavy velvet. The space was lit only by the soft glow of a single gas lamp.

Barely a minute later, the curtain rustled, and Isabel stepped through.

"Hello, wife."

"Hello, husband."

In two strides, he had her up against the wall, his mouth claiming hers in a brutal kiss. Her lips parted on a gasp, and his tongue brushed hers. She tasted of champagne. Sweet and sharp, like everything about her. His hands settled on her waist, pinning her in place while he devoured her, letting six months of marriage and years of wanting pour into the kiss.

"Isabel. Have I told you today how utterly you devastate me?"

She gave a breathless moan. "Once or twice. Though it was more an inarticulate series of grunts over breakfast."

"That wasn't talking. That was worship, little thief. What if I made you come right here with all of Vienna's elite just steps away? Would you be able to stay quiet, or would you scream my name until they all know exactly what I do to you?"

Her head fell back. The long line of her throat invited his teeth, his tongue.

"You're a vulgar man, Mr Volkov."

"That's why you married me, Mrs Volkova." He bent to nip at the lobe of her ear. "The knives. You're wearing them tonight?"

"Always."

He rewarded her with a slow grind against her. "How many?"

"Enough."

"Tell me. Or I'll start searching. Every. Inch."

"Better get started then."

Challenge accepted.

Ronan shoved his thigh between her legs, pushing up enough to make her gasp. His hands were already moving, aware of where to search. The hunt was half the pleasure.

His touch skimmed the outline of a small blade strapped to her thigh. "One. Did you strap this here thinking about me finding it later?"

Isabel arched into him with a shuddering sigh. Needy. "Everything I do is for you."

Something primal lit up in his chest. Heat flooded his veins as he slid his hand down to the hem of her dress. He bunched the silk, shoving it up until he touched the second blade on her opposite leg. "Two. Do you know what it does to me, knowing you're armed to the teeth under all this finery?"

"Why do you think I wear them?"

He moved to her bodice next. His hand dipped inside, and his fingertips traced the scars of his initials carved into her skin before locating the weapon nestled between her breasts.

"Three."

Her nipple pebbled against his palm, and he fought the urge to tear the whole damn dress off.

He found the fourth blade tucked into the small of her back. "Four."

Isabel's eyes fell shut. She was panting, a flush climbing up her chest. Callahan couldn't resist following the enticing path with his mouth.

"How—" Isabel broke off with a gasp as his teeth grazed her collarbone. "How do you know there's not more?"

He nuzzled the soft spot behind her ear that always made her shiver. "Because I know every trick you might think to hide one of your little darlings. Just like I know if I slipped my hand up your skirts right now, I'd find nothing between me and what's mine," he whispered, biting her shoulder softly. "God, I love you."

"I love you desperately."

He marvelled at the miracle of it. That this brilliant, fierce woman had chosen him. That she continued to choose him every day.

"I want you to come for me, little thief."

He brought her to completion in that alcove. He'd done this to her in the dark corners of half the great houses of Vienna – watched her come apart with his name trapped behind her teeth, her fingers leaving bruises on his arms. They'd cut themselves open for each other. Bled out their secrets. Found that their jagged edges fit together. He knew her body like his own – where to touch, how much pressure, when to slow down and when to push her over. Because he and Isabel Dumont had taken their broken pieces and stitched them into something stronger.

When she finally stopped trembling, he pressed his mouth to her temple. "Ready to get back to work, Mrs Callahan?"

"Lead the way, Mr Callahan."

Acknowledgements

THIS SERIES HAS led me on such a journey that leaving it here after seven years feels bittersweet. In many ways, it's changed my life.

First, I wanted to thank my agent, Danny Baror, for all the work he's put into putting my books out into the world. He's such a tireless defender of my work, and I'm so grateful to him every day.

And of course, I'm immensely thankful to the team at Head of Zeus, especially Aubrie Artiano, who have been so supportive of my books. Working with a publisher that feels like a supportive partner is such a joy, and the HOZ/Bloomsbury team has been this for me. A shoutout to my former editor, Rosie de Courcy, who I learned so much from over the years.

To my readers: thank you for going on this journey with me. I hadn't written romance before *His Scandalous Lessons* in 2018, and your embrace of my work as Katrina has been a profound joy. I love writing for you.

ABOUT THE AUTHOR

KATRINA KENDRICK is the romance pen name for *Sunday Times* bestselling science fiction and fantasy author Elizabeth May. She is Californian by birth and Scottish by choice, and holds a Ph.D. from the University of St Andrews. She currently resides on an old farm in rural Scotland with her husband, three cats, and a lively hive of resident honey bees.

Stories to fall in love with.

Aria

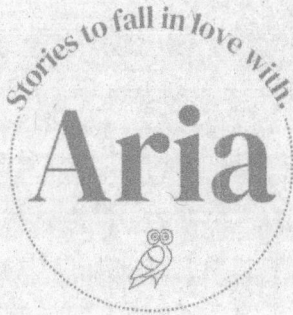

THANKS FOR READING!

Want to receive exclusive author content, news on the latest Aria books and updates on offers and giveaways?

Follow us on X @AriaFiction and on Facebook and Instagram @HeadofZeus, and join our mailing list.